The
Chatelaine
Kate

The
Chatelaine
Kate

B.B. Jones

Published by IM Books

THE CHATELAINE: KATE

ISBN 978-1-8384631-2-0

More from this Author

The Sundered Path

The Chatelaine Series

The Chatelaine series tells the story of Annie and two of her daughters. It spans a period of over fifty years and follows the three women as they face the challenges of living and loving in the twentieth century, whilst remaining true to both their obligations and their dreams.

The Chatelaine: Annie

The Chatelaine: Kate

The Chatelaine: Isabelle

The most beautiful things in life are not things.

They're people, and places, and memories and pictures.

They're feelings, and moments, and smiles, and laugher.

Chapter 1

August 1980

The rain lashed mercilessly, stinging Kate's face and making her screw up her eyes as she fought her way along the narrow and uneven path, lit only by the dim light from her torch. The wind howled through the trees, which swayed and bent with its force. The eerie sound echoed in the dark while the sea crashed against the rocks below. She could almost taste the salty bite of the water.

'Why tonight of all nights?' Kate muttered to herself.

***

Kate had arrived in Guernsey the week before to help look after her sister Elisabeth's two-year-old daughter, Fleur. Also, to help with the twins, Elisabeth was expecting in a few weeks' time.

Her sister and her family had moved out of the Camblez Hotel and into a rented cottage in the parish of Forest. The move was to give Elisabeth some respite from the pressures of running the hotel in the run-up to the birth of the twins. At the same time, Elisabeth's husband, Robert, supervised their apartment's renovation at the Camblez to accommodate the new arrivals. The rented stone-built cottage was beautiful but remote and isolated as it sat on the highest southern point on the island. What it lacked in modern-day conveniences, it made up for with the views across the sea and beyond to Jersey on a good day – except today wasn't a good day!

Kate had reflected that Elisabeth's call for help had come at just the right time. She was still smarting and remorseful after her marriage break-up with Andrew and wondering what to do with her life now that she was single again. Throwing herself into helping her sister with her growing family had seemed a perfect solution to take her mind off things. She had found solace in helping her mother with the art retreats at the Château; she had even developed her own enthusiasm for painting. But she felt the odd one out, the add-on, the long-term guest.

The final art retreat of the season at the Château had been about to finish when Elisabeth had rung and asked her to come and help. Her mother, Annie, had gone with her husband Maurice to Lyon to celebrate their wedding anniversary, leaving her nominally in charge at the Château. But, with no art retreats to organise, she would be left with nothing to do other than twiddling her thumbs.

Kate also confided all this to Elisabeth, with whom she'd grown especially close, when she agreed to come and help and that she missed Phillipe, her best friend, who was now married and preoccupied with his wife and family. Her sense of separation and being alone had perhaps been at its strongest.

Despite being busy running the hotel and a family, Elisabeth still found time to listen to Kate whenever she needed to talk. Kate also delighted in playing with her niece, Fleur. She looked like her mother: a delicate-looking child with blonde curly hair framing her chubby pink cheeks and big blue eyes. Their characters were similar, too – sweet-natured and happy. Even so, despite her sister's loving attention to her and her niece's playful distraction, Kate asked herself what she would do with her life at thirty-five?

'You have everything, Elisabeth!' Kate had blurted out one day as they sat over a cup of coffee in the kitchen, staring out onto the azure blue sea on the horizon. The seagulls swooped and danced over the waves, and Kate could see a ship in the distance. She wondered where it was going – somewhere exotic and romantic, perhaps? Oh, what she would do for some romance in her own life!

'What do you mean, I have everything?' Elisabeth asked.

'You have a husband, a family, a place of your own... What do I have?' Kate returned miserably.

'But you live in a beautiful Château in France where you run art retreats. I thought you loved helping to host them?'

'Yes, I do love hosting them. But seeing you here with Fleur plus twins on the way, I can't help but feel I am missing out….' Kate replied, her voice tapering off as she lowered her eyes to her empty cup on the table. 'You have *no* idea how much I envy you … how much I envy your family.'

'You may not say that when the twins come along! You know what they say: double trouble! Have you forgotten all those telephone calls you made to me when our little sister Isabelle was a baby? You were crying down the phone saying how hard it was and you were only coping with one baby then, not two and a toddler!' Elisabeth laughed.

'That was different – it was mother's baby, not mine, and yet she left the looking after Isabelle to Madame DuPont and me all the time,' Kate replied indignantly.

'I know, let's go out for a walk. It's going to rain later and there may be a storm tonight according to the forecast, so we'd better make the best of the sunshine while we can!' Elisabeth said brightly. 'Come on, Fleur, pop your shoes on. Aunty Kate and I are taking you out for a walk.'

'How about we take the car instead and go to Moulin Huet Bay? I don't think you'd be able to walk far anyway in your advanced state of pregnancy,' Kate suggested. 'And I want to see if I can pick out some of the scenes Renoir painted when he stayed there,' she added.

'That's a great idea, and we could pop into the café and have one of their delicious crab sandwiches for lunch. Then, if the tide is out, Fleur can play in the rock pools afterwards. That's, of course, if I can manage to waddle down to the beach,' Elisabeth giggled.

'I'd be happy to take Fleur down to the beach; you can rest up in the café and watch us rock-pooling down below,' Kate replied brightly.

Kate and Elisabeth sat down on a wooden bench after devouring their sandwiches of freshly baked wholemeal crusty bread with a generous helping of crab oozing out from between the slices. The view had taken Kate's breath away as she sat soaking up the warm rays of the late summer sun and admiring the stunning scenery. She could see why Renoir had been inspired to immortalise the rugged outcrop rock formations in his famous painting that she had admired for so long. The Pea Stacks, as they were commonly known, jutting out of the clear, deep blue sea.

'Elisabeth, when I look out onto all this,' Kate said, flinging her arms out wide, 'it makes me feel so alive. My time growing up was so insular and unhappy, and my time with Andrew was stifling. The Château is lovely – and somewhere I really needed to be. But I can't see what my future holds if I stay there,' Kate confided. 'I feel as though I've been in prison for so long and I still am, even though it's in a gilded cage now.'

'But what of the art retreats? You told me you're happiest when immersing yourself in your painting. That's what you've always said in the past; what has changed?'

'Nothing has changed; all of that is still true. But I can't help thinking about what else might be out there that I've yet to experience. The trouble is I don't know whether I am brave enough to go and look for it in case I fail!'

'Kate, follow your heart! Decide what you want to do and go for it,' Elisabeth replied, gently squeezing Kate's arm.

'You're right! Mother said something like that to me when we were in France the first time we went there together,' Kate replied thoughtfully.

'Then she was right, wasn't she? Remember, you have always got me and your family to fall back on no matter what happens. We are all here for you, Kate.' Elisabeth said, gently squeezing her arm once more.

'Thank you,' Kate replied softly, tears pricking the back of her eyes.

Kate continued to look out to sea with Elisabeth's words whirling around in her head: *we are all here for you.* After an unhappy childhood as an adopted child and being made to feel like the black sheep of the family. Finding Elisabeth and the rest of her biological family, who loved her for herself, had been like simultaneously finding a rainbow and its pot of gold. Elisabeth and her mother were right: it was time she discovered what the rest of the world had to offer. After seeing Elisabeth through the twins' birth, she resolved to bite the bullet and find that missing link in her life. Not that she expected it to be that easy!

On returning to the cottage, Kate noticed the signs of the forecasted storm approaching. The blue skies were turning a silver-grey, and the blue sea was now dark and choppy. The seagulls, a flash of white as they were being tossed around in the wind.

'I think we'd better batten down the hatches; there's more than just rain on its way, I think,' Kate said, pointing out to sea. 'There's a storm brewing by the looks of it.'

'Yes, I think the forecast must be right for once,' Elisabeth replied. 'Thankfully, we've managed to get home before it hits us. Being this high up, we'll know about it before anyone else! I might go for a lie down if you don't mind watching Fleur for me, Kate?' she added.

'Yes, of course, you go for a nap; I will start the generator, and then Fleur and I can start dinner,' Kate replied with a smile.

Kate took Fleur's hand and they followed the narrow path to the shed at the garden's end. Lying within, looming in the corner and standing like an iron statue, was 'The Beast' as they had nicknamed the generator. As the wind intensified, it slammed the shed door shut behind them, plunging them into near darkness, which made them both jump and caused Fleur to cry.

'Shh, Fleur, it's okay. It's only the wind; it won't hurt you. The Beast is working now; let's go back to the cottage,' she told her reassuringly over the roaring noise of the generator.

Returning to the house, they stopped momentarily and looked out to sea. The sky had grown darker; they could see lightning in the distance, followed by a faint rumbling sound of thunder.

Fleur grabbed Kate's hand, 'I not like this, Aunty Kate,' she said tearfully.

'Don't worry, darling, it's okay. Let's go inside and find Mummy,' Kate replied, putting her arm around her and leading her back up the path to the cottage.

Elisabeth was coming out of her bedroom as they entered the cottage.

'You didn't sleep for long. Is it this storm brewing that's keeping you awake? It's blowing a gale already out there,' Kate told her.

'No, it's not so much that… although I agree, it does sound a bit gusty out there; it's making the windows rattle! No… I've got a funny sort of pain in my groin and I can't seem to settle,' Elisabeth replied, clutching her bump.

'Oh my God, it's not that crab sandwich you had, is it?' Kate asked with a look of concern on her face.

'No, silly! I'm sure it's nothing …' Elisabeth replied, grimacing.

'Come and sit on the sofa and put your feet up.'

Kate put her arm around Elisabeth and guided her into the sitting room. Just as they entered the room, Elisabeth let out a loud 'Oh No!'

Chapter 2

'What do you want me to do?' Kate asked, feeling panic rising, seeing the tell-tale wet patch on the carpet where Elisabeth stood.

Even though she had already been in this situation with her mother when Isabelle was on the way. This was different. There was no help on hand here!

'B…b…but it's too soon! There are at least another th…th…three weeks to go,' Kate stammered.

'Perhaps officially, but twins often come early and these two obviously couldn't wait to meet their Aunty Kate,' Elisabeth attempted to make a joke. 'Help me change my clothes and onto my bed, would you? Then ring the midwife. Her number is on the pad, and Robert, too. Let them all know what's happening,' Elisabeth added.

'You can't have the babies here! We haven't got anything prepared for the birth! Let me drive you to the hospital,' Kate implored.

'I'm not sure we'd make it before the storm hits, Kate. Storms can descend very quickly here.'

'But we must try. First, I'll telephone Robert and the midwife to let them know we are going to the hospital and to meet us there. Then I'll bring the car up to the front door, get Fleur ready and into the car, then come back for you,' Kate replied.

Kate battled against the wind to reach the car and drove it as close as she dared to the front door. Fleur was in the kitchen, looking wide-eyed and scared as each thunderclap got louder.

'It's okay, darling. It's just God moving his furniture around up there. Let's get your coat on. We are taking Mummy for a little ride in the car to the hospital for them to look at the babies in her tummy,' Kate reassured Fleur.

Kate settled Fleur into the car and returned to fetch Elisabeth, who was sitting on the edge of her bed with her coat draped around her shoulders.

'Have you rung the midwife and Robert?' Elisabeth asked as Kate entered the room.

'Yes, don't worry. I got through to both and told them we were going to Princess Elizabeth Hospital. We'll be there in ten minutes, quicker if that wind out there is behind us,' Kate quipped, trying to make light of the situation.

Kate helped Elisabeth into the car's front passenger seat, checking Fleur was still safely buckled up in the back.

Despite it only just coming up to five o'clock in the afternoon, it was already dark enough to put on the car headlights to negotiate the narrow, un-made lane leading from the cottage to the main road. Kate drove slowly and carefully, but Elisabeth cried out each time they hit each bump or pothole.

'Are you okay, Elisabeth?'

'Yes,' she replied with a sharp intake of breath.

Finally, they rounded the corner to where the end of the lane met the main road. Kate slammed on the brakes, and the car abruptly stopped! A large tree lay across the route, blocking their access. Elisabeth let out a cry of pain; Fleur started to sob.

'Don't worry, I'll soon move that out of the way!' Kate announced with great bravado.

A massive gust of wind nearly knocked Kate off her feet as she stepped out of the car. She carefully approached the fallen tree with her head down against the wind. It was still light enough for her to see in an instant that, for all her boldness, there was no way she would be able to move it on her own! There was nothing for it: she would have to turn the car around, return to the cottage and ring Robert to let him know the situation.

Plan B!' Kate announced as she got back in the car. Elisabeth gasped as a gust of wind hit her face from the opened car door.

'What is plan B?' Elisabeth asked tentatively.

'We go back to the cottage, ring Robert and get him and some of his strong mates to come and move the tree blocking the lane. Robert can then take you to the hospital in his Landrover,' Kate announced, pleased that she sounded like she had the situation in hand.

Elisabeth drew a sharp intake of breath. Then, letting it out, slowly and quietly said, 'I see…'.

As Kate attempted to do a three-point turn in the narrow lane, Elisabeth's body stiffened each time she hit something at the back of the car and then again at the front. *It's lucky it's dark so Elisabeth can't inspect the paintwork.* Kate thought grimly as she rammed the gearstick into reverse and again in drive for the umpteenth time.

Eventually, Kate managed to turn the car around and drive back to the cottage. She helped Elisabeth undress and settled her into bed. She then sat Fleur down in front of the television with a big bowl of forbidden snacks she'd brought from France, hidden in her room so Elisabeth couldn't see them. Picking up the telephone, she dialled Robert's number at the hotel.

'The Camblez Hotel, can I help you?' a voice answered.

'May I speak with Robert please? This is Kate, his sister-in-law.'

'I'm afraid you've missed him. He's gone to the hospital. Elisabeth is in labour, we think.'

'Can you get an urgent message to him, please? We are still at the cottage; a tree is blocking the lane….' A bright flash of lightning illuminated the room, followed by a loud crack of thunder. The telephone went dead, and the lights went out. Momentarily, Kate stood rooted to the spot but was soon jolted back to reality by a scream, followed by sobbing which appeared to be coming from the sitting room. A tearful, frantic voice was calling, 'Mummy, Mummy!'

Kate rushed to Fleur. 'It's okay. It's probably God again, dropping something this time. Let's get the torch from the kitchen and ask Mummy where the candles are. It will look pretty with them lit, just like a birthday cake?'

'I not like this, Aunty Kate,' Fleur replied tearfully.

Kate took Fleur's hand and they set off to look for the torch in the kitchen. Finding two in a drawer, Kate turned them on, passing one to Fleur. A smile flashed across Fleur's face as she shone it around the room in delight.

'Like moonbeams,' she announced, smiling up at Kate.

'Yes,' Kate agreed, smiling. 'And now I'm just going to take my moonbeams to see if Mummy is awake and if she needs anything. Will you be a good girl and stay here for a few minutes with yours?' Fleur nodded, still preoccupied with shining the torch around the room and making patterns.

'Are you okay, Elisabeth?' Kate asked as she entered the bedroom.

'I'm worried, Kate; the contractions are getting stronger. You're right. I can't have the babies here!' Elizabeth's voice sounded panicked through the darkness.

Kate crossed the bed and laid her hand on Elisabeth's arm. 'The storm has knocked the generator and the telephone out. I managed to get a message to Robert at the hotel, albeit a garbled one. He'd already left for the hospital. So don't worry, I'm sure help will be on the way very soon. Fleur is fine; she's playing with the torch in the kitchen. Do you have any candles so I can leave you with some light in here before I go and restart The Beast?'

'There are some in the cupboard under the stairs, I think. Don't be too long, will you?' Elisabeth pleaded.

'I won't, don't worry,' Kate replied, smiling and patting Elisabeth's hand before threading her way back to the door, using the torchlight to guide her.

So here she was battling, bent almost double, to reach the shed and restart the generator. Torch in hand, Kate ran through the checklist in her head as she attempted to restart The Beast. Fuel valve on… choke out… turn on the ignition… pull cord… nothing! She tried again: nothing. And again, nothing. Panic was now setting in.

'Why tonight of all nights?' Kate yelled at the top of her voice, not that she could be heard above the deafening sound of the wind. For a moment, she felt terrified – defeated – she squared her shoulders. No! She wouldn't be beaten! Not now, she'd found a new focus in herself. 'Elisabeth depends on me and Fleur depends on me; I *am* going to get you going!' she yelled at The Beast before stopping short and laughing at herself. What did any of that matter to The Beast? She just had to persevere. She took a deep breath and gritted her teeth, giving it one more concerted try… The Beast roared into life!

With a great sense of satisfaction, Kate hurried back to the cottage through the wind and the rain, using the lights inside the cottage as her beacon. She edged along the cottage wall until she reached the back door. Inside, Kate breathed a sigh of relief. Fleur was still in the kitchen and complained it was too light now, so she could no longer see her moon-beams on the kitchen walls. Kate quickly made her a sandwich and a glass of milk and led her through to the sitting room. She sat Fleur down in front of the television for a second time, with the sound turned loud, before checking on Elisabeth.

As Kate entered the bedroom with a cup of tea for her, it was apparent that Elisabeth was now in advanced labour. With each contraction came a pain that appeared to dominate Elisabeth's entire being as her face contorted in agony. Yet, she made little sound. It wasn't an unfamiliar scene to Kate, having witnessed her mother's labour with Isabelle. But, unlike her mother's delivery, no one else was around to help this time. She sat on the side of the bed and took Elisabeth's hand.

'Elisabeth, while we wait for help, which I'm sure will be here anytime soon, I'm going to scout around the cottage and grab a few things like towels and sheets and boil some water. Is there anything else you'd like?'

'Where's Fleur?' Elisabeth asked anxiously.

'Fleur's fine. She's in the sitting room with a sandwich and a glass of milk in front of the television. I've turned the sound up loud,' Kate replied. 'How about I pop next door to the bathroom and get some warm water and a flannel to sponge you down for now?'

'Okay,' Elisabeth sounded hesitant. 'But don't be too long… I think the babies are coming…' she added haltingly between the contraction pains.

Kate dashed into the bathroom, telling herself she had to be calm for Elisabeth's sake, regardless of how she felt. Kate could see lightning flashing across the sky from the bathroom window, followed by the rumbling of the thunder in the distance. She counted the time between each one: she told herself the storm was going out to sea. But that was the least of her worries. The rain continued to lash against the window and if Robert and the midwife didn't get through in time, she was about to deliver twin babies!

'I need to push!' Elisabeth cried as Kate walked back into the bedroom, carrying the bowl of warm water. 'I can feel the baby's head,' she sobbed.

'Oh, God!' Kate could see that one of the baby's heads had crowned. She rushed to the bed, dumping the bowl down unceremoniously on the floor, slopping water everywhere. Then, as she reached across to Elisabeth, she caught the tiny head in her hands; its body followed. The first twin was born: a girl!

'Elisabeth, where are you?' Robert's voice came from nowhere as Kate wrapped the baby girl in a towel.

'We're here, in the bedroom,' Kate shouted with relief. 'Quick, I need help.'

Robert rushed into the room with the midwife close behind him. Kate's legs turned to jelly; she steadied herself before blurting out.

'You have a daughter, and the other baby is coming!'

The midwife gently moved Robert and Kate to one side, placed her bag on the bedside table and neatly arranged the contents. Then, with scissors in her hand, she cut and tied the baby's cord, re-wrapping her tightly in the towel.

'Baby number one. Meet your beautiful daughter,' she announced as she handed the baby girl to Robert, smiling warmly at Kate. 'Now for baby number two,' she added with a chuckle.

They didn't have to wait long before baby number two entered the world to join their sister. The midwife cut and tied the cord, bundled the baby in a second towel, and turned to Elisabeth, she said. 'Well done, you have a son!' before handing him to Kate.

Kate took the precious bundle in her arms and looked down at his crumpled little face. A wave of longing swept over her. *This is what is missing from my life. Something of my own to love and nurture,* she thought as she held him tightly to her chest.

After the midwife had attended to Elisabeth and helped her sit up, Kate handed the boy baby to Elisabeth. 'So, what will you call him?' she asked.

'Peter, I think, after my little brother who died, but I need to talk to Mother first to see if she minds,' Elisabeth replied. 'What do you think?' she asked, smiling at Robert.

He smiled back. 'Whatever you think. You've done all the hard work,' he teased. 'You definitely should get to choose the names! What about this little one?'

Elisabeth was about to reply when the telephone rang abruptly.

'The telephone's back on!' Elisabeth exclaimed.

'It's probably the hospital,' the midwife said, then turning to Kate, added, 'Would you be a dear and tell them all's well? Don't want them thinking they need to send someone out unnecessarily on a night like tonight.'

'Of course,' said Kate, rushing to answer it.

Some minutes later, Kate returned to the bedroom, ashen-faced with tears winding down her cheeks. Looking at the scene of happiness in front of her, she hesitated in the doorway. She wondered how she would break the news.

Chapter 3

'No one knows how the accident happened. Mother and Maurice's car was found overturned on the bend of a country road just outside Lyon.' Kate tearfully relayed the devastating news she'd just received by telephone of the car crash that had killed her mother. Her hands trembled as she held onto the glass of brandy that Robert had poured for her as she continued. 'Maurice is still alive but has been taken to hospital with serious injuries.'

In just those few minutes, the scene of happiness in the room that Kate had left to answer the telephone had been wiped out and replaced by one of immense sorrow. Elisabeth was comforted by her husband her newborn twin babies, beside her. The midwife was in the next room, cradling Fleur. Kate stood by herself, trying to keep it together, wondering how she'd be able to cope with Isabelle when she got back to France. Gone were all those wild, exciting dreams from yesterday; they were now buried under a burden of grief and confusion. As she turned away, Elisabeth called her back.

'Kate, where are you going?'

'I must pack. I must return to the Château as soon as possible to be with Isabelle.'

'Oh, of course. I'm so sorry we can't be there to help,' Elisabeth added.

'You have enough on your hands here.'

'Even so. We're here if you need us….'

***

The sight of Château des Vieilles Tours was both welcoming and daunting as Kate's taxi drove around the turning circle and drew up to the front steps. So much had changed since she left just a short while ago!

Isabelle ran down the steps with her arms stretched out wide and flung them around Kate on reaching her. 'Kate, Kate, Kate,' she chorused with delight.

Kate held her little sister tight, wondering what the future would bring for both of them with their mother gone and Isabelle's Papa seriously injured in hospital. Strange to think that, given there was a generation between them, she possibly felt just as lost as Isabelle at that moment.

Isabelle was an outgoing, vivacious child, bright and curious. Her light hazel eyes shone from under the blonde hair that fell in soft curls around her freckled face. Kate wondered how much her little sister would understand when she told her that their mother had died in an accident and how she would receive the gifts she had in her suitcase that Elisabeth had brought on behalf of their mother for her eighth birthday next week.

Kate climbed slowly up the steps with her arm around Isabelle to where Olivia and Madame DuPont stood. Olivia, the twenty-six-year-old English nursery nurse her mother had hired, hung back at the top of the steps. Olivia hadn't been her mother's first choice. She had thought of her as a little flighty. But Isabelle had taken to her immediately, so Olivia had been hired. She was an attractive girl with curly auburn hair and green eyes, easy-going and friendly. Still, Kate agreed with her mother and considered her a romantic and empty-headed – and no match for Isabelle when she was mischievous! Kate had asked Olivia and Madame DuPont, the housekeeper, to delay telling Isabelle the devastating news. She'd explained to them that with Maurice in hospital, it should be her, not anyone else, who told Isabelle the devastating news.

The next few days were difficult and emotional ones for Kate. Still, Kate found a surprising inner strength that she hadn't been aware she possessed as she explained gently to Isabelle what had happened to their mother. Although Kate had found it painful to think and talk about losing a mother she'd not long found, she reasoned it would be harder still for a child to understand. Tears began to spill from Isabelle's eyes as Kate told her that her Mama had gone to heaven and that she would be a new bright star in the sky, always watching over them both. Although they were clichés, Kate ironically drew comfort from her words as she hugged Isabelle tightly.

The next few days were challenging ones. Charlotte, Kate's mother's best friend, had helped her gather the necessary documents to register the death. She'd always been a shoulder to cry on since her mother suffered from severe post-natal depression after having Isabelle, supporting them through that difficult time, and she was no different now.

'Kate,' Charlotte asked one day after visiting Maurice at the hospital. 'Have you thought about what you might do if Maurice doesn't pull through?'

'But he will, won't he?'

'Hopefully, of course, but maybe he won't...'

'Oh,' Kate had considered this possibility but had tried to ignore it. She sat silently for a moment, then asked. 'What do you mean, what might I do?'

'About whom will look after Isabelle and the Château?' Charlotte replied.

Kate hung her head and stared into her lap: she had also thought about this but quickly pushed the thought away. She felt guilty that she was angry at the idea that she might be trapped again. What about what *she* wanted to do? She'd finally been set to escape her confines and find a life out there for herself, as her brother and sister James and Elisabeth had done, but if Maurice died…

'I don't know yet,' Kate replied carefully.

'I know this situation is hard for you. I know that you're still grieving for Annie, too. That's understandable,' Charlotte told her gently. 'But you do need to think about it,' she added.

'I know,' Kate replied quietly, then added sullenly, 'It's not fair. I had plans….'

Charlotte was silent for a moment. 'You must put those on hold if Maurice doesn't pull through. Isabelle needs you; you have to put her first.' Charlotte replied firmly. Kate continued to stare into her lap, thinking about what Charlotte said. 'You can always count on me for support, you know that.' Charlotte added, her voice softening and patting Kate's hand.

Kate nodded, forcing back the tears welling up in her eyes. She knew Charlotte meant well and was right, but she wanted sympathy, someone to see her side of things right then. Someone to hug *her* and tell *her* it was going to be alright. After all, she'd lost her mother too! But that clearly wasn't going to be Charlotte. She would take up her friend Phillipe's offer and let him drive her to the hospital next time instead. He was more her age, and he would understand how she felt.

Charlotte's words turned out to be premonitory. Later that afternoon, Kate got the call she was dreading Maurice had died from his injuries.

Chapter 4

Feeling totally devastated and lost at the news of Maurice's death, Kate picked up the telephone and called Phillipe, and holding back the tears, she told him the news.

'I'm so sorry,' Phillipe's voice was gentle and comforting. 'Is there anything I can do? Would you like me to come round?'

'Oh, please!' Kate could barely hold the tears back. Then, as an after-thought. 'Actually, I'd like to get out for a while. Can I come round to you?'

'Of course, come now if you like.'

Phillipe had set up home in his father's beautiful honey-stoned Château de Pierre Miel, where they had first met at his art exhibition. He was now happily married and had a young family, but they were still great friends. They often got together to discuss art over a glass of local wine. He hadn't changed much since they first met about seven years previously. He was still dashing, his long brown hair tied back in a ponytail and was still dressing in paint-splashed clothing as he had been when they first met. He greeted her affectionately as she rounded the back of the Château, where his art studios were.

'My poor Kate! How are you coping?' he asked, giving her a warm embrace. 'Come into the studio out of the sun. It's nice and cool in there,' he added.

Kate followed him into his studio. The familiar smell of oil paint engulfed her as she entered and immediately felt at home. The walls were covered with various vibrant pictures. Ordinarily, she would have studied each of them, but not today.

'Thanks for letting me drop in like this; I know you're busy,' she said, sitting on the bench before his makeshift desk strewn with sketches.

'Not at all. I'm never too busy for you; you know you're welcome here anytime, Kate,' reaching over the desk, Phillipe patted her hand. 'Would you like a glass of wine?' he added.

'Yes, please. I would,' Kate replied.

'I was so sorry to hear about Annie and now Maurice's death,' Phillipe said quietly. 'It must have been such a shock for all of you.'

'Thank you,' Kate replied, the lump in her throat building.

'What will you do now? With the Château, I mean?' Phillipe asked.

'That's just it. I don't know what's in store for me now. What should I do?' Kate replied.

Phillipe got up from behind his desk and sat beside Kate on the bench. He put his arms around her and cradled her head onto his chest. She sobbed so long and so profoundly that she felt her heart would break. Phillipe held her until her sobs subsided and Kate had composed herself.

'I'm sorry, Phillipe,' she said eventually.

'It's fine. That's what friends are for, to be blubbed all over,' he replied, laughing as he offered her a box of tissues.

'I didn't want to burden you with this, but I have no one else to confide in. I had made so many plans in my mind during the short time I was with Elisabeth in Guernsey and I was so happy with my life: a new niece and nephew to spoil ….'

'And you'll be happy again. I'm sure you will. Is there anything I can help you with?' Phillipe asked.

'I think Charlotte will help me with the notification of Maurice's death at the Town Hall. She helped with my mother's and she's already helping me with my mother's funeral arrangements. So, we will need to include Maurice's. I'll give you a call tomorrow and let you know the details. Thank you for the sympathetic shoulder to cry on,' Kate replied.

'I'm here if you need me,' Phillipe replied, kissing Kate tenderly on both cheeks. 'And you will know what to do. Things have a way of making the path forward clear; you'll see. And you're brave. I know you will find your way when the time comes, my brave and kind Kate.'

'Oh, I don't know about that – but thank you. I'll try to be.' And strangely, Kate did feel better – and brave and kind.

As Kate drove back to the Château, she couldn't help remembering the early days when she and Phillipe had first met. She had to admit that she had been quite struck by him in the past. Kate believed he was with her, too. But as she'd only just separated from her husband Andrew, it was too soon to be involved romantically with anyone. Now Kate was glad they had become and remained firm friends instead, and that Phillipe now had a lovely wife and a little daughter he doted on. They were too different from each other to have been romantically involved anyway and would have driven each other mad. She smiled to herself. As friends, they complemented each other perfectly. Phillipe was impulsive, imaginative and occasionally impractical; she was organised, determined and capable. Yet that slight nagging disappointment often came back to haunt her: Phillipe had found someone special. Elisabeth, too. Even Mother had found someone special. So why couldn't she find someone?

As Kate crossed the grand entrance hall in the Château, she could hear the familiar raised voices of Madam DuPont and Angeline, the new cook. Her mother had hired Angeline at the start of the season to help Madam DuPont. The latter, her mother believed, was now well into her sixties and felt she should have help with the cooking and housekeeping.

As a formidable figure dressed in black taffeta from head to toe, Madame DuPont disagreed and was difficult to argue with. Since Angeline had arrived, Madame DuPont would frequently point out, steadfastly, standing upright with her hands linked together in front of her. She didn't need a 'slip of a girl' coming in and interfering in *her* kitchen, as she had served the Marquis's father and the present Marquis all these years without help. However, Kate's mother had remained resolute and Angeline had stayed. Maybe that had been a mistake.

Kate sighed. It was the last thing she wanted to deal with today, of all days, playing peacemaker between Angeline and Madam DuPont. Angeline didn't help matters by being a hot-headed, twenty-eight-year-old southern Italian. Due to language differences, Angeline often misinterpreted situations and could be argumentative and abrasive. She was a stocky girl with striking blue eyes that would blaze when she was riled. Angeline would gesture wildly with her arms and chubby hands to illustrate her point. You couldn't describe Angeline as pretty, especially when she wore her blonde hair tucked under her chef's cap, accentuating her sizeable Roman nose. Still, she was undoubtedly handsome or maybe striking at a stretch. This added to the sense that the unstoppable force in Angeline had met an immovable object in Madame DuPont when they really started! According to Angeline's references, she was a skilful cook who had trained and worked at a list of impressive establishments. But her temper! It was undoubtedly ready to flambé at the slightest provocation!

'Whatever floats your goat, I do it my way,' Angeline shouted in a thick Italian accent.

'Non!' Madam DuPont replied resolutely.

'What's going on? I could hear you from the grand entrance hall?' Kate asked as she stepped into the kitchen to see the two women standing in front of each other, almost nose to nose.

'I bake Panna Cotta cake for the Bambina Isabelle and dress in chocolate. Sheez says no!' Angeline replied indignantly, wagging her finger at Madame DuPont.

Kate could sense that both women, still standing their ground, were waiting for her to say who was right and who was wrong. Instinctively, Kate did what she'd seen her mother do a thousand times in the face of a similar confrontation: ignore it.

'Ah, ladies, just to let you know. Charlotte will be coming tomorrow to sit down with you to discuss what food we can put on for family and friends after the funeral service.'

'Ah – oui, Madame Kate. However she needs, we will assist Madame Charlotte,' Madame DuPont replied, immediately appearing to feel deflated and turning to Angeline. The latter had also gone off the boil and nodded in agreement.

At least that's one battle avoided, Kate thought as she left and went in search of Raimond, the Property Manager. This was another confrontation Kate wasn't looking forward to, asking him to set up the tables and chairs in the Orangery, where the food would be served after the funeral. She was sure he didn't like her and that the feeling was mutual. At forty-three, Raimond was still single, moody and narrow-minded. He constantly watched her critically – or that was how it felt to her. When she'd pointed this out in the past to Maurice, he'd sprung to Raimond's defence and said that, on the contrary, he was skilful, hardworking and loyal. Perhaps Raimond was used to the ladies fawning over his ruggedly handsome face, his dark brown eyes matching his dark brown hair? Not that she'd noticed, of course. She most certainly wouldn't fall for his charm!

Kate lost herself in the practicalities of the funeral arrangements and the family arrivals, leaving everyone else to get on with it.

Finally, the day of the service arrived. Heading the cortège behind Annie and Maurice's caskets and walking side by side holding hands were Kate, Elisabeth and James, dressed in black and looking sombre and drawn. A simple spray of white freesias lay on each of the caskets. Following on behind were Charlotte and Madame DuPont, Phillipe and his family and other close friends. It was decided that Isabelle was too young to attend; despite her protests, she stayed behind with Olivia.

It was standing room only inside the local Catholic church, with additional mourners paying their respects lining either side of the path, leading the church. The caskets were placed reverently side by side on trestles in front of the altar. Two tall candlesticks flanked the caskets on either side. The flames from each white candle flickered like a draught coming from somewhere – *or was it her mother and Maurice's spirits watching them say goodbye?* Kate shook her head and tried to focus. She was becoming fanciful, and she couldn't afford to be that if she were to get through the day. *Too much time with Phillipe recently*, she scolded herself.

The gold handles on the cherry wood caskets gleamed in the morning sunlight that streamed through the stained-glass windows in the knave. It was Kate's first time in a Catholic church and she suspected it was Elisabeth's and James's first time also. As a distraction, Kate's eyes were drawn to the stained-glass window where the sun was streaming in. The picture of a lady in a blue dress appeared to glow in the sunlight; she was standing on a green snake with a bright red, ruby eye. Kate was momentarily mesmerised. Her eyes then drifted away towards the statue of Jesus below the window. He was hanging from a wooden cross, and blood was dripping down from each of his hands and his side. Kate shuddered briefly at the sight of it. A priest appeared from nowhere, swinging a silver ball attached to a chain; it emitted an overpoweringly strong-smelling smoke. It reminded her of the incense sticks she had bought once and burned in a moment of rebellion against her adoptive parents when they had refused to have anything 'hippyish' in the house. The church and the service were far removed from the Baptist religion she'd been raised in. Kate wasn't sure whether she was comfortable with it all or if she understood what was going on. Still, it was Maurice's religion and, therefore, had become her mother's too.

Kate was abruptly brought back to the present. The priest continued to swing the incense burner in and around the caskets whilst chanting in French. She was also aware that Elisabeth, sitting beside her, was sobbing quietly into her handkerchief. Kate took Elisabeth's hand and, at that exact moment, was overcome by the reality of what was happening. Not a strange imagery and stilted ceremony, but a final goodbye to her mother. It suddenly became all-engulfing and overwhelming. Giving away to the raw pain inside, she huddled up to Elisabeth, and tears coursed down her cheeks.

As Kate left the church after the service, it was with a sense of loss so great that she wasn't sure how she would ever fill the hole inside her. Her head was bent as she faced the bright sunlight outside and the sea of faces lining the route to the cemetery to say their final goodbyes.

The caskets were placed carefully, side by side, in the family crypt. Kate, Elisabeth and James each took turns putting a single red rose on each casket. Finally, the priest bowed in front of the open door, making the sign of the cross and intoning, 'Repose en Paix.'

As the doors closed on the crypt, the realisation hit Kate that she would never see her mother again. She had taken it for granted now that they had found each other, that her mother would be around forever and always be there if she needed her. As that reality hit her, she resolved to make her mother proud of her; she would live her life to the fullest no matter what!

Chapter 5

Following the internment, the three siblings sat silently in the back of the hired car on the way back to the Château. Each was deep in their own thoughts.

'What time is your flight in the morning, James?' Kate asked, breaking the silence.

'It's not till the arvo, sis. It's at six-thirty,' he replied. James was just on a flying visit; he had flown in the day before from Sydney and needed to get back to the surf school he owned there.

'It's a pity you can't stay longer,' Kate replied.

'Oh, well, them's the breaks. It's the start of our busy season, so no-can-do. I'm sorry I can't hang around longer to help. I will still be around to go to the Notaries' office in the morning for the Will reading, of course,' James answered.

'That's fine, James. I do understand.'

'Of course, if there's anything I can do from across the pond, you will let me know, eh?' James added. Kate nodded.

'I'll stay on if you need me,' Elisabeth offered.

Kate turned to Elisabeth. 'But have you got someone helping Robert with the twins and Fleur?' Kate asked.

'Yes, Nellie jumped at the chance. She's going to live in while I'm here. She's always been a hands-on Granny, but I wouldn't want to leave the babies too long. I'll stay for a little while, but if you don't need me….'

'Of course, I understand you can't stay. As a family, we have been lucky to have had Nellie and Edward's support all these years. Firstly, as mother's best friends when she arrived in Guernsey and now part of our family, now that you're married to their son,' Kate squeezed her hand. 'No, you go back home and be with your babies. I'll manage.'

'If, you're sure?' Elisabeth squeezed Kate's hand in return. 'Then I'll

catch the ferry back after going to the Notaries' office if that's okay?'
Elisabeth replied.

'Of course. By the way, you never did tell us if you've settled on names for the twins?' Kate added.

'We have. Peter Edward and Annie Kate,' Elisabeth replied.

'Oh! I'm touched! What lovely choices,' Kate replied with tears pricking the back of her eyes at the thought of her niece being named after her.

'You didn't get to meet our brother Peter, or Petey as we called him, of course. He died before you came back into our lives, but he was such a special little brother, wasn't he, James?'

'And a pain at times!' James quipped and chuckled.

'It took Mother a long time to get over his death if indeed she ever did. He was only five years old when he had his accident. The stump of the tree he fell from is still there as a reminder,' Elisabeth said quietly. 'We named Annie Kate after mother and you. You, because you delivered her into this world,' Elisabeth's voice quivered. 'And Annie, as she was born around the time Mother died,' she added solemnly with tears in her eyes.

After breakfast the following day, Raimond brought the car around and drove the three siblings to the Notaires' office. The office was next door to where their mother married Maurice seven years ago. Kate thought of that happy day as they drew up in front of the office. Mother had looked radiantly happy in her oyster-coloured satin gown and delicate French lace detailing. She was now lying in that same dress in her casket. Kate felt a cold shudder picturing seeing her in her casket the night before the funeral. She looked so serene and beautiful, lying there in her wedding dress. Maybe she *was* sleeping in peace like the priest had commanded her to?

Monsieur Duval, the Maître, welcomed them at the Notaries' office door and showed them into his wood-panelled room. It was dark and gloomy, sparsely furnished with a wooden cabinet and three chairs in front of an oversized desk strewn with papers. A fourth chair was found for Raimond, whom they'd brought along as a translator. Kate had been reluctant to ask him to come along, but she had no choice as none of them was fluent in French.

Monsieur Duval opened the bulging file in front of him. Loose sheets of paper spilt out onto the desk as he shuffled through the file before he came across a large document, its sheets of paper fastened by a silver clip. He proceeded to read from the document.

All three listened intently to the Maître as he read, in French, line by line, the document's contents before him. Although she'd worked on her French over the years, Kate only partially understood some of what he was reading aloud. Since Maurice had survived his wife, Annie, her share of the estate had reverted to him. A sum of money was to go to Madame DuPont in recognition of her service over the years. Also, she was to be given accommodation in the Château for her lifetime. A small legacy to Raimond was made for his loyal service. There were various other donations to Maurice's favourite charities and one to the church. To Kate, Elisabeth and James, the document provided a lump sum to each of them. The rest of the estate, including Château des Vieilles Tours, was to be held in trust for his daughter Isabelle until she reached eighteen years.

The Maître paused and then looked meaningfully across at Kate. 'Et de conclure,' he added before continuing as he caught her eye, 'je désigne Kate Sinclair comme gardienne de Isabelle de Paganel jusqu'à ce qu'elle ait dix-huit ans,' he concluded placing the document down on the desk in front of him.

Kate sat transfixed momentarily, then looked at Elisabeth and James, who shrugged. She asked Raimond, 'Please, would you translate that last statement?'

He hesitated and replied, 'The Marquis has designated you as Isabelle's guardian until she is eighteen, when the Château will pass to her in totality.'

As his words sunk in, Kate could feel the cold creeping down her body. From her open mouth, into her chest and stomach and then into her legs. Until the burden of what Maurice had handed to her overwhelmed her. She sat paralysed in her chair, her eyes on Elisabeth, who stared back at her, wide-eyed and sympathetic. She knew Elisabeth would understand what was going round and round in her head – above all else, *bang goes all my plans for a life of my own!*

Chapter 6

Kate drew back the curtains and gazed out of her bedroom window onto the garden below and the hills beyond. It was going to be a glorious October day; the sun was already up and shone on the trees in the distance, picking out the red and yellow hues of the autumn leaves. The last months had been difficult, but Kate, filled with renewed vigour, decided today was the day to start going through her mother's things.

'Good morning, sleepyhead,' Kate said as she entered Isabelle's bedroom. 'It's a beautiful day!' she added, pulling back the curtains.

'Argh! It's the school holidays. Why are you waking me so early?' Isabelle complained.

'I thought after breakfast, maybe you'd like to help me go through some of Mama's things? What do you think?'

'What are we going to do with them?' Isabelle asked, who was now sitting up in bed and looking more awake. Her blonde curls tousled, but her hazel eyes were bright with curiosity. The cherubic features didn't fool Kate, though. As much as her little sister could be an angel, she could also be a little imp. She needed to approach this carefully to ensure Isabelle understood and wasn't upset about seeing her mother's belongings packed up and given away.

'Charlotte has offered to take Mama's clothes for one of her charities,' Kate replied. 'Then we can divide her jewellery and other special things between Elisabeth and us.'

'Oh, yes! I'd love to do that!' Isabelle replied excitedly, jumping out of bed and hastily pulling on her clothes.

Kate knew Isabelle loved glittery things. She'd often seen her trying on their mother's jewellery when she was alive. She would undoubtedly be in her element today, going through their mother's jewellery box.

'Bonjour, Madame DuPont et Angeline,' Kate greeted them as she entered the kitchen, with Isabelle trailing behind her.

'Bonjour, Madame Kate,' they chorused back.

'Isabelle and I are going through my mother's things today,' Kate said, turning to Angeline. 'I will pack up her clothes into suitcases for Charlotte to collect. Would you be kind enough to carry them downstairs when I've finished and leave them in the grand entrance hall, please? They will be too heavy for Madame DuPont,' she added.

'Okey cokey,' Angeline replied, turning to Madame DuPont with a wry smile and a toss of her head as she walked towards the walk-in pantry. Momentarily, fire flashed in Madame DuPont's eyes. Then she lifted her nose as if something smelled terrible as Angeline flounced past her.

I really must do something about those two, Kate thought.

'Sébastien would like to see of you today,' Madame DuPont turned to Kate with quite a different expression on her face – kind and sympathetic.

'Thank you. I'll pop out to the garden directly after breakfast,' Kate replied.

Kate went in search of Sébastien, the young French twenty-something gardener Maurice had hired at the start of the season, leaving the next French rebellion site in the kitchen. He was becoming more of a hindrance than a help in the garden the past few months. Even though she was no gardener, Kate constantly had to remind him what needed to be done next – and often had to be told twice.

As a would-be poet, his head was in the clouds most of the time, no doubt composing some romantic epic, Kate suspected. He was also a distraction for Olivia. Kate would often find her in the garden on the pretext of taking Isabelle out for some fresh air. In reality, it was to seek out Sébastien to hang around him, making cow eyes at him! He was, as Kate had overheard Olivia confide in Angeline, a bit of 'eye candy'. With his shock of shoulder-length curly blonde hair, deep blue eyes and slim tanned body, he would make any young girl swoon, no doubt, Kate thought. That was just part of it, but the poetic stance undoubtedly helped, too. Unfortunately, Olivia was anything but level-headed.

Kate found Sébastien in the greenhouse in the walled garden, looking around in confusion.

'When I am planting these pleez?' Sébastien asked, holding up a large bag of onions.

Kate took the packet of onion sets from him and read the back of the bag.

'See, it says here, *plant September to mid-October, ready to harvest June,*' Kate replied, handing him back the bag of onion sets.

'Merci. My reading engleesh not very good, excusez-moi,' Sébastien replied, smiling charmingly at her.

'That's okay, don't worry,' Kate answered, taking pity since his face had gone bright red despite the charming smile. For all his faults, he was a sensitive boy, she thought. 'Don has prepared those last three beds at the back on the right to plant these in, okay?'

'Merci, je comprends.'

Being a Chatelaine is not all it's cracked up to be sometimes, Kate thought as she walked back to the Château. Dealing with people like Sébastien, the ever-warring Madame DuPont and Angeline and not forgetting Olivia off with the fairies most of the time – and then there was Raimond! She allowed herself to dwell irritably over how he constantly challenged her decisions and treated her like a child. She then realised the good mood she'd started the day was rapidly disintegrating. She sighed… 'What have I been let in for?'

She gave herself a little shake. At least some people were a source of support as opposed to trouble. She was now secretly thanking her mother for bringing Florence and Don over to help each year over the busy season. She wished they were still here now, but they'd had to return to Cornwall to finalise their house sale before returning to France to settle here permanently. They had been the first guests at the Château when her mother and Maurice had re-opened it after its restoration. They'd remained friends and regular visitors ever since. The gardens were still reaping the rewards of Don's last visit, Kate had noted; with the help of Sébastien, Don had transformed the grounds and the potager garden.

Don, originally from Louisiana, proved to be an expert garden landscaper and a professional filmmaker, producing documentaries in arts and culture worldwide. The potager garden was now arranged into orderly rows of fertile, well-tended beds growing fruit and vegetables and cutting flowers for the Château all summer. Kate had foolishly told her mother that she didn't need Florence's help to run the art retreats, but she didn't know how she would have hosted them without her by the end of the season. Florence, for all her scattiness, was an accomplished artist. She also had a way with people with her soft and encouraging demeanour. Kate wished she could be more like her and curb her inclination towards shyness, which often came across as abruptness. Kate had been observing and copying Florence to develop a gentler, more supportive approach; she was undoubtedly going to need it to steer Isabelle through the aftermath of both her parent's deaths.

Isabelle came running towards her, full of vibrant mischief. She wasn't much of a scholar but was happiest when she had her freedom. Despite her sad situation of being an orphan, being on school holidays had put an extra spring in her step and bounced her attitude.

'Madame DuPont has given me these scraps for the chickens. Do you want to come with me to feed them?' Isabelle asked, whirling into Kate and almost knocking her over.

'Yes, of course. Then we must start sorting through Mama's things, okay?' Kate replied, steadying herself and Isabelle at the same time.

Isabelle nodded, then abandoned her, skipping happily towards the chicken enclosure. A pang of melancholy came over Kate. She watched her little sister's curly blonde head bobbing up and down, swinging the bag of food in her hand that Madame DuPont had given her for the chickens. Despite becoming a foundling at such a young age, Kate marvelled at how resilient Isabelle appeared to be, still finding pleasure in little things, like feeding the chickens. Kate's grief came in waves and at random times; she suspected that was the same for Isabelle, but she was too young to share her feelings. Instead, hers manifested themselves in temper tantrums, of which there were many when she couldn't get her way.

Chapter 7

Kate and Isabelle climbed the stairs, holding hands, to Marquis's suite on the second floor at the front of the Château. After their marriage, Kate's mother and Maurice had taken over the Marquis suite, which had last been used by Maurice's father.

Kate loved this suite; it was the most elegant set of rooms she had ever seen. Its walls were covered in soft blue *toile de jouy* wallpaper; the windows dressed in grey linen curtains with powder blue swags gave the room an air of coolness and style. Inviting, elegant grey linen sofas, accessorised with plump blue cushions, placed on either side of a mahogany coffee table. *Oh, how she would love to sit here quietly, curled up with a book!* Kate thought, *But no! There's work to be done!*

Isabelle slowly followed Kate into the bedroom, suddenly looking subdued. The room was dominated by a large mahogany four-poster bed with carved details on the head and footboards. The tapered and turned posts supported the panelled tester above the bed. Heavy tapestry curtains were tied back either side at the head of the bed and a matching pelmet hung down from the canopy.

Isabelle wandered around the room. Kate watched her, alert for any signs of distress, but Isabelle appeared relatively calm. Kate opened the chiffonier drawers and started to pile clothes onto the bed. At the same time, she kept a surreptitious eye on Isabelle, who was standing in the middle of the room, just looking around. Kate noticed she'd picked up their mother's decorative jewellery box from the dressing table and had opened the box, revealing some of their mother's jewellery nestling inside the padded and buttoned duck egg blue silk interior.

'Can I have this please, Kate?' she asked, pointing to a sparkling pendant Maurice had given their mother two birthdays ago.

'No, not until I've had a chance to go through what's in there. Let's start with Mama's clothes, shall we, so we can get them ready for Charlotte?'

Still clutching the jewellery box, Isabelle sat on the edge of the bed with her chin dropped into her chest and pouting.

'You don't let me have anything,' Isabelle grumbled.

Sensing Isabelle was gearing up for one of her strops, Kate said brightly. 'I'll tell you what. Let's go through Mama's treasure box and see what we can find there for you to keep until we can properly look at Mama's jewellery. What do you think?'

At this suggestion, Isabelle jumped down from the bed. She raced to the window where her mother's large wooden chest sat. Kate, too, loved going through her mother's wooden chest. She'd been intrigued each time she'd seen her mother open the old laundry trunk and rummage around amongst the contents inside to find something to show her. It always reminded her of the Mary Poppins film. She would never have been surprised if her mother had pulled the odd coat stand, plant, or the like out of the chest like Mary Poppins had produced from her carpetbag.

Kate pulled up a small table alongside the chest to spread its contents. She sat on a chair while Isabelle, kneeling on the floor, brought out each item individually.

Hurriedly diving in, Isabelle randomly picked up and discarded items that didn't appeal to her. Bundles of letters, newspaper clippings and even an unfinished knitted garment, its needles still stuck in the ball of the wool. Along with several school exercise books that Kate had seen her mother write in, using them as journals. These were all tossed aside. The chest was a treasure trove but obviously not rich enough to interest Isabelle.

'I've stayed here,' Isabelle said, thrusting a brochure from Hôtel Lafayette at Kate, then diving into the chest again.

'I don't think so. This is where Mama and Papa stayed when they went to Lyon. They also stayed there on their honeymoon,' Kate replied, studying the brochure. At the same time, Isabelle piled more discarded items on the table. Flicking through the hotel brochure, Kate remembered her mother telling her that this was the hotel where she and Maurice had first made love and where Isabelle had been conceived. But she couldn't share *that* with Isabelle!

'Oh, isn't this pretty, Kate?' Isabelle was looking at a poster of La Fête des Lumières. 'What is it?' she added.

'It's the Festival of Lights held in Lyon. Mama and Papa visited the festival the year before you were born,' Kate replied, studying the poster. 'It does look magical, doesn't it?' she added. Still, Isabelle had already lost interest, moved on, and was now investigating a small envelope, yellowed by age. On the front of the envelope was a handwritten name and address faded by age. She opened the envelope and inside was a little embroidered Eau de Nil-coloured silk handkerchief.

'I don't know why she kept this old hanky,' Isabelle said, tossing it and the envelope onto the table.

Kate picked up the envelope and studied it: she could just about make out the slopping handwriting; it was addressed to her mother. The postmark was somewhere in France, but Kate couldn't determine the date. Still, she remembered her mother telling her that her father had sent it to her mother towards the end of the war when he was on a mission as a signal to her to show her that he was safe. It was also the last time she'd heard from him before he was sent back to his native Canada. Kate carefully placed the delicate handkerchief back into the envelope and slipped it into her slacks pocket.

Isabelle pulled out a large, heavy, leather-bound photo album. Struggling with the bulkiness of it, Kate took it from her and placed it on the table. Opening it up and flicking over each page, they studied each photograph. As they flicked over the pages, Kate explained to Isabelle who was who. Isabelle stopped at the picture of a young, curly-headed blonde child.

'Who's that? Is it me when I was younger?' she asked.

'No. That's Petey. He was your brother,' Kate replied.

'That's silly! I've only got one brother, James and he lives in Australia with the kangaroos,' she retorted.

'Yes, that's right. You only have one brother *now*, but you had another brother, Peter. They called him Petey. Unfortunately, he died when he was five years old,' Kate explained.

'Why?' Isabelle asked.

'Because he climbed a tree when Mama told him not to, and he fell from the tree and died,' Kate replied.

'Oh, I won't climb any trees, I promise,' Isabelle said solemnly, shaking her head. 'Cross my heart,' she added, moving her hand in the sign of a cross over her heart.

'That's good. I'm pleased to hear it!' Kate smiled.

They were now at the bottom of the chest and all that remained were two boxes. Isabelle picked them up and placed them on the table. She opened the first one.

'Oh, it's just a load of old buttons,' she exclaimed as she emptied them onto the table, allowing them to spill all over the floor. Kate instantly thought of the collection of buttons she'd had as a child, but she decided not to share this memory with Isabelle; she was too young to understand. Kate's button collection had been something for her to play with when she was sent to bed early with a blanket up at the window to darken the room and not even allowed to read. Her upbringing had been devoid of love and attention, unlike Isabelle's. The memory brought a lump to Kate's throat. How lucky Isabelle was in comparison. She carefully collected the buttons and put them back in the box while Isabelle dived into the other box.

'Oh, this is better! Look, shells! Lots of lovely seashells. Look at all the colours,' Isabelle exclaimed, interrupting Kate's thoughts as she thrust the box under Kate's nose. 'They still smell of the sea. Smell Kate,' she added.

'They are beautiful, aren't they?' Kate smiled. 'I think Mama may have collected them from the beach on Herm.'

'Herm? What is this Herm thing?' Isabelle queried, frowning.

'It's a small island off the coast of Guernsey's where Mama lived before meeting Papa and moving here. The beach is full of shells. Maybe we will go there one day,' Kate added.

'Can we make something with these shells, please, Kate?' Isabelle begged.

'I suppose we could…yes, I have an idea… Mama bought me a little box covered in seashells from Herm when I visited her in Guernsey a long time ago before you were born. So maybe we could do the same! Perhaps we could even cover the box the buttons are in. Would you like to do that?' Kate asked.

'Oh, yes! Can we, can we?' Isabelle replied, arranging the shells on the top of the button box. 'Then I can put my treasures in it, can't I? We can throw all of the horrible old buttons away.'

Sensing that Isabelle's quest to find a treasure for herself had been satisfied, Kate said quickly. 'Okay, let's put everything back in the chest, except for the box of shells and the photographs and go through Mama's wardrobe.' She quietly put the button box aside to retrieve it later.

Chapter 8

Kate was glad of Isabelle's company as a distraction as she sorted her mother's clothes. Emotionally, Kate thought she was ready for this task; however, handling her mother's clothes with her perfume still lingering on them made it emotionally difficult. Kate had to steel herself against plunging her face into the garments and trying to pretend the accident had never happened and that her mother was just downstairs and would call them any minute now to come down for lunch. But as Isabelle was sat on the bed watching, Kate contained her grief, folded the clothes carefully and placed them into the suitcases she'd put on the far end of the bed. As she closed each suitcase, she tried not to think of it as losing yet another piece of her mother.

Just at the right time, Isabelle broke into Kate's morose thoughts, both lightening and yet also intensifying her sadness. 'Look, Mama's favourite dress she wore when Papa asked her to marry him!'

Isabelle was dressed in her mother's long-sleeved green dress, dancing around the room, almost tripping over the oversized garment. Kate couldn't help but laugh at Isabelle's antics. *Ever the actress,* she thought.

Finally, Kate opened the blanket box at the bottom of the bed, packed with her mother's jumpers, all neatly folded and piled on top of each other. Carefully, she lifted them out and placed them into the remaining empty suitcase. At the bottom of the chest lay a beautiful handstitched quilt her mother had spent many years making. She vividly remembered her mother sewing the quilt as they sat together in the gardens at the Camblez Hotel. Kate lifted it from the blanket box. She stroked the soft material as she remembered those warm sunny days perched on the decorative wrought iron chairs on the lawn, drinking tea from delicate bone porcelain cups, eating dainty sandwiches and beautiful patisserie cream cakes. Kate placed the quilt to one side. She decided this was something irreplaceable, something she would keep forever, alongside all those lovely memories that could never be taken from her.

It had been a long morning and a mentally and emotionally challenging one. Kate turned to Isabelle. She was still draped in her mother's dress and playing on the floor with the shells, arranging them in patterns and then scattering them as a kaleidoscope mirror would.

'Come on, Isabelle. Let's go and see what Angeline has made for lunch,' Kate said as she gathered up and tucked the quilt and photograph album under her arm. 'Bring your box of shells with you,' she added.

'Can I take this too?' Isabelle asked, picking up the jewellery box to which she'd taken a shine.

'No, leave that there. I must go through Mama's jewellery properly another day,' Kate replied.

'You never let me have anything,' Isabelle's sunny mood changed in seconds. She stamped her foot and threw the shells onto the floor.

'I bet Olivia's never seen as many shells as you have there,' Kate said gently. 'Let's make her jealous and go and show her, shall we?'

Isabelle's face lit up at that idea. Scooping up the shells into the lap of her mother's dress she was still wearing, Isabelle raced on ahead to find Olivia to show off her shells. Kate hadn't the heart to tell her to take off the dress. She was relieved they had found something from the treasure chest to make Isabelle happy and allay another one of her tantrums. Slowly, she followed Isabelle down the stairs, deep in thought. There was still so much to go through, but not today. She couldn't face any more today.

Kate found Isabelle sitting next to Olivia in the kitchen, showing off the shells she'd found to her. Isabelle had taken off their mother's dress and it was draped over the back of a chair. She was picking the seashells out of the box and handing them to Olivia individually. Kate could see Olivia's eyes had glazed over as she muttered, 'very nice' to each of them.

'What's for lunch today, Angeline?' Kate asked brightly. She was famished after her emotionally draining morning.

'Today we 'ave pizza, the Bambina's favourite,' Angeline replied, placing a wooden platter piled high with pizza slices in the middle of the table with a flourish.

'Oh, goody!' Isabelle exclaimed, diving in to take a slice of pizza off the platter.

'Lovely. Thank you, Angeline. I'll just put this quilt and album away and I'll be back,' Kate replied. 'By the way, I've placed my mother's clothes into cases and left them on the bed in the Marquis bedroom. Would you please bring them down to the grand entrance hall after lunch?' she added. Kate collected the discarded dress from the back of the chair as she left the room, glad that Isabelle now had two distractions: the shells and food!

When Kate returned to the kitchen, Raimond and Sébastien had joined the others. They were also helping themselves to the pizza, which was now almost gone.

'I 'ear you've told Sébastien to plant the onion sets in the walled garden this morning?' Raimond said, turning to Kate.

'Yes, that's right. It's the right time of the year, I understand,' Kate replied.

'They should 'ave went in September, when the earth was still warm, before the frosts,' Raimond replied haughtily.

'The packet says they can be planted from September to mid-October,' Kate replied firmly.

'Well, don't be surprised if the bulbs go....' Raimond made a gesture like something falling apart, 'and disintegrate,' he said gruffly.

Kate merely shrugged her shoulders without replying. She took the last piece of pizza and slipped in alongside Isabelle, deliberately ignoring Raimond for the rest of the mealtime. *Why does that man have to be so picky, so critical of everything I do?* Kate angrily thought as she ground the pizza between her teeth, pretending it was Raimond she was chewing on.

Chapter 9

Sitting over their coffee after lunch and watching Isabelle, ever the performer, dancing around the table to the music on the radio, when suddenly the music stopped.

'Hey! Who turned off the music?' Isabella asked indignantly.

Raimond got up from the table and flicked the light switch. 'Another power cut!' he announced. 'That's two we've 'ad this week. I wonder how long it will be off this time?' he added, frowning at Kate as if it was her fault.

'I was thinking last time this happened that we perhaps should place some candles around the Château in case we have one at night.'

'No! They are too dangerous; they might have a fire,' Raimond interjected.

'But I wouldn't want any of us falling down the stairs in the dark,' Kate announced, ignoring Raimond.

'I will assister, Madame Kate,' Madame DuPont replied. Raimond shrugged and stomped out of the kitchen.

'Merci, I think we have some in the closet in the grand entrance hall and some holders. There may also be matches. Let me know if we need more,' Kate replied. 'Isabelle, would you like to help Madame DuPont find the candles and place them around the Château while I finish off some paperwork in the office?' she added.

'Yes, if I have to,' Isabelle replied sullenly. 'But I would much rather make my shell box?'

'I don't have time today, but maybe we can start it tomorrow?' Kate replied, hugging her as she got up to go to the office, just as the radio burst into life and the lights returned.

'Oh! Now we don't need them,' Isabelle announced. 'So, we can make my box instead!'

'Tomorrow,' Kate reminded her firmly. 'And we still need the candles in case we have another power cut… and think, you can make it look like our own Festival of Lights here. Under supervision, of course!'

'Oh, yes, yes!' Isabelle grabbed Madame DuPont's hand as they went together to find the emergency candles.

Once again, Kate was grateful for small mercies from those who supported her. Madame DuPont had been an integral part of Isabelle's life while growing up, from a tiny baby when her mother could not cope. The pair had a special bond, and Madame DuPont was adept at averting Isabelle's tantrums.

Isabelle and Madame DuPont found Kate a short while later to show her the selection of candles and holders, plus a box of matches they'd gathered. They'd placed them inside an empty cardboard box and were ready to be positioned around the Château.

'Look, Kate!' Isabelle remarked, picking up a large white candle. 'I've not seen candles this big before. The only ones I have seen are candles on birthday cakes.' She ran her hands up and down the smooth, waxy finish and smiled mischievously. 'We could make an amazing Festival of Light with them, couldn't we?'

'These not for you to lighted, comprends?' Madame DuPont warned, wagging her finger at Isabelle as she and Kate caught each other's eye.

'No, I understand. I won't, I promise,' Isabelle replied, turning from devil to angel as she nodded and smiled earnestly, as only she could.

***

Isabelle woke up, her heart pounding from a recurring dream. She was waving to her Mama and Papa as they passed her in their car. In her dream, she next heard a loud noise, their car somersaulting in the air, and the scraping of metal and coming to an abrupt halt after landing on its roof, with its wheels still spinning in the air!

She sat upright after finding her night light wasn't on, and it was pitch black.

'Kate!' She called out. There was no answer. 'Kate!' she called out loudly one more. Still no answer.

Shivering, Isabelle crept out of bed, feeling her way to the door. She flicked the switch – nothing! Then, remembering earlier that day, she and

Madame DuPont had left an emergency candle and matches on a small table outside her bedroom. She slipped out onto the landing.

She looked down upon the dark pit of the stairs. It looked like there were monsters slowly climbing up it – their shadows coming closer and closer. Isabelle sobbed back a scream. She tried calling for Kate again; nothing came out of her mouth this time. She felt for the table, candle holder, and box of matches. Isabelle knew she'd promised not to light the candle, but this was an emergency! She struck the match, lit the wick and watched, mesmerised, as the flame flickered and the wax around it started to melt and drip down its sides and onto the holder. With the candle in the holder in her hand and the candle alight, Isabelle took another look down the pit of the stairs. The monsters were gone!

Feeling braver and with the candle's bright light guiding her way, Isabelle decided to explore. She crept past Kate's room next to hers and ascended the stairs to the next floor, to her Mama's suite where she had been earlier with Kate. Now was her chance to look around better without Kate telling her off for touching things. Especially to get a better look through her mother's jewellery box.

She made a beeline for her Mama's bedroom and the jewellery box. She placed the candle holder on the dressing table. She opened the jewellery box, taking out and studying each piece: broaches, rings, and necklaces. She tried some of them on and peered at herself in the dressing table mirror, admiring how they sparkled in the candlelight.

'I will be a fine lady like my Mama and wear these one day,' she told herself as she posed in the mirror wearing the jewellery.

After a while, the candle's flickering made her eyes droopy and she began to feel sleepy. Isabelle closed the jewellery box lid. She picked it and the candle up and brushed past the drapes on the bed as she weaved her sleepily to the bedroom door, closing it behind her. Isabelle stopped momentarily and stood by the sitting-room window, looking out onto the night and at all the stars twinkling in the sky like Mama's sparkly necklaces and herself. Kate had told her that her Mama was also a star in the sky. She leaned further into the window, looking hard at the stars and wondering which star her mamma was.

'Ooh,' she whispered, 'Pretty…' leaning even closer to the window to see the moon, which was high in the sky but obscured by clouds.

Suddenly, she was aware of a smell like Sébastien's bonfire when he burnt paper in the walled garden. Then, out of the corner of her eye, she saw smoke. She turned her head. The curtain next to her was smouldering; small flames had started to appear where the candle she held in her hand had rested against the curtain. The curtain was on fire!

Dropping the candle, Isabelle screamed. 'Kate, Kate!' her voice rang out loud into the night as she ran out of the room, clutching the jewellery box.

Chapter 10

'*Kate, Kate.*' Kate woke up with a start on hearing Isabelle screaming out her name. *Isabelle's having another one of her nightmares*, Kate thought as she hurriedly got out of bed, grabbing her dressing gown.

Still half asleep, Kate felt her way to the door to turn on the light. She flicked the light switch, but nothing happened. She tried again… nothing. Kate sighed. Another power cut! She heard Isabelle still calling for her. Kate hurriedly felt for the door handle to open the bedroom door and retrieve the emergency candle on the small table outside her room.

Expecting to be met by darkness instead, she saw a flickering light coming from the floor above. She could see Isabelle's silhouette hanging over the railing, still screaming, '*Kate, Kate.*' She could also smell burning. *Oh, my God! It's a fire!*

'I'm coming!' Kate yelled to Isabelle as she raced two stairs at a time. On reaching the top of the stairs, Isabelle grabbed her and clung to her.

'I'm frightened,' Isabelle whimpered.

'I know, but we need to wake everyone up!' Kate gave her a quick hug and then pushed her towards the stairs. 'Go and wake Madame DuPont first and tell her to wake the others, then run and get Raimond. Quickly!'

Isabelle didn't move. She reached out wide-eyed and trembling and clung back onto Kate. Kate gently detached herself, pushing Isabelle towards the top of the stairs.

'Isabelle, go!' Kate shouted on seeing smoke coming from the Marquis suite.

'Madame DuPont, Madame DuPont!' Isabelle called out as she ran, her feet clattering on the stairs and echoing behind her.

Cautiously entering the Marquis suite's sitting room, Kate could see the fire had started to take hold of one of the curtains. A discarded candle lay nearby. Steeling herself against the smoke and the heat, she yanked hard on the curtain in an attempt to pull it down. It remained fixed. She reached further up the curtain and tugged at it again. The curtain and the pole came crashing down, missing her head as she managed to jump out of the way. A shower of sparks from the smouldering drapes shot into the air. Kate began to stamp on them to deaden the flames. She cried out in pain as her hand briefly touched the burning material while quickly folding the heavy volume of material into a mound to smother the flames.

'Oh, mon Dieu!! What is 'appening?' Raimond exclaimed as he raced into the room, holding a torch and was closely followed by Madame DuPont.

Kate sighed in relief. 'Quickly, help me grab the other curtain and put it on top of this one,' she yelled.

Without further discussion, Raimond helped lift the other curtain and heaped it onto the mound of material Kate was safeguarding. They both then stamped down on the pile of material to extinguish any remaining fire.

'How this started?' Raimond asked.

'I don't know, but I found a spent candle on the floor by the window. Isabelle and I were here this morning sorting out our mother's clothes, but as far as I know, no one has been here since,' Kate replied.

Raimond frowned. 'Let's take this top curtain off now and check if the fire 'as gone out,' he suggested. Together, they lifted the hefty volume of curtain material. 'If we pull back this curtain, we can see if it's still lighted and put water with it,' he added.

'I'll go and get some water,' Kate replied, hurrying off to the bedroom and the bathroom beyond, returning with the porcelain jug from the washstand filled with water.

As Raimond untangled the pile of material, Kate poured water over the still-smouldering areas. She rushed to and fro between the sitting room and the bathroom, refilling the jug as she went.

'I think it looks like it's out now,' Raimond said after a while.

'Oh, thank goodness!' Kate said as she sank to the floor, exhausted, cradling her burnt hand. She was trying to hold back the tears welling up behind her eyes, partly due to shock and partly due to her injury. Raimond looked across at her, his expression softened.

'Are you alright?' he asked, moving towards her.

Before Kate could answer, a voice whimpered from the doorway. 'Is it… is it alright now?' Isabelle stood wide-eyed in the doorway, trembling, with Madame DuPont behind her, trying to comfort her.

'Yes. Come downstairs to the kitchen; I think it safe to leave this now,' Raimond said kindly, scooping up Isabelle. He looked back at Kate. 'Are you okay to come?' he asked solicitously. She nodded back. 'Stay close then and 'old onto me going down the stairs if you need to. You no want to fall.'

In the light from Raimond's torch, as he raised Isabelle into his strong arms, Kate noticed she was clutching the jewellery box from her mother's dressing table. She caught Isabelle's eye and glared at her. So here was the culprit! Isabelle buried her face into Raimond's shoulder, clutching the jewellery box closer.

Shining Raimond's torch to show the way, Madame DuPont led them down the stairs to the kitchen. Kate held her throbbing hand to her chest, her face twisting with pain as Raimond turned to check that she was following. He was still carrying Isabelle, but he ushered Kate ahead of him.

'Madame DuPont, can you 'elp Madame Kate, s'il vous plait?' He called as Kate followed Madame DuPont into the kitchen. Madam DuPont lit the two candles in the holders on either end of the kitchen table.

'You hurt, Madame Kate?' Madame DuPont asked, rushing to her.

'My… my hand,' Kate stammered. 'I burnt it when pulling down the curtain to extinguish the fire. I didn't realise until afterwards,' Kate replied in excruciating pain, feeling a little foolish admitting how she'd hurt herself in front of Raimond.

'Why did you not say?' Raimond looked concerned.

'I… we had to extinguish the fire….' Kate replied awkwardly.

'Oh, non, non – this is important too!' he exclaimed.

'Sit, I look at,' Madame DuPont said, fetching the first aid box whilst Raimond settled Isabelle on a chair and collected cups to make coffee.

'And I will make your coffee – or would you like Engleesh tea – that is what you ladies ask for in an emergency, isn't it?' Raimond teased, his eyes twinkling kindly at her. Kate smiled despite her hand throbbing. *How long was it since she'd been teased by a man?*

Madame DuPont gently prised open Kate's clenched fist to reveal red, blistered areas on the palm of her hand and the tips of her fingers. 'Oh, la la! You could have been so badly hurt if Raimond hadn't been there. Come, we put it under the cold water,' she added.

Out of the corner of her eye, Kate noticed Raimond watching her. She quickly looked away before he could catch her eye, trying hard not to acknowledge the little buzz his concern for her had prompted.

Madame DuPont held Kate's hand under cold running water. Initially, the cold running water stung, causing her to cry out. Then, gradually, she began to feel relief as the cold water soothed her injured hand. Madame DuPont gently dried her hand and dressed it with a gauze dressing held on with a bandage.

'Thank you, Madame DuPont. That does feel a little better,' Kate said wearily when Madame DuPont had finished.

She suddenly felt drained and couldn't stop trembling. She huddled in on herself, cradling her bandaged hand and gratefully accepted the coffee Raimond placed in front of her. Kate glanced across to Isabelle, now curled up fast asleep on the big leather chair in the corner, covered by the rug Raimond had placed over her.

'Here, Madame,' Madame DuPont said, handing Kate a small glass of brandy and moving the coffee to one side. 'You drink. It makes you feel better than coffee.'

'Thank you. I am feeling a little shaky,' Kate replied.

Cupping her hand around the glass, Kate took a sip of the amber liquid. She could feel it burning the back of her throat as she swallowed, then the warmth of it as it travelled down into her body. Slowly, Kate relaxed. She was about to take another sip as the lights came back on. Everyone cheered.

'Thank goodness,' Kate said, breathing a sigh of relief.

'Oui and per'aps, we can do away with those candles now, Madame DuPont?' Raimond added. 'I say they're too dangerous to 'ave around, didn't I? I'll find more torches instead later.'

'Yes, yes, thank you,' Kate mumbled. She was uncomfortably conscious that Raimond had been right that candles were dangerous, and she'd gone ahead with them anyway.

Chapter 11

'You think this candle is 'ow fire started?' Raimond pointed to the discarded candle they'd found in the Marquis suite.

'I'm not certain, but it could have been. It was on the floor by the window,' Kate replied.

'But no one was in there, you say? They must've been and gone without making the candle safe. I will ask everybody tomorrow,' Raimond announced, jutting his chin out the way it did when he was incensed about something. 'They should 'ave been more careful.'

'Let's leave it to me, Raimond. I will look into it in the morning,' Kate replied firmly, glancing across at the sleeping Isabelle. She didn't want to tell him that she thought Isabelle had started the fire. It would be better for her to talk to Isabelle and deal with her, especially as she was meant to be her guardian!

'Well, if you 'ave not pulled down the curtains, so it was not spreading, all the Château would 'ave went poof,' Raimond said, turning to Kate. He smiled. 'That was very brave,' he added softly, his eyes twinkling. She felt a strange warmth in the centre of her chest that she hadn't felt in a long time.

'Oh… thank you, Raimond,' Kate replied, blushing. It was the first nice thing or, indeed, the first compliment that Raimond had ever given her.

'I will go check the fire all out and make it safe for you to go to bed,' he added. 'Then you need sleep.' He gave her a mock-stern look and she smiled back.

'Thank you. ' I am ready for my bed,' Kate replied, staving off a yawn. 'And so is this little one,' she added, gently rousing Isabelle and leading her back upstairs.

But try as she might, Kate couldn't get to sleep. Her hand throbbed as she lay in bed, exhausted but wide awake. The events of the evening were tossing around in her mind. What if this and what if that! Finally, she fell into a deep yet troubled sleep, dreaming she could not put the curtain fire out. Instead, in her dream, the fire had taken hold and the room had rapidly become an inferno. The heat inside the room was intense; the fire had engulfed the windows and spread to the room's middle. The ceiling above the window had collapsed. Charred beams, wooden joists and other debris had fallen. They were strewn about in the room, burying artefacts damaged in its path. She'd run to grab the door handle; she knew she *had* to shut the door somehow to stop the fire from spreading, but the heat from the room and the choking smoke had forced her back. In her dream, she stood outside in front of the Château. Tears were streaming down her face as she watched the flames rising high into the night sky and engulfing the Château building that had been entrusted into her care.

'I can't do it, I can't do it, I can't do it,' she was shouting as she awoke with a start, tears streaming down her face.

Momentarily, she was confused. The fire in her dream had been so real – had it really happened? Kate put on her dressing gown and climbed the stairs to the Marquis suite. She lingered outside the door. Yes, the fire had been real enough; she could smell smoke hanging heavily in the air. Cautiously opening the door, an acrid smell hit her, automatically trigger-ing her to cover her nose and mouth with her hands. She stood transfixed in the doorway. Her eyes were drawn to the floor area in front of the window. The elegant, grey linen curtains that had once hung from the windows were blackened by fire and piled on each other. Saddened by the sight before her, Kate left the room, shutting the door behind her, and returned downstairs. She needed that coffee she hadn't drunk last night – maybe even another brandy!

'If she thinks I clear up zee mess in that room, then sheez wrong! Fire has nothing to do with my job. She always wants me to do things other than my cooker,' Kate overheard Angeline announce as she approached the kitchen.

'I think Madame needs all the 'elp and support we can give 'er right now,' Raimond retorted.

Surprised by Raimond's reply, Kate hesitated before entering the kitchen, then plunged in, a forced bright smile on her face.

'Bonjour, everyone,' she said casually, glancing at Angeline before heading for the empty chair at the table. Angeline tossed her head and started to bang pots and pans around.

Madame DuPont sniffed and made a disapproving sound as she made space for Kate.

'How is your hand?' she enquired.

'It's fine, thank you,' Kate replied briskly. She didn't want any fuss in front of the staff this morning as she still had to deal with Isabelle.

'I will clean the Marquis room today,' Raimond announced. 'You must take care of your hand.'

'Huh,' Angeline huffed in the background.

'Thank you,' Kate replied, trying to ignore Angeline. 'But I think we need to get a building expert in to assess if there is any damage before we touch anything. I noticed this morning that a lot of plaster has come down where the curtain pole was,' Kate replied.

'I know someone who can do the plaster,' Raimond offered.

'Thank you, but I still think I'd like an expert to look at it. There's a big crack across the top of the window,' Kate replied.

Was this what Maurice would have done? Or her mother? She wasn't sure, but the burden of doing the right thing made her anxious. *Undoubtedly, the right thing was to get an expert in, wasn't it?* She reasoned. Raimond gave her a gallic shrug and said nothing, his expression reverting to the usual sullen broodiness she was used to from him. Angeline made more clattering. 'Angeline!' Madame DuPont admonished her.

Kate listened to the usual bickering between Angeline and Madame DuPont starting to ramp up, which set Kate thinking that maybe that was better than the highly uncomfortable silence between herself and Raimond. Kate quickly finished her coffee and got up to make a phone call. As she was closing the door, Kate overheard Raimond grumble to Angeline.

'Only trying to be 'elpful.'

'Maybe she doesn't want your help? You're only the handle man to her, after all!'

'I'm not the handyman, I gestionnaire de propriété!' Raimond retorted.

Kate hesitated. That wasn't true. Maybe she should have explained why she wanted an expert to check first? She was still unsure what to do as the guardian of the Château, Isabelle and everything! What if she got it wrong and made it all much worse? That was what she'd like to say to Raimond. She half-turned to re-enter the kitchen to explain when she heard Raimond continue, 'Well, if Madame isn't grateful, I won't offer to 'elp again! Non! She isn't like Madame Annie – so gracious. And she knows nothing. Let 'er find out 'er own way, then….'

She paused mid-turn, incensed at the unfavourable comparison. No! Why should she explain herself to him? Raimond was her employee, as was Angeline. Mother would have urged her to rise above it and not react and accept her role. And so, she would, whatever Raimond thought of her.

Kate rang Charlotte and relayed the story of the previous night's fire to her.

'Oh, my goodness! Are you alright?' Charlotte asked when Kate had finished telling her about the ordeal.

'Yes, I'm okay, thanks. I was a bit shaken and I've burnt my hand, but I'll be fine,' Kate replied, trying to make light of last night's events.

'Should I take you to the hospital for them to look at it?' Charlotte asked.

'No, it's fine, truly. Madame DuPont has put a dressing on it,' Kate replied.

'But how did the fire start, do you know?' Charlotte asked.

'I'm still looking into that,' Kate replied. 'But I think it was Isabelle.'

'What! Why?' Charlotte exclaimed.

'I'm still piecing it all together. I'm going to have a talk with Isabelle after this phone call,' Kate replied.

'Oh, poor lamb. Don't be too hard on her,' Charlotte replied.

'Well, we could all have been killed…' she started but soon changed the subject. After all, she didn't know for sure yet and Charlotte would always take Isabelle's side, anyway. 'Do you know of someone who could come and look at the wall above the window where the curtain pole was? There's not only plaster missing but also a big crack has appeared,' she added.

'As a matter of fact, I do. A friend of mine currently has a nice young man working in her Château. He's a conservator over from England. Would you like me to see if he's free to come and look?' Charlotte asked.

'Yes, please! That would be marvellous. I'll wait to hear from you,' Kate replied.

One problem down, one to go, she thought as she put the phone down. Isabelle – now, how to tackle that one? Food… food and firmness, perhaps?

Kate took a tray of croissants and milk up to Isabelle. She'd not come down for breakfast and was no doubt still asleep after her escapade last night, Kate thought. However, she was none too pleased with her, and she would tell her so in no uncertain terms.

Chapter 12

'Good morning,' Kate briskly announced as she entered Isabelle's bedroom, expecting to find her asleep.

But Isabelle wasn't asleep; she was sitting up in bed, wide awake.

'Hello,' she replied, looking sheepish.

Kate put down the tray in front of her. On the tray with her breakfast was also their mother's jewellery box.

'Well? What do you have to say for yourself?' Kate asked sternly. She hadn't meant the question to come out that way, but all the pent-up irritation with Raimond found its way into her voice.

Isabelle stared at her, then cast her eyes down before replying haltingly, 'I had a bad dream. It was dark; my night light didn't work. I called for you, but you didn't come,' Isabelle mumbled and started to cry.

The sight of Isabelle's tears melted Kate's heart for a moment. *She's only a child. She's lost both of her parents*, Kate told herself. Maybe Isabelle was too young to understand what might have happened if she'd been unable to put the curtain fire out.

'So, what were you doing with the candle in Mama's sitting room?' Kate continued, more gently this time.

'I was just looking at the twinkling stars from the window; they were like Mama's glittery necklaces. I tried to see Mama's star. It wasn't my fault. The candle just touched the curtain….'

'Hmm. Come with me, Isabelle,' Kate said.

'Where are we going?'

Taking Isabelle's hand, Kate led her up the stairs to the Marquis suite. She opened the door.

'Oh, no!' Isabelle exclaimed and burst into tears.

They stood side by side for a moment, viewing what was once their mother's favourite room that had now been reduced to a smoke-damaged mess.

'You were the cause of this!' Kate turned to Isabelle, pointing her finger. 'This is what happens when you disobey and play with lighted candles!' Kate added sternly, her irritation rekindled by the state of the room and the thought of the responsibility of setting it straight when she hadn't the faintest idea how to renovate a building like the Château.

'But it was dark. I was frightened. And you didn't come when I called,' Isabelle replied tearfully.

'We'd had another power cut and I'm sorry I didn't hear you call, but that doesn't excuse what you did,' Kate replied firmly.

'I miss Mama so much. I just wanted to look at her pretty things,' Isabelle replied tearfully. 'She let me when she was here,' Isabelle added, looking up at Kate from under her eyelashes, a large tear rolling down her cheek. But Kate was resolute.

'Yes, I know you miss her, but what you did last night was very naughty and dangerous. You could have caused a huge fire. People could have got seriously hurt. I want you to promise me that you will never use matches to light anything again. I mean anything, ever again – will you promise?' Kate said firmly.

'I won't, Kate. I promise. I was very frightened when I saw the flames.'

'And when I tell you not to touch things, you don't! I am going to keep Mama's jewellery box in my room for the time being. If you want to look at it, you must ask me, okay?' Kate asked.

'Okay, I will. I promise,' Isabelle replied, crossing herself as she did in church. 'But it wasn't my fault….'

Kate sighed. She wondered how you disciplined a child without being too heavy or soft-handed? Clearly, she would not get Isabelle to see the severity of her actions – or admit she'd been in the wrong. She would have to tackle it at some point, but not today. Today, she felt too tired, too disheartened.

Kate was finishing her lunch when the phone rang. It was Charlotte, as bright and breezy as Kate felt tired and jaded.

'Hi, it's Charlotte. I've just heard back from my friend about the man I told you about doing some work on her Château. He can see you in the morning on his way to her Château. Nine o'clock, does that suit you?'

'Yes, that will be fine, thank you!' Kate replied with relief that someone else might shoulder the burden of the renovation – someone who knew what they were doing.

'His name is Stephen Andrews, by the way,' Charlotte added. 'And my friend says she thinks you'll like him,' she said meaningfully.

With some trepidation, Kate went to find Raimond to inform him of Stephen Andrews' impending visit. Raimond was in the Orangery putting some finishing touches to a minor repair he had been doing.

'Well, if he's from London, he'll charge you fancy prices. What's wrong with 'aving a local man?' Raimond retorted on hearing about the impending visit.

Kate sighed. She should have known she'd get no cooperation from Raimond after what she'd overheard earlier that morning. Okay, she would have to toughen up – starting with Raimond.

'Just thought I'd let you know. I would appreciate it if you could make the meeting too,' Kate replied, 'so you're kept in the loop.'

She knew Raimond could be agreeable. He'd shown that last night and initially backed her up this morning to Angeline, but now he was back to his old moody self. She left the Orangery feeling even more disheartened, unsure why Raimond's attitude was getting to her so much right now. Maybe it was because she'd had a brief glimpse of a different man behind the hostile façade – a man who might be quite agreeable underneath.

Chapter 13

'Turn that noise off. It makes my head go boom!' Madame DuPont yelled over the music that was blaring out from the radio.

'It's *'Disco Bambina'* for Isabelle. She likes, don't you cara?' Angeline turned to Isabelle, whose body was gyrating in time with the music and singing along loudly.

'I do! It's fun!' Isabelle replied with a broad smile on her face.

'Italian absurdité!' Madame DuPont walked over to the radio and turned it off. '*Pah!* See! That's what I thinks,' she said loftily, tossing her head.

Kate had walked into the kitchen in the middle of yet another set-to between Madame DuPont and Angeline. Wearily, she sat down at the table. With the music off and before the next war of words, she announced, 'We have a visitor coming today at nine o'clock to look at the damage in the Marquis suite.'

'I show him into the Grand Salon?' Madame DuPont enquired.

'Yes, please. His name is Stephen Andrews,' Kate replied. 'Then perhaps you'd organise a tray of coffee to be served?' Kate added.

'Oui, Madame,' Madame DuPont replied.

'Merci,' Kate nodded, getting up to prepare for Stephen's visit.

Having put the finishing touches on her makeup, Kate gazed at herself in the full-length mirror whilst tucking her pale blue check shirt into her jeans. Her eyes caught sight of the clock as she reached for her hairbrush. *Oh goodness! It was nine o'clock already.* Her hair would have to remain as it was, hanging loose; she didn't have time to find a hairband or pins to pull it back into the business-like chignon she usually wore. Briefly, she acknowledged to herself why Phillipe had once remarked that her hair looked better hanging loose anyway. She did look less stern, with her hair tumbling around her shoulders in thick, heavy waves. Maybe even not bad for a thirty-five-year-old – no, wait, almost thirty-six-year-old! The hall clock chimed nine, alerting her that she was already late. The clock always ran two minutes slow, no matter how often she corrected it. She'd better get a move on if she didn't want to get off on the wrong foot with Stephen Andrews!

As she descended the stairs, Madame DuPont was disappearing into the Grand Salon with the visitor. She rushed in after them.

'Hello, I'm Kate Sinclair. Please do call me Kate. How do you do,' Kate announced with slight breathlessness to the tall stranger standing alone by the fireplace. *So, no Raimond in attendance to stay in the loop, then?* Kate acknowledged to herself. She squared her shoulders, trying to set her irritation aside.

'Good morning, I'm Stephen Andrews. It's very nice to meet you, Kate,' the visitor replied, smiling broadly. He stepped forward, hand extended to shake, then hesitated when she didn't reciprocate.

'I'm sorry, I would shake hands, but….' Kate extended her bandaged hand apologetically. 'The fire…'

'Ah,' Stephen looked from Kate's injured hand to her face. 'You tackled it yourself? That was very brave.'

'Or foolhardy,' Kate replied, shrugging. She was already warming to this good-looking man.

'Well, I'm delighted that only your hand got hurt. This is a lovely Château you have here. Tell me, where does the name Le Château des Vieilles Tours come from?' he added.

'Loosely translated, it means 'many towers',' Kate answered with a smile, hoping he wouldn't ask too many questions about the history of the Château.

'It must be wonderful to own and live in such a beautiful property,' Stephen remarked.

'I'm only the custodian of the Château, actually. And to be honest, it's quite daunting! It's in trust for my sister Isabelle until she's eighteen. Unfortunately, our mother and her father were killed in a car accident a few months ago,' Kate's voice trailed off. Then, sensing she may have made Stephen feel awkward, she continued, 'Please do sit down. Madame DuPont, our housekeeper, will bring us some coffee shortly. Meanwhile, I'll give you a brief outline of what I'd like you to assess before I show you up to the Marquis suite where the damage is,' she added brightly.

Kate surreptitiously studied the clean-cut, somewhat sophisticated, good-looking stranger facing her as they discussed the project. Kate noted how refreshing it was listening to Stephen's English accent. She guessed Stephen was in his early forties. Kate wondered if he was married, then quickly dragged her deliberations back to the subject in hand, chastising herself for getting distracted. Still, she did that a lot these days. Her thoughts were interrupted again as she realised Stephen was asking her a question.

'How did the fire start, do you know?' he asked.

'Oh, yes… unfortunately, a lighted candle was put too near a curtain in the sitting room. So, we've banned all naked flames from now on,' Kate replied.

'A good move. These places go up like tinderboxes. You were lucky that no one else was hurt.' Then, glancing over to Kate's bandaged hand, he added, 'Or I assume they weren't?'

'Oh, no, no one else was hurt and this is nothing really; it just got a little burnt when I pulled down the curtain that had caught fire,' Kate replied, blushing.

'Then, I was right. It was courageous of you to tackle the fire by yourself and you probably saved the Château by your swift actions,' Stephen declared.

'Well, I did have some help,' Kate added quickly, thinking about Raimond's help and how he'd taken charge when he'd arrived. She didn't deserve to be considered a heroine. 'If you've finished your coffee, shall we go and look at the damage?' she added.

'Of course,' Stephen immediately depositing his half-drunk cup of coffee on the table and jumping to his feet.

As they climbed the two flights of stairs to the Marquis suite, Kate caught herself acting as a tour guide as she relayed a brief history of the Château. On reaching the suite, Kate swung open the door, releasing the nauseating, pungent smell of the fire, which made her gasp. Stephen let out a long, low whistle.

'We've not touched anything, as you can see,' Kate explained. 'I wanted to check with you first whether you thought the rest of the plaster above the window was safe and not likely to come down onto someone underneath. I'm also worried about that big crack above the window,' she added.

'Yes, I can see the crack; it does look quite deep. I must return with my ladder to get up there to assess the damage. Then we can discuss what work might be needed. Can I come back tomorrow at about the same time?' Stephen asked.

'Yes. That will be fine, thank you,' Kate replied.

After Kate had shown Stephen out and watched him disappear in his car down the drive, she went to find Olivia. Kate found her, as she expected, in the walled garden, sitting on the wheelbarrow, talking to Sébastien. Isabelle was chasing a chicken, trying to catch it.

'We could try that new bistro in town on Saturday night,' Kate overheard Olivia saying to Sébastien as she approached.

'I think I busy on Saturday,' Sébastien replied.

'Oh? Doing what?'

Kate interrupted, rescuing Sébastien, who appeared to be struggling to think of a reply from the look on his face. 'Olivia, isn't it time for you to take Isabelle to her ballet class?'

'Oh, yes, sorry! I lost track of time,' Olivia's cheeks coloured almost as red as her hair as she looked at her watch and hastened off to fetch Isabelle, who was now right down at the back of the garden, still trying to catch the chicken.

Sébastien turned to Kate. 'Merci,' he muttered as Olivia rushed away.

'De rien. You're welcome anytime,' Kate replied, grinning. 'Ah! While I'm here,' Kate added, 'Angeline has asked if you could pick her some chard for the kitchen?'

'Oui, I take it to her,' Sébastien nodded.

'Merci beaucoup,' Kate replied with a smile.

So, Olivia was setting her cap at Sébastien, was she? The phrase her mother had used to describe girls who chased after a man had always made her smile. It also made her think about her mother, so the smile was also tinged with sadness. Kate strolled back to the Château, deep in thought about the intricacies and difficulties of relationships. They all seemed to pass her by and probably always would do now she was stuck here. At times, she felt she was being swallowed up by the all-consuming responsibility of guardianship of the Château and Isabelle. Oh, for some time out! And why not? Why shouldn't she? Isabelle would be at her ballet class and there was nothing more she could do about the Marquis suite. She would ring Phillipe!

'Hi Phillipe, are you busy this afternoon?' Kate asked when she heard the familiar voice answering the phone.

'Hi, Kate, how are you?' Phillipe replied brightly.

'I'm fine, thanks. I'm at a loose end this afternoon and wondered if I could pop over?'

'Of course, you know you're always welcome. I'm just working on some sketches in the studio for my next exhibition. Come on over and give me some ideas,' Phillipe replied.

'Thanks, I'd like that. Plus, a bit of wine and sympathy?' Kate laughed.

'You got it. See you later,' Phillipe replied.

Kate went upstairs to tie her hair back. It was annoying her now, flopping around her face. She also needed to change into clothes more suited to sitting in Phillipe's studio. Even if she wasn't painting today, she was bound to get *some* paint on her one way or another. It seemed such a long time since she'd picked up a paintbrush. Kate calculated that the last time must have been before she went to Guernsey. She longed to be able to paint today, but looking down on her bandaged hand, like escaping her ties here, that was impossible too.

She found Phillipe in his studio, head bent over a sketch he was doing. 'Hello there,' Kate sang out as she entered the studio.

'Hello back to you,' he replied. He straightened up and stared at Kate's bandaged right hand. 'I thought you told me you'd only slightly burnt your hand. So, what's with the big bandage, trying to gain sympathy?' he asked, chuckling whilst kissing her on both cheeks.

'Oh, ignore that; it's just Madame DuPont being over-cautious, but it does mean I can't paint at the moment, as it's my right hand,' Kate sighed.

'You've got another hand, haven't you? Use this one!' Phillipe replied, grabbing Kate's left hand.

'What! Paint with my left hand? You are joking, aren't you?' Kate laughed.

'No, loads of great artists are left-handed. Michelangelo, Escher, for instance,' Phillipe replied.

'Yeah, but I'm naturally right-handed; that's the difference,' Kate replied, nudging Phillipe's arm playfully.

'So? Rumour has it Leonardo Da Vinci could write, draw and paint with both hands,' Phillipe quipped.

'Well, I'm no Da Vinci, am I?' Kate chuckled.

'Look, joking aside. Unlike scissors, knives and so on, paintbrushes are not made specifically for right-handed people, are they? So, let's test the theory, and both of us have a go at painting something left-handed?' Phillipe beamed.

'Okay, why not? I like a challenge,' Kate agreed. She was starting to feel better, already having this time out for herself.

Phillipe set up an easel and canvas for each of them. He then squeezed out a selection of oil paints onto two palettes, placing them beside each easel.

'This feels weird,' Kate remarked as she picked up the brush in her left hand. She mixed a little grey, white and blue and daubed some splodgy strokes at the top of the canvas.

'What's that?' Phillipe asked, laughing.

'It's going to be a stormy sky; go away, it's not finished yet. Anyway, what's yours supposed to be? It looks like a rainbow of colours arranged in a non-descript pattern across the canvas,' Kate replied.

'That's because it is a non-descript pattern. It's called *abstract* art, Kate,' Phillipe responded, laughing.

Kate couldn't remember the last time she'd enjoyed an afternoon so much. Phillipe's company, the laughter, the banter and most of all, she had enjoyed the challenge of painting with her left hand.

'Okay, it's not a masterpiece,' Kate announced, holding up her painting. 'But it's a passable landscape picture, right?' she enquired.

'I like it. I like it very much. You've managed to capture the hills' ruggedness in the background and I love the lawn in the foreground rolling down towards the line of trees. It reminds me of … I know … that view from the room at the back of the Château that leads out to the terrace where we've often sat and watched the sunset,' Phillipe replied.

'You've guessed it! It can't be all that bad, then. It's not my usual detailed painting style, but I must admit I quite like this more abstract look. I love yours too, Phillipe,' Kate said, squeezing his arm. 'Thanks for a lovely afternoon; I really do feel uplifted and ready to tackle life's battles once more,' she giggled.

Stephen arrived at the Château the following morning as arranged, right on the dot of nine. Kate had seen him coming up the drive, his ladder perched atop his car. She opened the door to him and watched him struggle up the front steps: ladder in one hand, a large toolbox in the other.

'Good morning,' Kate greeted him brightly.

'Hello, Kate! Can I bring these in and leave them somewhere for a moment, please? I've got a couple of other things to fetch from the car,' Stephen asked. He paused, studying her face intensely. 'Sorry for staring at you. You look quite different with your hair up.'

Kate could feel a warmth spreading across her cheeks as he gazed at her. 'Yes. Yes, of course, you can leave them here in the grand entrance hall,' Kate replied, flustered as she gestured to the area just inside the door.

Stephen returned with a briefcase in one hand and a small bag in the other. 'You don't believe in travelling light, do you?' Kate said, laughing.

'Oh, sorry. I do seem to have a lot of stuff, don't I? All tools of the trade!' he laughed.

'Let's go into the Grand Salon, and I'll order some coffee before you make a start,' Kate replied.

Kate rang the bell by the fireplace. 'Do sit down,' she added, pointing to the sofa behind where Stephen was standing as he hovered indecisively. 'Coffee won't be long.'

'You rang, Madame?' Madame DuPont appeared by the door, cheeks as pink as Kate's. Kate guessed there had been another contretemps in the kitchen. Still, she felt too flustered after Stephen's comments about her hair to tackle that right at that moment.

'Yes, Madame DuPont. Could we have coffee for two, please?' Kate replied.

'Oui, Madame,' Madame DuPont replied.

'So, Stephen, are you permanently based in France?' Kate asked, attempting to recover some sort of composure.

'No. I used to work for the National Trust in England. At the moment, though, I'm freelancing, working worldwide on historic buildings in the public and private sectors,' Stephen replied. Sitting opposite Stephen, Kate noticed that he was studying her again.

Madame DuPont returned with a tray of coffee. She placed the tray on the table between the two sofas, eyeing up Stephen before she swept noiselessly out of the door.

'Thank you, Madame DuPont,' Kate called out after her.

'That sounds very interesting. It must be wonderful visiting and seeing new places all the time,' Kate remarked as she poured a cup of coffee for each of them. 'Cream and sugar?' Kate asked.

'Black, please. Yes, that is a plus side to the job, but living out of a suitcase and not being in one place for long does play havoc with your private life,' Stephen admitted.

'Yes, I suppose it must, especially if you are in a relationship.' Kate replied, looking thoughtful.

'That's very true. I was married, but because I was rarely home, it put a strain on our marriage. Sadly, it ended in divorce last year,' Stephen added, sipping his cup of coffee.

'I'm sorry to hear that. Going through a divorce can be painful. I, too, have been divorced. We didn't have children, so at least the divorce was quite straightforward,' Kate added. She was amazed at herself sharing this information with a total stranger. Yet, she felt a strange kind of affinity towards him.

'Luckily, in hindsight, we didn't have children either,' Stephen added.

'Oh, dear. We've gone a bit maudlin. Let's change the subject. What do you like to do in your leisure time, Stephen?' Then, realising Stephen's cup was empty, she added, 'Would you like another cup of coffee?'

'Yes, please,' he replied. 'I love museums and art galleries. In fact, I think there's an art gallery not far from here in Laval? I've heard it's excellent,' Stephen added.

'Yes, there is and yes, it is first-rate. There are several of Henri Rousseau's paintings hanging in that gallery. He was born here in Laval, did you know?

'No, I didn't know how interesting,' Stephen replied.

'Yes, he was a great friend of my stepfather's father. We have a copy of one of his paintings hanging in the bathroom of the Chambre de Rousseau,' Kate explained.

'I know of his work. Which painting do you have?' Stephen asked.

''*The Dream*' I'll show it to you when you've finished your inspection today if you like? It's a beautiful painting. It's just a copy, of course, but it's signed by Rousseau on the back. My mother discovered it in the attic when she first moved here,' Kate answered.

'I would love to see it and it would be wonderful to go to the art gallery with you sometime if you would like to go with me?' Stephen suggested.

'Yes. I would like that, Stephen,' Kate beamed, feeling her cheeks colouring again.

'Good. Meanwhile, I'd better get going and look at that damage upstairs,' Stephen added.

'Oh yes, of course! Would you like me to take up your briefcase and bag to save you from coming back down for them?' Kate asked.

'Yes, please, that would be most helpful. Thank you,' Stephen replied, indicating for her to lead the way.

Stephen followed Kate up the stairs to the Marquis suite. Kate placed his briefcase and bag on the coffee table. 'I'll just leave these here for you. Is there anything else I can help you with?' Kate asked.

'No, I think that's all for now. Where will I find you if I need to talk to you? It's a big place to try and hunt you down in!' Stephen said, laughing.

'Ah, good point. If you return to the Grand Salon, where we've just had coffee and ring the bell by the fireplace, I'll find you,' Kate replied. 'Lunch is at twelve o'clock today. I hope you'll be able to join us?' Kate added.

'Thank you. Yes, I'd love to. I will probably have done the preliminary checks by then,' Stephen replied.

'Great! See you down there for lunch then.'

As Kate descended the second flight of stairs, she heard whispered voices from below. She slowed as she got closer to the bottom. She couldn't see anyone, but she recognised the voices. Reaching the bottom of the stairs, Kate advanced towards the kitchen. Standing out of sight under the stairwell were Raimond and Angeline, standing very close to each other. She had intended to pretend she hadn't seen them, but they sprang apart on seeing her, forcing her to stop and acknowledge them.

'Ah, Angeline, just the person,' Kate improvised awkwardly. 'When you have a minute, can we discuss today's lunch menu in the kitchen, please?'

'Si, Madame,' Angeline replied, looking flustered, her face flushed.

Raimond stared back sullenly at Kate as he commented, 'I see the *expert* 'as arrived?'

'Yes, and he is starting work today,' Kate replied testily. 'But then you would have known that if you'd joined us at our meeting yesterday as I suggested.'

'Hmmm,' Raimond grunted. 'I saw no point since Madame had already made up her mind whatever I said.'

Angeline led the way to the kitchen, with Raimond following on behind. Kate could feel Raimond's eyes boring into the back of her. Aside from the discomfort caused by his obvious irritation that she'd engaged Stephen, she wondered why finding the pair of them together had made her feel so unsettled.

On a whim, Kate had decided to have lunch with Stephen in the dining room. She'd not taken meals in there for what seemed like months. She asked Madame DuPont to set the table for Stephen and herself as Isabelle was having lunch with Olivia in town after her dance classes; Madame DuPont nodded without comment. On being informed that lunch would be served in the dining room, Angeline pointed out, quite forcefully, that it would cause extra work, especially as it was only for two people. Kate suspected her response was most likely a cover-up for her embarrassment at being caught canoodling with Raimond. Kate smiled, thanked Angeline for her extra efforts, and left her to it. There had to be some perks to being the Chatelaine – albeit only nominal ones!

Kate left the kitchen to seek some quiet time in her office. She had to finish off the plans for next year's Châmbre d'hôte bookings and schedule the dates in the calendar for the art retreats. Although it was only late October, Kate knew her mother would have had this and the advertising organised by now. Oh, how she missed her mother at times like these! Kate felt out of her depth and restless. She looked at her watch. It was only eleven-thirty, but she'd had enough of the paperwork and decided to go and see how Stephen was getting on.

'Hello, is there anything you need?' Kate asked as she entered the room.

Stephen was perched high up on the ladder with a strange-looking instrument in his hand up against the wall.

'It must be telepathy as I was about to come and find you,' Stephen replied. 'I've almost completed the initial assessment and structurally, I think this wall is sound. I want to get a second opinion, though. I have a friend who is a structural engineer and he's in the area next week. Are you happy for me to call him to look at it?' Stephen added.

'Yes, please do. Just let me know when to expect your friend,' Kate replied. Then, on impulse, 'As it's nearly lunchtime, and if you're finished here, would you like to join me for an aperitif in the Grand Salon before lunch is served in the dining room?'

Everyone else was setting their cap at someone; why shouldn't she? Stephen was certainly attractive enough! Kate was rewarded by Stephen's enthusiastic affirmative response and somewhat taken aback by his question.

'By the way, why have you tied your hair up like that today?' Kate put her hand self-consciously to her neat chignon. 'It looks lovely loose – like you're a Rossetti maiden.'

'Oh,' Kate was lost for words. She blushed furiously. 'I've never thought of myself as anything like that before.'

'Then you should look in the mirror more often,' Stephen teased her, 'and let your hair down too,' he added with a wink.

Kate laughed awkwardly and led the way out of the room. As he followed her downstairs, she mused that maybe she was not so much setting her cap at him as encouraging an already existing interest!

'What would you like to drink?' she asked when they reached the Grand Salon.

'A dry sherry if you have one, please,' he replied, leaning against the fireplace and looking for all the world, the Château owner.

'One dry sherry coming up,' Kate replied, smiling, deftly pouring the pale liquid into a small lead-cut crystal glass and passing it to him. Briefly, their hands touched, and a frisson of excitement rushed through her.

Stephen raised his glass, 'Á votre santé!'

'Á la votre,' Kate replied, beginning to enjoy herself.

Chapter 14

Despite her shortcomings, Angeline was an excellent cook, and she produced a mouth-watering three-course lunch served efficiently and quietly by Madame DuPont to Kate and Stephen in the dining room.

'So, what are your plans for the rest of the day?' Kate artlessly asked as they finished their first course.

'As it's Friday, I have the next few days off. So, I thought I'd find a local Châmbre d'hôte in Laval and stay around there for a few days until my friend can come and look at your wall.' Stephen hesitated, then added, 'And maybe if you're not too busy, we could go to the art gallery one of those days?'

'Oh…yes,' Kate blushed and covered herself by gulping down a large mouthful of wine. It rushed to her head, making her feel lightheaded and giggly. 'That would be lovely,' she gushed. 'If you're free this afternoon then, would you like me to give you a tour of the Château and show you the Rousseau painting I mentioned?' she added. Kate was beginning to imagine how nice it would be to spend more time in this charming man's company. She was really starting to enjoy herself now. Maybe she should have 'set her cap' at someone sooner?

'I'd like that very much, thank you,' Stephen smiled, leaning towards her and raising his glass to her, 'as long as you let your hair down again!'

'Oh…' she giggled. 'Well, if you insist!'

After lunch, Kate led the way up the main staircase to the two restored guest suites in the central part of the Château on the first floor. The door at the top of the stairs led to the Chambre de Fleurs.

'Stunning!' Stephen exclaimed as he entered the sunlit bedroom. The afternoon sun poured in through vast windows directly ahead, bathing the room in a vibrant glow and onto the yellow-striped wallpaper of tiny yellow sunflower daisies. Framing the windows were drapes of soft yellow silk, held back with gilded metal tie-backs. The arched doorway in the corner led to the bathroom, its walls decorated in cream with green accessories.

'What a magnificent suite,' Stephen added, clearly impressed.

'Thank you,' Kate replied, showing him out the door and along to the next suite. 'Next, we have the Chambre de Hugo,' Kate announced as they stood outside the large cream-painted door. In contrast to de Fleurs, the room was much darker and more manly. Stephen pulled out and studied a few of the books from the bookcase underneath the window.

'Most of those Victor Hugo books – *Les Misérables, The Hunchback of Notre Dame* – my mother found in the attic and around the Château,' Kate told him. 'It gave her the inspiration for the theme of this room.'

'Another wonderful room – so much atmosphere. I can imagine Victor Hugo sleeping in that bed,' Stephen marvelled.

'Now for the last suite: Chambre de Rousseau. It's at the back of the Château and a bit of a climb, I warn you!' Kate laughed.

Kate led the way up the steep spiral staircase.

On reaching the last bend, Stephen slowed and stopped. 'Phew! You're right – that's some climb up here. Have you ever thought of putting in a lift?' He asked, panting.

Kate laughed. 'I'm often asked that question. You do get used to it,' she replied, giggling. 'Take a look at the bathroom through there,' Kate added.

Stephen entered through the arched doorway in the corner of the room, which led into the turret bathroom. The walls were painted soft green – a muted backdrop to the room's centrepiece: a luxury, antique gold-painted cast-iron claw foot bath.

'Henri Rousseau's *'The Dream'*!' Stephen exclaimed as he spotted the painting. 'How wonderful it looks in these surroundings,' he added, gazing out through the turret's curved window down to the terrace court-yard below and the magnificent views of the forest and the sweeping hills beyond.

'It is rather splendid, isn't it?' Kate agreed. An impish whim came to her. 'Look, I've had an idea. All three suites are unoccupied at the moment. Would you like to stay here for a few days instead of trying to find a Chambre d'hôte in town?' Kate added.

'Really? That would be wonderful, thank you!' Stephen beamed.

'Splendid! That's settled, then. Except, which suite would you like?' Kate asked.

'No contest! It has to be this one, please. If it does nothing else, it will keep me fit climbing up and down those stairs,' Stephen laughed.

'I will get Madame DuPont to make up the room for you. Okay, onwards for the rest of the tour. Attic next,' she announced.

'Excellent! Lead the way!' Stephen laughed, cupping her elbow solicitously and urging her gently on.

Her mother had told her that the attic was an untapped treasure trove which had hardly been touched in years. It still hadn't, by the looks of the mounds of dusty and cobwebbed *treasures* that had laid there for years. If Kate had *her* way, it would all be dumped. On the other hand, Stephen appeared fascinated by many of his finds. So much so that Kate, on several occasions, had to urge him to hurry along.

'I think we'd better start making a move downstairs. Olivia and Isabelle will be home soon,' Kate suggested eventually, much as she wished their tour could have lingered longer. 'But we can always come back up here another day to go through this junk if you like,' she added with a coy sideways look.

'Now that would be great! There's some fascinating *junk*, as you call it,' Stephen laughed, setting aside what he was looking at and joining her by the door.

'Okay, it's a deal,' Kate agreed, smiling. 'But now, if you like all things old, I'll show you a room downstairs that's not been restored or used in years. It's at the back of the house, underneath your suite.'

'Lead on!' Stephen replied.

On reaching the bottom of the stairs, Kate led him down to the end of the corridor and a well-worn pair of double doors. She pushed open the doors to reveal a large quarry-tiled room and a strong, musty smell that took Kate's breath away.

Suspended from the middle of the ceiling was a majestic chandelier hanging down from a plaster Fleur De Lys ceiling rose. The same Fleur De Lys pattern continued on the cornice, running around the room. The papered walls were faded and partly hanging off in places. A tall marble fireplace on the far wall showed signs of damage and wear.

'This room makes me feel so sad to look at it; it looks so unloved. Yet, underneath all the deterioration, it's a very special room. You can watch the sun setting over the forest and the hills beyond from these glazed doors. It's a spectacular sight. My mother and stepfather had planned to restore it during the closed season this year and turn it into a Winter Salon. Sadly, it's beyond my capabilities to do it alone,' Kate sighed.

They stood side by side in companionable silence, gazing out of the glass double doors at the majestic vista before them. With their arms almost touching, Kate could feel the heat of Stephen's body. Stephen turned to Kate.

'You need a partner,' Stephen said softly, looking intently down at her. 'Kate… I've got a proposition for you.'

Chapter 15

The clock in the grand entrance hall struck eight o'clock as Kate descended the stairs. Through the bannisters, she noticed that Stephen was already sitting at the dining room table, head bent over the newspaper spread out before him and a cup of coffee in his hand.

'Good morning,' Kate greeted him, her heart pounding fast on seeing him. Kate noticed he was dressed casually in a black roll-neck jumper and jeans. She brushed her hair away from her face, suddenly feeling self-conscious that she'd not tied it back as usual. He'd said he liked her hair hanging loose, but maybe she'd taken it the wrong way?

'Good morning,' Stephen replied, looking up from the newspaper and smiling. His eyes appeared to linger appreciatively on her. Maybe she hadn't taken it the wrong way after all.

'You're up and about early for a Saturday,' Kate remarked, trying to sound casual as she allowed her loose curls to swing across her face to hide her reddening cheeks. 'Has Madame DuPont been looking after you?' she added.

'Yes. Thank you. As you can see, I've already eaten some delicious croissants and pastries. However, I still have some coffee left in this cafetiere if you'd like a cup?' Stephen replied, picking up the cafetiere.

'Mmm, please.' Kate sat opposite him, her cheeks settling into a rosy glow and her heart steadying into a more regular rhythm.

'Good. Now I'm going to set you to work, even though it's the weekend! What's a French seven-letter word for a shared annuity?' Stephen asked, looking back down at his newspaper, then back up at her with a twinkle in his eyes.

A shared annuity? Was he teasing her or flirting with her? Either way, she was enjoying the buzz it was giving her,

'It's a bit too early in the morning for riddles,' Kate laughed.

Stephen put the newspaper down. 'Oh, sorry. I always do the crossword over breakfast; it gets my brain working,' he replied with a grin.

'I must admit, I'm no expert with crosswords, especially cryptic ones, but I'll have a go. Do you have any letters?' Kate asked.

'The third letter is N and the last is E,' Stephen replied.

Kate sat down at the table and gazed into space for a moment. 'Tontine!'

'Tontine? Well, it fits, but what *is* a Tontine?' Stephen asked, filling in the letters in the crossword.

'In French law, a couple buying a property can use an en tontine. On the death of one party, the surviving partner becomes the sole owner and is regarded as having been so since acquiring the property. It can also be a sort of mortality lottery dating back to the seventeenth century,' Kate added.

'A seventeenth-century mortality lottery?' Stephen quizzed with a wry smile.

'It works a bit like an investment plan, a sort of annuity. Each subscriber invests a sum of money on which they are paid dividends. As each subscriber dies, their share is redistributed amongst the surviving subscribers. The entire investment is passed to the remaining survivor,' Kate explained.

'Lucky last man down then!' Stephen laughed.

'Yes, but I wonder if they spent their days looking over their shoulder?' Kate laughed out loud, then added, 'not so funny, really, though. My mother and Maurice wouldn't have thought so, at least.'

'Oh, is that what happened to them?'

'Sort of – a bit more complicated, though.'

'Ah, well, that leads nicely into what I wanted to talk to you about. You mentioned at our first meeting that you don't own this Château, that it's in trust to Isabelle until she's eighteen? Does this allow you, as guardian, to make changes to the Château?' Stephen asked.

'Are you referring to your proposition yesterday?' Kate asked.

'Yes. I did wonder afterwards whether I might have got a bit carried away with my suggestions for the Winter Salon. You may not have the authorisation to carry out such plans?' Stephen asked.

'I think I'd probably need to ask our solicitor if I wanted to start knocking walls down. What you are suggesting, though, should be fine as its internal cosmetic improvements to the Château. If we have the funds to do the work,' Kate replied grimly.

'Ah, well, if money's the issue….'

'No, no, I'm joking. Carry on with the plans, please,' Kate put down her coffee and settled back in her chair to imply he had her attention.

'Okay then, I'll start putting together some proper plans and estimates for you. Does that suit you?' Stephen asked.

'Yes, that's fine, but not today: it's the weekend. You mentioned you'd like to visit the Museum and Art Gallery in Laval. Would you like to go today?' Kate asked, mentally crossing her fingers that she didn't sound too forward.

'Yes, I would love to,' Stephen grinned, then copying her earlier move, 'but don't you have to look after Isabelle?' he added.

'It is Olivia's day off, but Isabelle has a dance workshop all day, so I don't need to watch over her today. She's due to be picked up shortly, so I need to ensure she's got everything and see her off first, though. I'll see you downstairs in about an hour?' Kate replied.

'Sounds a great idea, thank you,' Stephen replied, folding up his newspaper and downing the coffee in his cup. 'I'll be ready and eagerly waiting!'

Kate stifled a giggle and went to look for Isabelle. She found her in the kitchen, eating breakfast and holding court on her aspirations of being a dancer to everyone around the table. From a very young age, Isabelle had said she wanted to be a dancing girl when she grew up. Their mother had thought Isabelle would grow out of it, but there were no signs of that happening yet.

'Hurry up with your breakfast, Isabelle and go and get ready; you're being picked up in about fifteen minutes,' Kate interrupted Isabelle in full flow.

'I *am* ready,' Isabelle retorted, her mouth full of toast.

'What about your hair?' Kate replied, giving her long curly locks a flick. 'I need to put it into a chignon.'

'Oh, yeah. I forgot…'

Kate breathed a sigh of relief as she waved goodbye to her little sister. Isabelle waved back enthusiastically through the car window, grinning from ear to ear, clearly excited about the day ahead. It wasn't so much that Kate wanted to see the back of her for the day. Looking after her was a delight; however, getting through to her was sometimes a struggle. Today was one of those days! Isabelle often reminded her of the Henry Wordsworth Longfellow poem:

"There was a little girl,
Who had a little curl,
Right in the middle of her forehead.
When she was good,
She was very good indeed,
But when she was bad, she was horrid."

Kate climbed the stairs to the sanctuary of her bedroom for ten minutes of peace and quiet after the whirlwind, getting Isabelle out of the door on time. She studied herself in the mirror. Was this outing a date she was going on with Stephen? When she'd dressed earlier, she'd not given much thought about the day's plans and had thrown on her favourite jeans with a sloppy multicoloured jumper and loafers. But now… would this do for a trip to the gallery and museum, she asked herself. Yes! Stephen wasn't exactly dolled up, she reasoned. Anyway, given that it was late November, she would be putting on her trusty hooded sheepskin duffle coat to keep her warm. It wouldn't matter what was underneath it, she argued with herself. But what about if they stopped for lunch? Maybe a different top?

Ten minutes and a complete outfit change later, Kate found Raimond hovering at the bottom of the stairs.

'I noticed a damp patch in that unused backroom that overlooks the terrace,' Raimond said brusquely.

'Yes, Stephen and I noticed it yesterday, too, when we were deciding what to do with the room,' she replied frostily.

'Oh? Are you planning to be doing something to it then?' Raimond asked, frowning.

'Yes, Stephen is drawing up some plans for me to look at,' Kate answered.

'Don't you think…' Raimond started to say but stopped as Stephen joined them in the grand entrance hall.

'Well, I'm ready. I hope I haven't kept you waiting,' Stephen said brightly, nodding politely to Raimond before standing next to Kate. He, too, appeared to have changed. He was now sporting a well-pressed pair of trousers and an expensive-looking cashmere V-necked jumper over an open-necked check shirt and sports jacket.

'No. Not at all,' Kate replied, smiling up at him but aware that Raimond's expression was far from a happy one.

'Let's go then,' Stephen said gaily, offering his arm and steering her towards the door.

'Raimond, would you mind letting Madame DuPont know I'm going out with Stephen for the day, please? Also, we'll probably have lunch out,' Kate added. She tried to stop the mischievous grin she could feel brewing from spreading across her face as she looked back at Raimond's outraged one. She turned back to Stephen, smiling before Raimond could reply. 'Your car or mine?'

'Yours, I think. You know your way around here!' Stephen replied. 'And I can admire the scenery and you whilst you drive.' Kate linked arms with Stephen as they went out of the door. She could feel Raimond's eyes boring into her back, allowing the impish grin to finally spread across her face. She, too, could flirt with someone. Let's see how *he* likes it, she thought to herself!

Kate felt a bit like her little sister – excited at the prospect of a day out with Stephen and being able to share her love of art with him. As they drove along, she pointed out landmarks and places of interest. It didn't seem that long ago that she had taken the same journey herself for the first time with her mother, who had pointed out the same landmarks. Finally, they approached the multi-arched, medieval bridge crossing the Mayenne into the town. Kate directed Stephen's attention to the Château de Laval, sitting on a rocky spur overlooking the city and the river.

'That's where we're heading, up there,' Kate explained, pointing to the Château.

'Is that the art gallery then?' Stephen asked.

'No, that's Château de Laval. Inside the castle grounds is *Le Musée de Laval*, which has the most beautiful collection of naive art in Europe, several of which are by Henri Rousseau,' Kate replied.

'I'm really looking forward to seeing it all,' Stephen remarked enthusiastically.

They parked the car and made their way to the castle, which served as a backdrop to the museum.

'There is also a tour of the castle available,' Kate explained as the castle came into view. 'Including a trip up a never-ending steep flight of stairs to an unusual fortified wooden tower right at the very top. See it up there? I did it once with my mother,' Kate added, laughing nervously.

'Well, after climbing up the stairs to my suite back at the Château, I shouldn't find it too much of a problem. I'm game to climb up there if you are?' Stephen said, laughing.

'I'm afraid I will have to sit that one out. I'm not very good with heights,' Kate replied with a nervous laugh. She still remembered climbing up there with her mother and having a panic attack at the top when she realised how high up it was.

'What, no head for heights?' Stephen teased.

'That's right. I suffer from acrophobia,' Kate replied, feeling embarrassed admitting her weakness so early on in what – maybe – could be a budding relationship.

'I'm so sorry. I wouldn't have joked if I'd have known,' Stephen placed his hand lightly on her shoulder and left it there.

'No, not at all. My mother said next time would be easier,' Kate answered.

'Well, I could hold your hand if you want to try?' Stephen asked. 'Any excuse,' he added, winking at her.

Kate laughed nervously. 'I'm not sure I want to try, to be honest. My mother thought it's always easier the second time you do anything because it's no longer the unknown. Even if it is still tricky to accomplish.'

'Well, the offer stands. I'll help you if you'd like to try?' Stephen offered, giving her arm a comforting squeeze.

'Okay, maybe today *is* the day to test her theory!' Kate replied, mentally crossing her fingers behind her back so she didn't make a fool of herself like the last time she attempted it. Much to her relief, they were told at the information desk that the tower tour was not operating that day. Still, Stephen's offer and his throwaway comment about holding her hand stayed on her mind.

'Well, bang goes your chance to test your mother's theory!' Stephen declared. 'And mine to hold your hand, although…' he playfully held his hand out.

'Yes, it seems it wasn't meant to be,' Kate laughed, inwardly glad that she didn't have to potentially make a fool of herself in front of Stephen. 'This way to the art exhibition. I think at least that is open,' she added, wondering whether to take his hand.

Stephen solved her dilemma by tucking her arm through his. 'It looks like it, come on,' he replied, striding out with Kate tagging along to the entrance. 'It looks as though this place has everything: sculptures, paintings and drawings, and it's so well laid out,' he gushed, pointing to the gallery map on the wall next to them.

'Yes, I agree. As I mentioned earlier, it's a wonderful place,' Kate responded as Stephen steered her around, pausing here and there to study some of the paintings in greater depth.

'Look at this Rousseau painting. It says it's the view of the Pont de Grenelle. Do you know this bridge?'

'Yes, I think I do. I'll take you there one day if you like?' Kate replied.

'That would be great.' He paused and smiled down at her; she could feel her cheeks reddening again. 'This painting is quite different from *'The Dream'*, the one in my suite, isn't it?' he continued as if he hadn't noticed her blushes. 'That one is painted in rich reds, greens, blues and more dreamlike,' Stephen observed. 'This Grenelle Bridge is very architectural, symmetrical, and painted in muted creams and browns. I could spend all day here; it's so different from some of the art galleries in London,' he added.

'I agree. This is certainly one of my favourite galleries,' Kate replied, smiling then looking at her watch. 'I think, though, we should get some lunch before they stop serving. Anyway, I'm famished, aren't you?' she laughed.

'Okay, you've twisted my arm. Lead on, show me the best place for lunch. My treat!' Stephen replied, grabbing Kate's arm again.

They followed the towpath alongside the river Mayenne until they reached the centre of the medieval town, where a bustling street market was operating in the cobble-stoned market square. Rows of local food producer stalls were laid out under a sea of blue and white canvas awnings. The tables were laden with plump fruit, fresh vegetables, cheeses, sausages, salamis, olives, and assortments of loaves of bread and pastries.

'Oh, wow! Just looking at all that food makes me feel hungry!' Stephen remarked.

'Well, just as well you are hungry because here we are,' Kate laughed, pointing to the little sidewalk café where she and her mother had first met Maurice.

On entering the café, they were greeted by the garçon and shown to a table. Once Kate and Stephen were seated, the garçon disappeared. He returned with a basket of bread and a carafe of water, which he placed on the table, leaving them to study the menu.

'How good is your French?' Stephen asked, perusing the menu and frowning.

'Passable,' Kate replied, laughing. 'I've eaten here several times, so I could suggest what to order or order for you if you like?' she added.

'Okay, maybe I'll leave the ordering to you, but no snails, oysters or frog's legs!' Stephen replied, pulling a face.

'I'm totally with you there!' Kate replied, giggling.

Kate rattled off their order in French to the garçon while Stephen looked on in awe.

'So, what have you ordered? It sounded impressive,' Stephen asked, leaning closer across the table.

'I thought we'd stick to something simple – French onion soup with crusty bread, followed by Sea Bream and a salad. Plus, a bottle of Pinot Grigio. We can decide on dessert afterwards,' Kate replied.

'That sounds parfait,' Stephen returned, his eyes displaying amusement as he spoke. Kate wasn't sure if he was teasing her or was just happy. Whichever it was, she liked it!

They sat sharing stories over lunch like two old friends. Kate recounted parts of her life story: how she'd been adopted, then found by her mother and ended up in the Château. Stephen talked about the work that took him around the world and his painful breakup with his wife. They became so absorbed in sharing their stories that they lost all track of time until they realised they were the only ones left in the café. Apologetically, Stephen paid the bill and they hurried out of the café giggling like two naughty children. Kate linked her arm with Stephen's, and he pulled her close as they walked back along the towpath to collect the car. Kate felt relaxed and positive for the first time in a long time. The burdens of the past few months were forgotten momentarily. She had felt comfortable sharing her inner thoughts with Stephen and suspected he'd felt the same about her. Was she fantasising, or could it be she'd met her soul mate? She wondered.

Chapter 16

Over the next few weeks, there was a buzz of activity, but not so much of the romantic kind. Work had commenced in the Marquis suite after Stephen's structural engineer friend had given the all-clear for the renovation work to go ahead. Kate also spent hours discussing and fine-tuning the plans with Stephen for the Winter Salon renovations. Sometimes, she wondered if the closeness they had shared during the trip to the gallery had been a figment of her imagination. Stephen was so business-like with her now. She tried to set aside the closeness they had shared and concentrate on the task at hand. And anyway, perhaps it was good to work alongside someone before you got romantically involved with them – learn how to respect each other, she told herself.

Having been forced to be the guardian of the Château, Kate was determined to leave her mark on it and create something awe-inspiring. It was an exciting time with so much going on, except for Raimond constantly challenging Stephen's decisions about the work to be carried out, the materials and costs. Still, on some occasions, Raimond had proved correct to challenge Stephen and relished telling Kate to tell her what he had exposed.

'You should use lime plaster on those walls to fill between those laths!' Raimond snapped at one of the workmen one day after picking up a trowel of plaster and studying it.

Stephen walked through the door. 'What's wrong?' he asked.

'These men are using the wrong plaster. They're using ordinary plaster, not lime,' Raimond retorted.

Stephen studied the plaster on the trowel Raimond was holding. 'You are right. They were instructed to use lime plaster. There's obviously a case of poor communication somewhere,' he sighed.

'Ha!' Raimond responded with a wry smile.

On another occasion, Raimond caught sight of Stephen's latest invoice that was on Kate's desk.

'Is that zee bill for all the plasterwork in the Marquis suite?' Raimond inquired.

'No. It doesn't include the fibrous plaster repairs to the cornice over the window. Stephen is waiting for a quote from another company to do that part,' Kate replied.

'You are being overdone. That's too much. I could 'ave done it a lot cheaper. They see you coming!' Raimond criticised.

Kate picked up a piece of paper and pretended to study it. She wasn't going to get into a war of words with Raimond today.

'How much 'e charge you for the room at the back?' Raimond questioned.

'Do you mean the Winter Salon?' Kate replied.

'Yes. What fancy plans 'as that Stephen got for that room?' Raimond taunted.

'Stephen hasn't got all the costs back yet,' Kate replied. And anyway, she told herself, what business was it of Raimond's?

'Pah!' Raimond retorted, leaving the office and shutting the door noisily behind him.

'Why do I let that man get under my skin?' Kate voiced out loud. She sighed heavily. After that exchange, Kate lost concentration on the paperwork before her. She hated doing it anyway; she would much rather go to her studio and paint. Flinging the paperwork back onto the desk, Kate stood up in resolution: and paint, she would!

Kate was on her way to her studio when she spotted Raimond helping Angeline carry a tray of crockery into the kitchen. She couldn't make out what Raimond was saying but guessed it was something intimate by his soft and low tone and body language. In turn, Angeline was giggling and fluttering her eyelashes at him. Kate could feel her teeth starting to grind. Why did she feel jealous watching him being so attentive to Angeline when he'd just been so obnoxious to her? And what was Angeline playing at? Only the other day, she'd caught her sidling up to poor Sébastien in the kitchen, doing much the same thing as she was doing to Raimond now!

Kate marched over to the old coach house that her mother had converted into an art studio, deliberately putting the pair out of her mind. Whilst it was bright and sunny, she doubted it would be warm enough to sit and paint in the studio today. Still, it would be away from everyone – all the demands, all the confusing relationships, and pressures…

On entering the cavernous building with its high vaulted ceiling of oak beams meeting in a series of arches and its thick, uneven stone walls and cobble-stoned floor. Kate found the studio was like an icebox. Picking up some art supplies, she took them back to the Château and set up a temporary studio in the Winter Salon and hid in there instead.

It was fast approaching Christmas; maybe she could make some little cards for the staff or splatter away with her left hand and do more of her 'splodge' style paintings. Her hand was much better now, but the skin still felt tight and sensitive and she wouldn't want to risk irritating the burn scar with oil paint. Yes, that's what she would do; that would cheer her up. She was deep in thought as she painted an imaginary landscape of the view from the double glass doors. The Winter Salon door burst open noisily, making her jump.

'I've lost another tooth! Look and this one is loose too,' Isabelle yelled, rushing into the room.

'Oh, yes, I can see!' Kate replied, laughing once she recovered from the surprise.

'That means the little tooth mouse will come again tonight like he did last week, won't he?' Isabelle asked.

'Yes, yes, I imagine he will. You'd better put it somewhere safe then, hadn't you?' Kate replied, giving Isabelle a hug.

'I know; I'll put it in that empty matchbox Madame DuPont has in the kitchen,' she replied, skipping out of the room.

Kate made a mental note to remember to 'play' the tooth mouse later after she'd made her Christmas cards.

Over breakfast the following day, it seemed Christmas was on Isabelle's mind, too. Kate wondered how she would celebrate her first Christmas without her Mama and Papa.

'Do you like Christmas, Angeline?' Isabelle asked.

'Oh, yes. I'm so excited; I already needed a pee in my pants,' Angeline replied, followed by one of her loud and infectious laughs.

Madame DuPont raised an eyebrow and, turning to Angeline wagging her finger, uttered, 'Tsk, Tsk.'

Angeline shrugged and flounced off to the far end of the table, muttering about *vecchie signore*.

Kate intervened before an argument could gather momentum. 'Isabelle, how about we go foraging around the grounds after breakfast for foliage, berries and whatever else we can find to decorate the dining room and Grand Salon?'

'Oh, I'd love that. I used to do it with Mama,' she replied with a grin that showed off her dimples.

'Yes, I did too, before you were born,' Kate replied. 'Madame DuPont, do we still have those old trugs?'

'Oui, Madame. I'll get Sébastien to bring them to you,' she replied, giving Angeline a stern glance as Angeline perked up at the mention of his name. 'Whilst *we* are clearing up,' she added pointedly. Kate stifled a giggle at Angeline's affronted expression and whisked Isabelle out of the kitchen to find their coats.

Once Sébastien delivered the trugs and they were wrapped up warmly, Kate and Isabelle set off. Isabelle ran ahead excitedly, swinging her trug in her hand. Kate strolled leisurely behind with her trug slung over her arm and a pair of secateurs in her gloved hand. Then, spontaneously, Kate burst into song: '*Good King Wenceslas looked out on the feast of Stephen!*' Isabelle stopped, turned around, giggled and joined in.

Kate and Isabelle returned from their mission rosy-cheeked from the cold and with their trugs overflowing with ivy, holly branches laden with berries and pinecones. They hungrily finished a welcoming bowl of hot vegetable soup and crusty bread before setting about decorating the dining room fireplace and the Grand Salon with just as much enthusiasm as they'd had for foraging,

'It looks wonderful, doesn't it?' Kate remarked, standing back to admire each room now filled with a sweet, citrusy aroma.

'It does, yes. Very pretty,' Isabelle agreed, snuggling in closer to Kate. 'Are we going to have a tree?' Isabelle asked with great anticipation.

'Yes. I've asked Sébastien to bring it into the Grand Salon tomorrow for us to decorate,' Kate replied.

'Oh, goody,' Isabelle replied, holding Kate's hand and swinging her around.

'I think an early dinner and bed for you tonight, young lady, so you're fit and ready to decorate the tree tomorrow,' Kate announced.

'Will you read me *The Little Prince* then? It's my favourite book,' Isabelle implored. 'Papa bought it for me last Christmas. He used to read it to me in French,' she added.

'Yes, of course I will, but my French won't be anything like Papa's!' Kate replied, laughing as she drew her sister close and wrapped her arms around her.

There was a hive of activity in the kitchen the following day. During breakfast, Madame DuPont announced to Angeline that she would make the family's favourite traditional Christmas Bûche de Noël.

'Okey Cokey. Whatever floats your goat, but you stay on your side of the table. I make my Nona's Panettone today,' Angeline retorted.

'Can I help decorate the log with chocolate icing, please, Madame DuPont?' Isabelle begged.

'Yes, of course, ma chérie,' Madame DuPont replied, smiling at Isabelle.

'Come, Isabelle. Let's leave the ladies to their cooking and go and see if Sébastien has delivered the Christmas tree and the box of tree decorations to the Grand Salon yet.' Kate suggested as she ushered Isabelle out of the way of an impending war between Madame DuPont and Angeline.

Standing in the far corner of the Grand Salon stood a ten-foot-tall, lush-green pine tree. Its slender top fanned out into a wide girth down to the bottom. The sweet pine smell filled the room.

'Oh, wow!' Isabelle exclaimed.

'It *is* a magnificent tree, isn't it?' Kate marvelled. 'Okay, let's set to and decorate it,' she added.

The log fire crackled in the grate. Christmas music played on the radio as Kate and Isabelle selected ornaments from the box and carefully placed them on the tree. Hanging each of her mother's decorations she'd collected over the years, Kate was overcome with a tinge of sadness as she shared some of her mother's stories behind them with Isabelle.

'Oh, look at this one, Kate. It's a kangaroo dressed as a Père Noël,' Isabelle giggled.

'That was one James sent to Mama the first Christmas he was living in Australia,' Kate replied, smiling.

'It's got a baby in its tummy!' Isabelle added.

'That's called a joey,' Kate replied.

'Look at this one! What's that supposed to be stood by the Christmas tree and the pile of presents?' Isabelle asked, handing Kate a sparkling white disc hanging from a gold ribbon.

Kate laughed. 'It's a Guernsey cow. I think Aunty Nellie sent it to Mama to remind her of her time when she lived in Guernsey,' Kate replied.

'I miss Mama and Papa, Kate,' Isabelle said, tears starting to well up in her eyes.

'I know, I do too, but we're going to have a lovely Christmas together, aren't we?' Kate replied, giving her a hug. 'Don't forget, when we've finished here, you promised to help Madame DuPont ice the yule log.'

'Oh, yes. I get to taste the chocolate icing too; yummy,' Isabelle replied, visibly brightening at the thought.

With the tree fully decorated and groaning under the number of ornaments and lights they had placed on it, they stood back, hand in hand, to admire their handiwork. At the top of the tree was a silver star nearly touching the ceiling. Tiny, twinkling red, green, white, and blue lights bounced off the white garland wrapped around the tree and glistened on the ornaments.

'Parfait!' Isabelle exclaimed.

'Yes, it is and when you get up on Christmas morning, Père Noël will have left piles of presents under the tree. If you're good, of course,' Kate added, winking.

'I will be good, promise,' Isabelle replied, skipping off happily out the door towards the kitchen.

The following day, Kate woke with a start: she opened her eyes and saw Isabelle standing beside her bed.

'Wake up, wake up!' Isabelle was shouting. 'It's Christmas. Let's see what Père Noël has left under the tree!' she exclaimed excitedly.

'Breakfast first. Then, when everyone is downstairs, we can all go into the Grand Salon and open the presents,' Kate mumbled, still half asleep.

Isabelle pulled a face and plopped herself on Kate's bed, watching her get dressed with a sullen look.

'Joyeux Noël, Madame DuPont et Angeline,' Kate and Isabelle chorused together as they entered the kitchen.

'Merci, Joyeux Noël,' Madame DuPont replied.

'Buon Natale,' replied Angeline.

One by one, the rest of the household joined them around the table, including Stephen, whom Kate had persuaded would be welcome to join them for Christmas. Madame DuPont and Angeline served breakfast. Kate was pleasantly surprised that they appeared to be working together for a change.

'If we're all finished, shall we go through to the Grand Salon and open up the presents?' Kate announced.

Kate hung back to collect the last-minute gift she'd hidden for Isabelle as the rest of the household filed out of the kitchen and into the Grand Salon.

'Are you coming, Madame?' Raimond asked.

'Yes, I'm coming now,' she replied, following him out the door.

In the half-light in the corridor, Kate noticed that Raimond had stopped and turned to face her. His face was so close to hers that she could smell alcohol on his breath. Without warning, he pulled her roughly towards him – Kate let out a scream.

Chapter 17

'Kate, are you okay?' Stephen called out as he advanced down the corridor at speed.

'Yes, I'm fine … I think,' Kate replied, looking flustered.

'Madame wasn't looking where she was going. She would 'ave walked into that trolley if I 'adn't moved her out of the way,' Raimond interjected after steering Kate around the food trolley.

As she lowered the present she was carrying, she saw it had been directly in her way.

'Thank you, Raimond. I didn't know it was there. It would have been awkward getting past it carrying this box,' Kate replied. 'Will you move the trolley somewhere out of the way before someone else trips over it, please?'

'Pah!' Raimond replied as he unceremoniously grabbed the trolley and noisily pushed it down the kitchen corridor.

'Here, give that box to me,' Stephen said, reaching for the box Kate was carrying and ushering her in front of him. 'Are you really okay?'

'Yes. I am now, thank you. Raimond just startled me. I wondered what he would do for a moment – silly of me!' Kate replied. 'Let's go and join the others,' she added, trying to compose herself.

Isabelle had settled herself under the tree surrounded by the presents. 'Is that for me?' she exclaimed excitedly, flinging her arms wide on seeing Kate.

Kate sat down on the floor next to her. 'This is a present from Mama and Papa. They bought it for you for Christmas,' Kate replied as she placed the brightly wrapped box in Isabelle's lap.

Isabelle sat for a moment, frowning and staring at the gift-wrapped present. 'But they got killed in their car. So how can they buy me a present?' she asked defiantly, jumping up, sending the box tumbling onto the floor. 'You're a liar!' she yelled, barging past Kate and dashing out of the room.

Kate grabbed the box and ran after her. She saw Isabelle heading into the garden room, her favourite place to hide behind the assortment of coats hanging up, boots and other paraphernalia. Kate followed, shutting the door gently behind her.

'Isabelle, I know this must seem very confusing to you,' Kate gently said as she spotted Isabelle crouched behind a box in the corner of the room. 'Mama and Papa bought this present for you a while ago and gave it to me to hide. So, this is a very special present for you from them. Won't you open it?' Kate added encouragingly.

Isabelle hesitated. 'They went away and didn't say goodbye to me. I hate them!' she yelled tearfully.

'I know they left you, but they didn't want to. It was an accident,' Kate replied softly, placing the box on the floor next to Isabelle and crouching beside her. Kate put her arms around Isabelle, wiping away the tears streaming down her face with her handkerchief. Her own grief of spending her first Christmas without her mother paled into insignificance. 'I know they would have given anything to be here today, but sadly, they can't. I am sure they are looking down on us and would want us to be happy. Shall we try?' Kate urged.

Isabelle sniffed and wiped her nose with the back of her hand. 'Okay, I'll try.'

Kate passed the handkerchief to Isabelle without comment and pushed the gift-wrapped present towards her.

'I can't wait to see what's in here, can you?' Kate said brightly. 'Shall we open it together in here, where no one else can see?'

Isabelle remained silent but nodded, still sniffing. She carefully started to unwrap the box, her hands trembling as she picked away the sticky tape sealing the paper. Kate wondered what was going through Isabelle's mind. Generally, her little sister would unwrap presents at breakneck speed by grabbing and tearing away the paper as she went. But today, Isabelle was unwrapping the box slowly, carefully and thoughtfully. Kate wondered if she would ever get to the gift at the rate she was going. With the wrapping paper finally off, Isabelle removed the lid, gently pushed the tissue paper inside the box aside and sat staring at its contents.

'Oh, she's beautiful,' Kate exclaimed on seeing a doll with its bisque porcelain head appearing to gaze up at them. Its dark hair was arranged into two braids that fell onto its shoulders. Kate picked up the doll. 'Look, the doll's bonnet matches her dress. What a pretty lilac it is! And look, she's wearing pantaloons which match her frilly apron. Oh, feel how soft her body is! You'll be able to cuddle her,' Kate added, smiling, passing the doll to Isabelle.

Isabelle took the doll and studied it. She traced its painted-on button nose with her fingers, its brown eyes and the freckles on its cheeks. Then, without a word, she pulled the doll close into her chest, burying her face into the doll's face and hair.

Kate sat silently beside her. Finally, and quietly, Kate asked, 'What shall we call her?'

'Jacqueline. I will call her Jacqueline,' Isabelle answered, her head suddenly popping up with a smile stretching across her face.

Kate lay in bed that night, pondering over the day's events. It had turned out to be a special day after all, albeit tinged with sadness that her mother and Maurice weren't there to share it. She'd had long telephone calls with her siblings, James and Elisabeth, her only remaining close relatives. Still, somehow, that didn't make up for the void she'd felt not having her mother around. After a shaky start, Isabelle had bounced back to her usual buoyant self. She had gone to sleep, exhausted, holding onto Jacqueline and tomorrow – albeit without their mother – was another day.

And so it was. Even though it was Boxing Day, Kate returned to work. Progress on the Winter Salon was gathering pace: the marble fireplace surround had been restored and a new log burner had been installed. 'Just the thing for those chilly evenings,' Kate had reasoned with Charlotte when she'd dropped by to see the progress. 'I plan to use this room often in the winter when we have no guests. It's much cosier and a more convivial room than the Grand Salon,' she added.

'I can't wait to see it finished,' Charlotte remarked as she wandered around the room, surveying it from different aspects.

'Well, I'm not sure when that's going to be. It's been a major project. First, Stephen found dry rot and mushrooms growing out of the woodwork, so he had to rip out the wall panelling and the floor in the corner to replace the joists,' Kate explained.

'Now you've stripped the walls; are you re-papering them?' Charlotte inquired, pausing by a window.

'No. The walls are going to be painted. This is the colour in this paint pot,' Kate replied. 'Stephen thought painted walls would work best.'

'It's red!' Charlotte exclaimed.

'Well, more of burgundy, really. It will complement the terracotta tiles, don't you think? And it will make the room feel warm and more enveloping?' Kate responded.

'Well, I'll withhold my judgement until I see it finished. I don't have the same vision or design flair as you or Stephen,' Charlotte added pointedly. She paused, then added, 'So, I guess you'll be hanging onto Stephen for a while yet?' The casual comment was belied by the knowing look that went with it.

'I think it may be a while, yes,' Kate replied, lowering her eyes and blushing.

She didn't want to share with Charlotte that she'd started to get close to Stephen and would miss his company when he moved on. Yet, the temptation to tell someone about her feelings towards Stephen grew as time passed. Even though their relationship hadn't moved on from the closeness they had shared on their outing to the gallery, other than Stephen's occasional teasing remark and appreciative look. Sometimes, Kate felt he was deliberately keeping her at arm's length while making it clear he might want to do otherwise. With Stephen blowing hot and cold and Raimond mainly blowing hot, heavy and moody, life was confusing!

Chapter 18

Kate had lain awake for hours listening to the dawn chorus through her partially open bedroom windows that morning. The sun's early morning rays streamed through them and bounced off the walls. The March winds were winding down. Spring was here at last – and maybe it was time to think about the future?

Kate stretched and went over the day's plans in her mind. The past few months had kept her busy and occupied: the Winter Salon restoration, keeping the peace between Madame DuPont and Angeline, and fending off Raimond's never-ending negative and argumentative comments had all been exhausting – not to mention looking after Isabelle!

'This life is not exactly the one I had planned,' she grumbled out loud, 'But how can I change it?'

At least there was light at the end of the tunnel with Don and Florence's impending arrival later that day. They'd sold their house in Cornwall and were coming to stay and help for the summer. Don in the garden to sort out the unkempt look that had befallen it since being left in Sébastien's care, especially the potager garden. Florence to help run the art workshops as she'd done over the past few years. They'd also acted as surrogate grandparents to Isabelle over the years. *At least!* she thought, *their presence will take some pressure off me!* Kate's mood lifted considerably at the prospect of their company.

In fact, she'd lingered so long thinking about life, problems and Isabelle that the dawn chorus had long been overtaken by the smell of breakfast and Isabelle's scampering feet on the stairs. Kate dragged on her clothes before popping into the suite of rooms she'd prepared for Florence and Don, ensuring it was all in order. It passed inspection. The rest of the morning soon disappeared in minor tasks and paperwork until she was dragged away from her morning drudgery by Isabelle calling out from the grand entrance hall doorway.

'They're here! Quick, come quickly, Kate! They're here!'

Kate saw Florence and Don's car coming up the drive, just as Isabelle had announced. She hurried from the office to greet them at the main entrance but found that Isabelle had beaten her to it.

'Papi! You're here!' Isabelle cried, racing down the front steps to meet the car as it drew to a halt in front of the Château.

Don was the first to step out of the car. He was smartly, yet casually, dressed in a light green cashmere jumper over his multi-coloured check shirt and light camel-coloured slacks. His short, greying hair was smoothed down with oil, which Kate suspected Don also used on his pencil-shaped moustache. He picked up Isabelle and swung her up in the air as she squealed with delight.

'You're getting mighty too big for this *ma gurrl*,' he drawled, putting her back on the ground. She giggled and shook her wayward curls mischievously.

'I'm going to be nine years old in August, Papi,' she announced proudly.

'Almost into double figures!' Florence called as she stepped out of the passenger's side of the car, nearly getting caught up in her long flowing floral skirt. Her deep-set blue eyes twinkled, lighting up her rounded face framed by her unruly, silver-white curly hair. *As bohemian as ever*, Kate thought kindly as she watched the happy little scene from the top of the steps.

Florence held out her hands to Isabelle. 'Come, let me look at you!'

'Hello, Grandy, I've missed you,' Isabelle gushed, falling into Florence's arms.

'I have missed you too,' she replied, squeezing Isabelle tightly.

Kate descended the steps and joined them. 'Welcome, both of you. It's so good to have you back here at Le Château des Vieilles Tours.' She gave them each a hug and a kiss on each cheek in turn. 'Let's go in and have some refreshments. I'm sure you could do with some after your journey,' Kate added. 'Did you travel overnight on the ferry?'

'Yes. As you know, we always like to get an early start,' Don replied jovially, directing Sébastien where to unload the luggage from the car. 'What's your English saying – the early worm catches the bird?'

'The early bird catches the worm,' Kate corrected, laughing, then noticed Don was winking at her and she relished his leg-pulling with a feeling of joy inside her. Things would be so much more light-hearted now Florence and Don were here!

Kate helped carry some of the luggage that Sébastien had piled up in a mound at the bottom of the steps as he retrieved them from the car. Florence, as usual, looked as though she'd come for the duration.

'Don't worry, I'm not moving in permanently. You know me, I never did travel light. And now I'm married to my dear Don, I don't have to worry how much luggage I have,' Florence said with a tinkling laugh.

'I wish you were staying here forever, Grandy,' Isabelle said, grabbing Florence's hand.

'One day, one day,' Florence replied, laughing.

'I'm putting you and Don in the Chambre de Fleurs suite just until we re-open,' Kate said as she directed Sébastien to take the luggage to the suite. 'There's lots of work going on in the Château now, so I'm not opening the bed and breakfast side of things until around July time,' Kate explained.

'Oh, thank you! I love the view from the window in that room; it inspires me to paint it – one day perhaps,' Florence replied.

They all made their way to the kitchen and sat down to the lunch prepared by Madame DuPont and Angeline. Kate was relieved to find that calm had now prevailed between the two of them. She'd been aware of them running around the kitchen like headless chickens all morning, getting in each other's way and arguing about the ingredients in some of the dishes.

'I no listen to you. I bury my head in the ground!' Kate had heard Angeline yell.

Kate hadn't hung around to hear Madame DuPont's reply. Instead, she deliberately stayed clear for fear of interfering and worsening things. To this end, Kate kept her fingers crossed that the lunch would turn out edible without too many cooks spoiling the broth.

Kate need not have worried – Angeline and Madame DuPont had prepared a feast. The table was well set with a significant number of dishes for everyone to help themselves.

Despite her best intentions, Kate found herself next to Stephen over lunch. Although their conversation was confined to discussions about work and the Winter Salon restoration, Kate caught Don watching them each time she looked up. Finally, when lunch was over, Don drew her to one side.

'Stephen seems a nice man?' Don observed.

'Yes, he is very knowledgeable,' Kate agreed, smiling.

'So, nothing more than a working relationship then?' he asked, grinning.

'Of course not!' Kate replied indignantly, but she could feel her cheeks colouring. 'Unfortunately,' she added ruefully under her breath.

Don shrugged. 'Never say never,' he grinned, glancing meaningfully towards Stephen and winking at her. 'Maybe in time....'

'Maybe ....' Kate sighed.

'By the way, I've been approached by an acquaintance of mine, Marie Schmidt, about submissions for her next exhibition. I met her the first time I visited France when I made a worldwide arts and culture film. She has an art gallery in Paris and is looking for new painters to exhibit. Would you like your work to be considered?' Don asked.

'Me?' Kate gasped. 'Surely my work isn't good enough to hang in a gallery?'

'Both Florence and I think you're good enough. Why not let Marie decide? She's happy to come and look at your work whenever it's convenient for you.'

'Well, I'm under no illusions,' Kate replied sheepishly, 'but thank you for thinking of me,' she added with a smile.

'Think about it and let me know what you decide in the next day or two,' Don grasped her shoulder in his big, confident hand and squeezed it reassuringly.

'Yes, I will. Thank you again,' Kate replied, her head buzzing.

Her gut instinct told her to forget it – she had enough on her plate for now – but she would call Phillipe and see what he thought.

'Of course, you've got to take up the offer!' he gushed when she told him. 'Isn't this something that both you and I have strived for? To get recognised. I've got my work exhibited; now it's your turn,' Phillipe's excitement almost made the phone vibrate as they discussed what Don had said.

'Well, she's not seen my work yet, of course,' Kate giggled.

'Then she's in for a treat to my mind. Good luck, Kate – and let me know how the meeting goes, won't you?' Phillipe replied.

'I will do. Thanks, as always, for listening,' Kate said, hanging up the phone but already worried about what she would show the prominent gallery owner.

Don arranged the meeting with Marie Schmidt for the following week. Florence had helped Kate choose a selection of her paintings and together, they'd hung them in the art studio.

'Why aren't you including these ones?' Florence had asked.

'Oh, they're no good. Those paintings were just an experiment painting with my left hand when I burnt my right one in the fire. Phillipe egged me on one day to try painting left-handed,' Kate chuckled. 'I call them my *splodges*.'

'Well, I think you should include your *splodges*. Look at this one. I think I know the landscape –the view from the room you are restoring. I recognise the lawn sloping down to the line of trees and the hills beyond. And what about this one. A field of red poppies – how gloriously vibrant they look.'

'Well… okay if you think so. I'll include a couple of these then,' Kate replied, shrugging her shoulders.

Assuming it would result in nothing, Kate wasn't apprehensive about the upcoming appointment until the day of Marie Schmidt's visit arrived. Kate was filled with nerves.

Kate had imagined Marie Schmidt as an outgoing, flamboyant artist in her fifties, dressed like Florence, in a long flowing skirt or dress and sandals on her feet. She'd imagined her hair would be pulled up in a make-do chignon, with wispy pieces of hair hanging down at the back that had escaped the elastic band. However, apart from being right about her age, Marie Schmidt was nothing like Kate had pictured her. She was, instead, a tall, stocky lady with a Pinocchio nose. A shock of ginger afro hair protruded under a colourful turban, matching her wrap-around dress. She was vibrant and infused with a kind of power Kate had never experienced before – the power of self-belief. Kate was bowled over and in awe; she was glad Don was there to do the introductions.

'I'm pleased to meet you,' Marie said with a heavy German accent, shaking Kate's hand vigorously.

'Likewise,' Kate replied quietly, feeling intimidated and wishing the ground would swallow her up.

Don turned to Marie. 'If you'd like to follow me, we'll go to the studio and look at Kate's work.'

Marie nodded curtly and gestured for Don to lead the way. Kate followed them, as timid as one of the mice they'd ousted from the Winter Salon at the start of renovations.

Marie walked around the studio, stopping at each of Kate's paintings before moving on to the next one without comment. She completed the entire circuit, all without saying a word. She paused for a moment before setting off on the second circuit of the studio. This time, the paintings were either dismissed briefly or studied for what appeared to be an age. Kate, in turn, held her breath, waiting for Marie's comments, but still, Marie remained silent.

Finally, she spoke. 'I particularly like these,' she said, pointing at Kate's left-handed painted pictures. 'They show such a wonderful expression of style and technique. Such depth and vision. I want to offer you the opportunity to get your work noticed by exhibiting them in my gallery if you agree?'

Kate stood transfixed. Had she heard Marie correctly? She wanted to hang her *splodges* in her gallery.

'What do you think, Kate?' Don was asking, bringing Kate back down to earth.

'Um… well, yes. Thank you, that will be fine,' Kate replied, trying not to look amazed.

'Good,' said Marie, her clipped tones indicating the end of the discussion. 'I will be in touch with the details and you must do many more – you understand? More, in case these sell. Now I must go.' She nodded to Kate and then strode out of the studio with Don, leaving Kate bemused that her *splodges* might be displayed in a well-known Parisian Art Gallery!

Kate began to have doubts. Was this something she really wanted to do? Putting herself out there in the limelight? Was she ready for that? She had wished for change, but this?

Chapter 19

On hearing the news over lunch later that Kate's paintings were to be hung in a gallery in Paris, congratulations were voiced all around. Stephen pressed her hand and whispered to her 'special lady', leaving her flustered and heady but still as confused about how he felt about her; she blushed and threw him a questioning look. To everyone else, Kate smiled politely and nodded her thanks.

Still, she chastised herself, never mind introductions to Parisian gallery owners to confuse her. She needed to concentrate on the more important matters, the art retreat and Florence, who sat across from her at lunch and was here to set up the first art retreat of the season. As Raimond got up from the table, she called after him, 'Raimond, what are you working on now?'

'I 'ave my checks to the Château to do,' he replied gruffly.

'Okay. Over the next few days, would you get all the easels out of storage, please? Then check them all over, making any repairs needed and then give them a light sanding and revarnishing, please?'

'That's not my work. I gestionnaire de propriété – I look after Château, not bits of wood,' Raimond replied, scowling.

'Yes, I know your primary work is that of Property Manager. Still, I think it was agreed with the Marquis that you would also help with anything else needed.'

'That was an agreement with the Marquis. As he no longer 'ere, I just gestionnaire de propriété now since my advice is so inutile pour Madame!' Raimond replied, storming out of the door and slamming it behind him.

The room went quiet; everyone stopped talking and turned to look at Kate. She sunk down in her chair, red-cheeked and embarrassed.

Madame DuPont broke the silence, 'If you have all fini, I clear!' She announced stridently.

With that, there was a deafening sound of chairs being scraped across the flagstone floor as the household departed hastily. Don turned to Kate. 'Do you have a minute? I want to talk to you in the Grand Salon?' Don asked.

Kate nodded in agreement. Anything to get out of this room!

Don gestured for Kate to sit next to him on the sofa. The fire in the Grand Salon hadn't been lit and the room felt chilly. Kate shivered.

Don took Kate's hand, 'So what was that all about from Raimond?'

'Uh, we just don't see eye to eye about Stephen's work.'

'Ah, Stephen again. Just about his work or something else?'

Kate frowned. 'What else could there be?' she asked, surprised.

'Florence and I are worried about you, Kate,' Don said, putting his hand over hers.

'I'm fine. There's no need to worry,' Kate replied with a half-smile. She was still reeling from Raimond's outburst but didn't want to show her vulnerable side to Don.

'In the short time we have been here, I can see that you are doing an excellent job. I know looking after Isabelle and running the Château can't be easy. However, I think you are trying to take on too much,' Don declared. 'You're not your mother, and no one expects you to be,' he added.

'And what choice do I have?' Kate snapped indignantly, then could have bitten her tongue. She didn't mean to show how much she resented his comments. But after all, she'd run the Château and looked after Isabelle for the past six months reasonably successfully. Yet here was Don comparing her with her mother, finding her wanting without even being here to see what she had achieved!

'I'm not criticising you. I only want to help. As a suggestion, why don't you consider employing an Estate Manager? They would work directly with you to plan and execute the overall projects and manage the Château and the staff, including Raimond. That would free up your time to concentrate on Isabelle and your painting,' Don urged in a caring tone.

'Ha! I can't imagine anyone managing Raimond,' Kate replied haughtily.

'How about Stephen? You seem to get along well together – would he not be an ideal choice for Estate Manager? Or is there more to your relationship with him than a work colleague, despite what you said earlier?'

'No. I have already told you Stephen and I work together. We don't have a close relationship. I thought we did....' Kate replied, her cheeks beginning to colour, 'but as it turns out, we don't,' she continued to his hopeful expression. If only Don knew how much she wished it otherwise.

'Maybe it's Raimond you're too close to? Despite his outburst at lunch, maybe he's tipping his cap at you. Perhaps deep down, he admires you. That might explain his awkwardness – he is trying to get your attention. Do you know what his feelings are towards you? Are they reciprocated?' Don inquired.

'Feelings for Raimond? Ha! That's a crazy notion,' Kate exclaimed. 'That gruff Frenchman can't stand me. You saw that for yourself today.'

'Oh, I wouldn't be so sure of that. I've seen how Raimond looks at you when he thinks you're not looking,' Don replied.

'No, I think you're definitely wrong there, Don!'

'We'll see. Think over my suggestion about employing an Estate Manager though Kate?' Don added, standing up and leaning over slightly to kiss her forehead.

After Don had left the room, Kate remained in the Grand Salon, mulling over Don's idea of employing an Estate Manager. As much as she hated to admit it, it did make sense. Managing everything on the estate, looking after Isabelle and now – if she were to take up Marie Schmidt's offer – it would stretch her to the limit. And then there was Stephen, or rather, there wasn't Stephen… something *would* have to give. Her art, perhaps? Oh, she didn't know! She would see if Phillipe was free for supper tonight and discuss it with him.

As it was a balmy evening, Kate arranged for supper to be served on the floodlit terrace that led out from the Winter Salon's double doors at the back of the Château. Kate sat with a glass of wine, anxiously awaiting what Phillipe would advise.

'This is like old times,' Phillipe remarked as he rounded to the Château corner and found Kate sitting on the terrace drinking a glass of wine.

Kate smiled. 'Yes, isn't it? We've sat and watched a few sunsets from this terrace, haven't we? And on the odd occasions after a late party, sunrises too?' she replied, giggling and staring at the slowly sinking sun. 'Would you like a glass of wine?'

'Yes, please,' he replied. 'So, what's this all about? Your visit from Frau Schmidt?' he asked with a wink.

'Frau Schmidt, yes….' Kate sighed. 'She was a little scary,' she continued, draining her glass and refilling it before relaying her meeting with Marie Schmidt.

Phillipe raised his glass in a toast. 'But inspirational, too, huh? What paintings has she suggested you exhibit?' he added.

'My left-handed ones, my *splodges*, would you believe? That's if I take her up on her offer,' Kate replied.

'*If* you take up her offer? Are you *seriously* having second thoughts?' Phillipe queried.

'Well, yes and no. I'm feeling a bit out of my comfort zone, to be honest,' Kate replied. 'I am pulled as to which way to go. Don has suggested I employ an Estate Manager to free up my time for my art,' Kate added, 'and Stephen would be the obvious choice….'

'That's a great idea! So, what's stopping you?' Phillipe cried.

'I agree, in principle. I know I've complained to you in the past about always being the bridesmaid, never the bride, and it's silly, really – I've now got the chance to change all that. So, what's stopping me?' Kate replied, turning to him, her expression puzzled.

'You tell me? I'd jump at the chance,' Phillipe said, studying her. 'Was it Frau Schmidt who was scary, or was it what she suggested scary – stepping out into the limelight?'

'I knew you'd understand!' Kate exclaimed, turning to Philippe. 'That's exactly it! I'd be jumping out of the safe haven of my life in the Château into the spotlight. Am I brave enough to seize this once-in-a-lifetime opportunity?

Chapter 20

'Summer holidays are the best!' Isabelle announced, bounding into Kate's bedroom. 'What are we going to do today?' she added excitedly.

'It may be the first day of the summer holidays for you, young lady, but it's not mine. I have an art retreat to run with Grandy, remember?' Kate replied, laughing at Isabelle dancing and skipping around the room.

'Can't you forget that boring old art retreat and take me somewhere instead?' pleaded Isabelle.

'I'm afraid I can't take you anywhere today. I'll try and take a day off, maybe later in the week, and we can go out somewhere for the day then. How does that sound?' Kate asked.

'Boring!' Isabelle replied, slumping herself down on the end of Kate's bed.

'Olivia is back from her long weekend tomorrow; I'm sure she will take you out. So that's something to look forward to, isn't it?' Kate reasoned.

'Oh, she's soppy. She's only interested in Sébastien and shopping,' Isabelle replied, pouting and picking at the edge of the bedcover.

'Come on, cheer up. Look, it's a lovely day outside.' Kate gently drew her off the bed and away from the bedcover, which was beginning to fray. 'Let's go down for breakfast – Angeline is making pancakes today. Afterwards, you can come over to the art studio with me, help Grandy set up, and then chat with the ladies in the art group. What do you think?' Kate added with a smile.

'I suppose,' Isabelle mumbled. Kate propelled Isabelle, still pouting, through the door and downstairs to the kitchen. After a plateful of Angeline's pancakes, Isabelle returned to her gregarious self, skipping on ahead of Kate and heading for the art studio. The long school holidays stretching out before her filled Kate with dread. There was still so much to do without the worry of entertaining Isabelle. Not that she should *have* to babysit Isabelle – that should be Olivia's job. Isabelle was right, though – Olivia's head was in the clouds most of the time!

As if I don't have enough to think about, Kate thought. Although the Winter Salon was nearing completion, there were still rooms to get ready to reopen the Chambre d'hôte. There were the art retreats to run, the day-to-day running of the Château and the staff.

'I really need to think seriously about Don's idea and employ an Estate Manager,' Kate found herself saying aloud.

'Pardon?' a voice from nowhere inquired.

'Oh, Pat, I didn't see you there,' Kate replied, laughing, noticing one of the art group perched on a stool in the rose garden. She was painting one of the deep pink roses on the canvas resting on her easel. 'I was talking to myself, as one does,' Kate chuckled.

'I do that all the time,' Pat replied, laughing.

'You've started painting early this morning?' Kate commented.

'Yes. I wanted to capture this rose while it still had these tiny rain droplets from our shower of rain overnight.' Pat replied, continuing to painstakingly outline a droplet on one of the petals.

'It looks delightful – you've captured how the droplets glisten in the sun beautifully,' Kate admired.

'Thank you, Kate,' Pat replied, blushing. 'I copied how you did it on one of your still-life paintings hanging in the studio. Yours looks so life-like; I'm not so sure about mine,' Pat giggled.

'Thank you, Pat,' Kate replied, now her time to blush with the compliment. 'I'd better get going before they send out a search party,' she added before heading off through the rest of the rose garden towards the art studio.

The air was pungent with the heady perfume of the roses post-rain, and Kate breathed it in greedily, relishing the sense of being at one with nature that the outside gave her. On reaching the studio, Isabelle was nowhere to be seen. Several of the art group had already set up their easels and equipment in the gravelled area outside. Florence met her in the doorway.

'Good morning, Kate,' she greeted Kate brightly. Florence was nothing like a conventional sixty-something – she stood all of five feet, and there was nothing of her. She was as vibrant as the rose Pat had been painting. Her bright red-painted toes peeked out from the end of her battered-looking sandals. She wore a bright yellow tee shirt with a large flower motif blazoned across its front. The vivid orange and black diamond-patterned skirt completed the uncoordinated ensemble. Kate also noticed a streak of red oil paint on her cheek.

'Good morning, Florence. I see you've already got the group started. Thank you. It's been a slow start for us, being the first day of the school holidays,' Kate said with a frown. 'Have you seen Isabelle?'

'Yes, she's been here, but I'm afraid she was getting in the way a bit, so I've sent her over to *help* Don in the walled garden,' Florence replied with a smile.

'Good plan! I wonder how long that will last,' Kate replied, laughing.

***

'Hello, young lady, where are you heading?' Don asked, falling in beside Isabelle as he headed toward the walled garden.

Isabelle grabbed his hand and swung it to and fro as they walked. 'Grandy says you need some help, so I've come to help you, Papi,' Isabelle replied with a big grin.

'Oh, but shouldn't you be in school?' Don inquired.

'It's school holidays, silly, so I can help you *all* day if you like?' Isabelle replied.

'Thank you. That would be wonderful. I could do with another pair of hands. How would you like to start with some weeding? Then there's planting out some lettuce plants and watering them in?' Don asked. 'Oh, and Sébastien also needs some help to spread some mulch,' he added as an afterthought.

'That all sounds like hard work. I want to help with fun things,' Isabelle replied, kicking some loose soil into one of the garden beds.

'It's a busy time of the year and they are all the jobs I need to do today. Perhaps when I'm not so busy, we could find you a piece of the garden of your own to grow something in – radishes or carrots, maybe. What do you think?' Don asked.

'I don't like radishes – yuk! Will there be worms? I don't like worms,' she replied, pulling a face.

'What's wrong with worms? Earthworms are a gardener's best friend,' Don laughed.

'That's just silly, Papi. How can you have a worm as a best friend?' Isabelle asked, scowling.

'They are not just a best friend for you and me; they also play an important part in other ways. For example, they help improve the soil in the garden, so they are a plant's best friend. They are also a best friend of the wildlife. See that Robin over there? Well, they will make a delicious dinner for him and his family.'

'Oh, yuk!' Isabelle exclaimed, screwing up her nose. 'That's disgusting! If you haven't got any fun things for me to do, I'm going back to the studio to see if Kate has any fun things she needs help with!' Isabelle exclaimed, giving the loose soil in the garden bed a final kick with her foot before scampering off.

Don stood smiling and scratching his head as he watched her disappear around the corner of the garden wall, then shrugged and carried on weeding.

***

'Can I help with anything, Kate?' Isabelle asked, interrupting her sister, who was in conversation with one of the art group participants.

'Oh! Just a moment, Isabelle. I'm busy with Barbara at the moment,' Kate replied, gesturing to Isabelle to wait. Kate continued her conversation with Barbara while keeping one eye on Isabelle, whom she noticed had stormed off to the far end of the studio, pouting. Once finished with Barbara, Kate turned and glanced around the studio for Isabelle. She found her outside, sitting on a pile of logs, head in hands, looking sullen and swinging her legs. As she was about to go over to her, she heard her name called.

'Ah, Kate. Just the person,' Stephen said as he rounded the corner of the studio, walking straight past Isabelle without acknowledging her. 'I need your decision on these curtain rods for the Winter Salon windows,' he added, pushing the brochure in his hand before her.

'Oh great, you've got the leaflet. Let's go into the studio out of the sun and have a look,' Kate replied excitedly. 'We're almost there now, eh?' she added with a big smile.

'We are indeed!' Stephen grinned back as he ushered her on ahead of him. 'The proof of a great partnership!'

Kate glowed with delight. She'd almost forgotten Isabelle until one of the logs from the log pile she was sitting on tumbled noisily and rolled onto the pathway as she walked ahead of Stephen. She turned and glared at Isabelle.

'Isabelle,' she began, but Isabelle scowled back at her and hunched herself almost double. 'I won't be long,' she continued, leading the way into the studio. Kate hoped that Isabelle couldn't get into too much mischief just sitting on the logs, even if she did kick some of them around.

When Kate had gone, Isabelle got up from the log pile and went to the studio door. She peered in and saw Kate and Stephen sitting close to each other, heads bent over the brochure and seemingly oblivious to her.

'I only came to see if you wanted some help,' she called to them. 'I'm going to see if Madame DuPont does instead,' Isabelle announced huffily, kicking the doorpost. Kate half-rose to call her back, but Isabelle was already stomping out the door.

'She's just bored – school holidays and nothing to do. Madame DuPont will find something for her – cookie-making or … well, something.…' Isabelle heard Kate say to Stephen.

'Huh!' Isabelle said, marching across the lawn towards the Château.

Chapter 21

Isabelle found Madame DuPont and Angeline in the kitchen. They were standing face to face, practically touching noses. Angeline had her hands on her hips, and Madame DuPont's indomitable figure was squared onto her, with her hands clasped in front.

'Just cos you do church doesn't make you holy, like same if you stand in a garage doesn't make you a car!' Angeline yelled.

'If I agree with you, we'd both be wrong!' Madame DuPont retorted.

'Do you need any help?' Isabelle asked timidly.

'Oh! cara, come, sit. I fetch you some milk and biscotti I bake today,' Angeline smiled, beckoning Isabelle to sit at the end of the table.

'Thank you,' Isabelle replied quietly, cautiously squeezing past Madame DuPont, who stood with her hands clasped in front of her and glowering at Angeline.

'Angeline, do you need help with anything?' Isabelle asked, her mouth full of biscotti.

'Non. Why want work? You enjoy your holiday, cara,' Angeline replied, smiling as she headed for the walk-in larder.

'Madame DuPont, I'm bored! Do you have anything for me to do?' pleaded Isabelle.

'Olivia left that book you have to read for school. Have you done that?' Madame DuPont replied, looking up from the household account books and peering over her glasses.

'No, that's boring, too!' Isabelle grumbled as she got up from the table. She stuffed the last biscotti in her mouth, and then she had an idea! Rifling through a pile of glossy magazines in the basket near the kitchen door, she grabbed a handful and headed for the door.

'Well, if everyone will be boring and treat me like I'm invisible, I'll show them. I will hide out in my secret place and stay there forever. It will serve them right if they can't find me. And when it gets dark, they will start to worry,' Isabelle declared aloud as she stomped out of the kitchen, hoping Madame DuPont or Angeline would hear. But they were already about to start round two.

***

'What are you doing 'ere ma chérie?' Raimond asked, spotting Isabelle curled up on a large cushion tucked away in the corner of the garden room she'd sought sanctuary in several hours later. She'd been so excited when she got up that morning; it was the first day of the long school holidays. Finally, she would be able to do anything she wanted. No schoolbooks, no homework. Freedom! But it wasn't turning out to be fun; everybody was busy and ignoring her. It was as though she didn't exist!

Startled by Raimond standing over her, Isabelle replied defensively, 'I'm not doing anything,' her voice trembled. He was another grown-up who could get cross with her sometimes. But Raimond surprised her – he pulled up a chair and sat beside her.

'Why are you hiding away 'ere?' he asked kindly.

'Because everybody is busy and I'm in everybody's way,' she replied sullenly, casting her eyes down and trying to hide what she had on her lap under her skirt.

'Oh dear,' Raimond pulled a face and stuck out his lower lip as they did in the cartoons when they were sad. 'What 'ave you got there?' he gently asked as she shuffled the magazine as far under her legs as possible. Isabelle reluctantly pulled the magazine out and showed him.

'One of Olivia's magazines. I'm looking at the pictures; I'll put it back before she comes home from her weekend away, promise,' she replied quickly. Then, seeing he still didn't look cross, she added, 'Look at this one; these are dancing ladies. They are so pretty. I think their sparkly costumes are so pretty too, don't you?' she asked.

Raimond took the magazine from Isabelle and studied the picture. 'Oui. I do think they are très bien. These dancers are très fameux, Folies Bergère in Paris,' Raimond replied, smiling the magazine back to Isabelle.

'I'd like to go there one day and watch them dance,' Isabelle said, admiring the picture before her. She had been daydreaming that she, too, would be a dancer like them one day.

'It's not a place for little girls, ma chérie,' Raimond replied with a frown. 'Pretty dresses or not.'

'Why not?' Isabelle demanded.

'When you're grown up, you comprendre that some places aren't right for jeunes dames like you,' Raimond replied, squeezing Isabelle's hand lightly.

'I don't care what you say! I *will* be a dancing girl like them when I grow up!' Isabelle replied, jumping up and flouncing towards the door. 'You just watch me!' she shouted as she ran out of the room and raced up the stairs before Raimond could follow.

Isabelle stood at the door leading into the Marquis Suite, her Mama and Papa's rooms. With her hand poised on the doorknob, she hesitated before turning it. Her recurring bad dreams of the night of the fire were still fresh in her mind. Her nightmares, at times, got mixed up with the ones she had about her Mama and Papa's car accident. They were not in a car in those dreams but caught up in a fire, screaming for her to help them, but she couldn't save them. At other times, she could see herself standing in the middle of the sitting room in the Marquis Suite. The flames were *so* big, much bigger, and hotter than Papa's flames he made when he lit the Grand Salon fire. The ceiling was falling on top of her and she was too frightened to call out for help. Because of these dreams, she had been too scared to return to the Marquis Suite after the fire – this would be the first time.

She gingerly opened the door and glanced around the room. There was no sign of the blackened walls over by the window. New curtains had been hung to replace the ones her candle had set fire to. The furniture had been put back to where it had always been. She didn't know what she had expected to see and breathed a sigh of relief that there were no signs of the fire and that her Mama and Papa's room was back to normal. She went to their bedroom, making a beeline for Mama's treasure chest. Since she was a small child, she'd often gone through her Mama's treasures at her invitation. *'Go see what you can find in my treasure box, chérie'* whilst she'd waited for her Mama to either get dressed or write her letters.

In her imagination, its contents would change when she opened the wooden chest. One day, it was a pirate's chest full of gold like the one she had seen in the Peter Pan book they'd read in school. Or maybe it would be a Mary Poppins chest when she would pull out priceless treasure each time she put her hand in. But on opening the lid today, she was met by a musty, sweet smell. Crammed in the chest were an assortment of objects, all shapes and sizes. *But there must be priceless treasure in there, too*, she thought. Isabelle rummaged around in the box. Tucked away in one corner of the chest, Isabelle found a small oval silver trinket box. Its lid was embroidered with a simple spray of flowers. Inside the unlined box were two tiny identity bands; she could just make out some of their writing – *Le Page 28/08/1972.*

'That's my birth date, but that's not my surname?' she said aloud. Sitting under the trinket box were her Mama's journals, each marked with its year on the front cover. She shuffled through the pile until she came across the one marked *1972*. Making herself comfortable on her Mama's bed, Isabelle flicked over the pages until she reached ....

28/08/1972.

My waters broke at 10:00am. Contractions were strong. Kate drove like a maniac to get me to the hospital on time. Despite my protest, I was taken by a wheelchair to the delivery room. How embarrassing! Nearly a whole day of labour and not progressing. I was told by the doctor that the baby was in distress and I needed an emergency caesarean. This is what you get for being an older mother! Kate stayed with me while I was rushed to the theatre on a trolley. Poor thing, she looked just as frightened as I was. As much as I appreciated her being there, I wished Maurice could have been with me. I wondered if I'd actually get to see him at all today. His wife's funeral on the same day as our baby was to be born was ill-timed! I was wheeled into the theatre without Kate. The last thing I remembered was a kind doctor dressed all in white. He put a needle in my hand, and then I woke up to someone leaning over me saying, 'Hello, Madame Le Page. It's all over and it's all gone well.'

'But Mama's name isn't Le Page. It's La Paganel, like my name. So, whose Mama is this, and where is her baby?' Isabelle cried out, flinging the journal to one side and tears welling up in her eyes.

***

Kate, who had sent out a search party to find Isabelle, found her fast asleep on her mother's bed.

'Isabelle, wake up. It's time for lunch,' Kate said gently, stroking Isabelle's arm until she stirred.

Isabelle woke up startled. 'I had a dream. I dreamed Mama wasn't my Mama,' she exclaimed, throwing herself into Kate's arms and bursting into tears.

Kate dabbed Isabelle's eyes with her handkerchief. 'Shh now. Of course, Mama is your Mama; whatever gave you the idea she wasn't?' Kate replied with a little laugh.

'I read it in this book. Here, look here,' Isabelle replied, picking up the journal. 'Look, it says Madame Le Page. That's not my Mama's name!'

Kate glanced over the journal entry. It hadn't crossed her mind for one moment that her mother hadn't explained the family history to her little sister – and why would she have done that yet? Isabelle was still very young to be able to understand.

'Mama was writing about *your* birth, silly. I was there. Look what she said about you when she first saw you,' Kate replied softly.

'Nurse tells me I have a girl. I'm still a bit woozy from the anaesthetic. The nurse said I couldn't hold her yet, but she held my baby near me. I could see my daughter's beautiful little face peering from the blanket. She was perfect, and I immediately fell in love with her. Maurice came later to see us and was delighted with his daughter. I've never seen him so emotional. He was crying with happiness as he held her so gently and so carefully, as though she might break. We decided to call her Isabelle.'

'But Mama's name isn't Le Page!' Isabelle insisted.

Kate held Isabelle close to her. 'Mama married someone else before marrying Papa when she lived in Guernsey. Her surname became Le Page,' Kate explained gently.

'Where's that husband now?' Isabelle asked wide-eyed.

'He died, sadly. He was James and Elisabeth's Papa,' Kate explained.

'So, he's a star in the sky with my Mama and Papa?'

'Yes, that's right. When Mama met Papa, they fell in love. They couldn't get married immediately because Papa already had a wife who was very, very poorly. Papa looked after her until she died.'

'So, she's a star now, too?' Isabelle interrupted.

'Yes, she is a star, too,' Kate replied, smiling. Isabelle had undoubtedly taken her story to heart about people who died becoming stars.

'I think there are some photographs of Mama and Papa's wedding in the drawer over here. Did Mama show them to you?'

'No, I've never seen their wedding photos,' Isabelle replied eagerly.

'Would you like to see them?' Kate asked.

'Oh, yes, please! I love seeing ladies in pretty dresses. I bet Mama looked pretty in hers,' Isabelle sighed.

Kate crossed over to her mother's dressing table. She wondered why her mother hadn't shown Isabelle the wedding photographs. Could it have been that some of them included pictures of Isabelle as a baby? That she had been waiting for the right time to explain Isabelle's presence as a baby at the wedding? Now, it seems the responsibility of clarifying her mothers' and Maurice's relationship was left up to her, too. Would she ever get off this emotional roller coaster? Kate took the photo album from the drawer and sat beside Isabelle on the bed.

'Mama looked *sooo* beautiful,' Isabelle gushed as she gazed at her Mama's photograph taken at the top of the steps at the Château. 'Look how happy and beautiful she looked in her pretty bride's dress, Kate. She looks just like a princess. Where is Mama's bride's dress now? Can I try it on?' she added.

Kate decided that it was calling too far on her role as guardian to explain Isabelle's parent's relationship at her birth. Also, she hadn't the heart to tell her little sister that her Mama had been buried in her wedding dress.

'I think we'd better leave the rest of these photographs to another day; otherwise, we will be late for lunch. Come on, I'm hungry, aren't you?' Kate said, banking on the fact that food could always distract Isabelle, just like it had been for her brother, James!

'Yes. I'm starving! Race you down to the kitchen!' Isabelle replied, giggling.

Chapter 22

'It's hard to believe, isn't it?' Florence remarked to Kate over breakfast one morning. 'Here we are, nearly at the end of July and nearing the end of another successful art retreat.'

'And the Winter Salon is all but finished, too!' Kate added brightly.

'Yes, another big achievement!' Florence agreed with a smile. 'So, we can all look forward to a well-deserved break,' she added, cupping her mug of coffee in both hands and sighing.

'That's all true, of course; however, don't forget that we start the next art retreat in a few weeks and open the Chambre d'hôte,' Kate replied, laughing.

'Oh well, a bit of a break first, though,' Florence replied, always managing to find a positive slant.

'That reminds me, talking of the end of the retreat and Winter Salon restoration. I must get the numbers for Madame DuPont for those attending the collective exhibition and Winter Salon opening. She will need to give them to the outside caterers. Have you got your numbers, Florence?' Kate added.

'Yes, they are over in the studio. I'll give them to you when you come over later,' Florence replied.

'Let me know the numbers as well, Kate and I'll organise the wine, as agreed,' Don remarked.

'Thanks, Don. I will indeed,' Kate replied.

Kate turned to Florence. 'Phillipe is coming over tomorrow morning to help us hang the canvases if Raimond has *finally* finished putting up the temporary stands. Phillipe has not only got a good eye on how to display them to their best advantage but also the height we both lack,' she giggled.

'All good things come in …' Florence replied with a tinkling laugh.

'*Small packages…* Yes, very true,' Kate replied, chuckling. 'Meanwhile, we need to decide which paintings we include in the exhibition with the group,' Kate added.

Although this was the fifth annual exhibition Kate had been involved in, it was the first exhibition she had organised on her own. Previously, they had been run by her mother and Florence. Raimond had been a willing helper with each of them in the past. Kate was apprehensive that his cooperation this year might not be as forthcoming, given his attitude towards her lately. Still, she had been pleasantly surprised by his response when she'd asked him to bring down the temporary stands from the attic.

'I can 'ave them down and erected straight after lunch today,' he'd told her when she'd asked him over breakfast.

'Thank you, Raimond, that's most helpful,' Kate replied, giving him a warm smile, hoping he'd overcome his recent sulks.

'Not at all, Madame Kate. 'Appy to 'elp,' Raimond had replied with a slight nod.

He went off whistling, leaving her smiling after him. Whether or not Don had been right that he did have a soft spot for her after all, it was still nicer to have a good-humoured Raimond than the sour puss he'd been over the last few months. However, when Kate went to the studio the next day, there was no sign of Raimond or the temporary stands. Instead, Stephen greeted her as she arrived.

'Oh, I was expecting to find Raimond getting the art stands ready,' she said, faintly surprised to find Stephen there.

'Oh yes, he was here when I arrived, then he took off, muttering something when he saw me,' Stephen chuckled. 'I don't think he likes me much.'

'Oh, I'm sure that's not so...' Kate began, but who was she fooling? 'Well, I suppose I'd better try to find him and remind him then....' she paused. 'But why are you here?' she asked, smiling.

'Just curious as to what you get up to over here.'

'About my paintings?' Kate blushed with pleasure.

'No... well... yes... of course, but mainly what you use the other parts of the Château for,' he shrugged. 'And whether they need renovating, of course,' he added, laughing. 'But your paintings are lovely, too,' he said hurriedly.

'Oh,' Kate felt suddenly deflated – and irritated. What with Stephen being more attentive and Raimond being downright elusive – men!

Despite several reminders, there were no signs of the art stands over the following week, or Raimond came to that. Come to think of it, he'd carried on making himself conspicuously absent all week. Whilst Stephen had carried on making himself conspicuously obvious. But something had to be done urgently. There would be no exhibition for the art retreat participants without the stands. Kate made a mental note to do one final chase.

On her rounds in search of Raimond, Kate found the studio a buzz of excitement. The art group and Florence sat in a circle, surrounded by canvasses, discussing which paintings should be included in the exhibition. This retreat had been a much smaller group than usual, but they had integrated well. She'd enjoyed working with them and would miss them when the retreat ended.

'Which ones have we decided to include in the exhibition so far?' Kate asked as she approached the group.

'I think we've done more reminiscing over when and where the paintings were done than actually doing any selecting.' Florence replied, letting out one of her loud, tinkling laughs. 'We think Pat's single rose with the raindrops is a must. Barbara's Châteaux resident's ginger cat curled up asleep amongst a bed of catmint is a definite too,' Florence added. A chorus of *oohs* and *aahs* from the group agreed when Florence held Barbara's cat painting up.

'Oh, yes, I love that one, too. It's *so* adorable and *so* lifelike. It looks as though you can reach out and stroke it. Well done, Barbara,' Kate said, turning to her and smiling.

'Thank you.' Barbara replied, blushing demurely and shuffling uneasily in her chair. Kate had found her to be a modest and agreeable sixty-something whom she'd taken under her wing. Much to Kate's delight, Barbara had blossomed over the weeks, not only in her art but also in herself.

'We thought we should definitely include this one of Jenny's!' Jean exclaimed, balancing a large canvas on her knees. It was a painting of a sidewalk café scene. In the background was a white-washed café with a red and white striped awning over its large front window. A handful of tables covered in red and white tablecloths were positioned on the wide pavement in front of the café. A wooden framed blackboard menu propped against a large wooden barrel planted with an olive tree in the foreground.

'I agree,' replied Kate. 'That was such a fun day out, too!' she giggled,

'I think we caused chaos when we set up our easels and stools outside the café. Not to mention the passers-by obstructing the pavement by stopping to watch us at work, painting,' Jenny reminisced.

'Still, the owner was very gracious despite the chaos and even supplied refreshments. I don't know how much fun it was for Rebecca, though, sitting at one of the tables for hours pretending to be a customer for Jenny to paint her! How many cafetieres and pastries did you get through that day, Rebecca?' Kate asked, laughing.

'I lost count! But I do remember I had problems sleeping that night!' she replied, bursting into laughter. Rebecca, the youngest, most outgoing and enthusiastic group member, shared with Kate and Florence how much she enjoyed the retreat. Even though she was the baby of the group at just thirty years old, she had integrated well with the more senior members. She had confided that she found it exhilarating and, at times, very educational!

As each canvas was selected and carefully placed to one side, Kate marvelled at how each created a special memory for its artist. Memories of long, warm sunny days, soaking in their surroundings' atmosphere and beauty, along with the companionship of their fellow group participants. Maybe such lasting memories were as good as the fleeting illusions of love and romance? To achieve and be proud of your achievements without relying on a partner to make them a reality? She shook her head. But what did she know? She hadn't achieved anything for herself yet, with or without a partner!

She suddenly caught sight of Raimond and Stephen walking past the studio, apparently in deep – but not altogether – convivial conversation. All philosophical thoughts were forgotten as she chased after them.

'Oh, Raimond!' she called out. 'Do you remember I asked about the temporary art stands a while ago? Would you please bring them down from the attic and put them up in here by tomorrow morning? Phillipe is coming over at nine o'clock to help hang the paintings,' she added. She pitched her voice to sound friendly rather than demanding and added a winning smile for good measure.

'I could do that if you show me where they are?' Stephen jumped in before Raimond could reply. Kate stared at him – why hadn't he offered before?

'She asks me,' Raimond interjected gruffly. 'I say, I will do it when I 'ave time!'

'Thank you,' Kate said, smiling sweetly at Raimond, then retreating before she was tempted to add sarcastic comments. She could see Stephen eyeing the pair of them curiously out of the corner of her eye. Still, he said nothing, just hurried to catch up with Raimond again as he strode abruptly away. She watched them continue with their heated conversation as they disappeared around the corner of the barn. And what had that all been about? Clearly, neither planned to include her in it, whatever it was!

Kate breathed a sigh of relief when she found that the stands had been erected later that evening. She knew Phillipe would be prompt, so the temporary stands needed to be ready for him.

'Did you get your exhibition stands sorted after all?' Stephen asked ingenuously that evening over supper.

'Oh! Yes – they are all ready now. Thank you for putting up the stands in the studio, Raimond,' Kate added as an afterthought.

'I said I would when I 'ad time,' Raimond mumbled. He toyed with the food on his plate, glancing sourly at Stephen but avoiding Kate's eyes. Angeline was serving that evening whilst Madame DuPont rested, struck down by one of her *'heads,'* as she called them. Since Angeline had arrived, this was an increasingly recurring problem. Angeline sidled up next to Raimond and offered him a second serving. She stepped away as he shook his head, ignoring Stephen's hopeful glance towards his nearly empty plate.

'Could I...' Stephen began. Angeline gave him a look like thunder and dumped the serving dish on the table.

'I 'ave to see to the dessert. Serve yourself,' Angeline replied curtly and marched off. Raimond smiled, returning his gaze to his plate and deliberately ignored everyone. Kate concentrated on her own plate and changed the subject. Obviously, there was bad blood brewing between Stephen and Raimond. Kate hoped it wasn't because of the art stands.

Chapter 23

As predicted, Phillipe was at the studio on the dot of nine the following morning. *At least I can always rely on Philippe*, Kate thought. As usual, she had been racing around dealing with a hundred and one things before doing a mad dash to meet him in the studio at five minutes *past* nine!

Phillipe worked with Kate, Florence, and the group throughout the morning, arranging which paintings would be hung on the temporary stands or walls.

Don, who was on his tea break, wandered into the studio. 'There are some mighty fine pieces of art here, Kate,' he marvelled. 'Are you also going to include some of your *'splodges'*, as you call them?' he laughed, surveying the paintings that had been chosen to be exhibited.

'Yes, Florence and I are going to exhibit some of our work too, if there's room,' Kate grinned, pointing to the number of canvases waiting to be hung.

'We will have to find skinny ones,' Florence replied, collapsing into laughter.

At last, the grand opening and exhibition evening had arrived. Kate found Raimond and Isabelle standing in the grand entrance hall as she descended the stairs, ready to greet the guests in the Winter Salon. She was struck by how ruggedly handsome Raimond looked that evening – just as she had the first time they'd met – *if you liked that sort of thing*, she thought. But Kate hurriedly reminded herself *that she didn't!* Even though tonight, she hardly recognised him. His thick, wavy, dark brown hair had been combed back and slicked down with gel. He was freshly shaven and wore a smart suit, shirt and tie. If she didn't know how much of a grumpy old *salaud* he could be, she might have felt a flutter of excitement as he held her gaze, openly admiring her as she descended the stairs.

'You look beautiful, Kate,' Isabelle cried.

'Magnifique!' Raimond smiled and whispered loudly to Isabelle. 'She's so de toute beauté.' Kate couldn't help but hear what he whispered to Isabelle; he'd whispered so loud. Isabelle nodded in agreement.

'Where did you get that red dress? I've not seen it before,' Isabelle asked.

'It's actually one of Mama's dresses that I kept. She wore it on the night of her engagement party to Papa. I am wearing Mama's engagement ring too, see?' she added. Kate extended her right hand towards Isabelle to show their mother's ruby and diamond ring on her finger.

'How come you can wear Mama's ring and I can't!' Isabelle demanded before pushing past Kate and nearly knocking her over as she raced up the stairs.

'Isabelle… Isabelle…' Kate called after her. But Isabelle continued running up the stairs without even a backward glance. She had wanted to share with Isabelle how wonderful their mother had looked that night when she had worn the same red dress and had worn the same ring. How happy both her Mama and Papa had been that evening. Now, that brief magical moment was lost. She bit her lip.

Raimond looked across to Kate, giving her a sympathetic smile. She saw warmth in his eyes for the first time. Momentarily, she relaxed.

'Should I go after her?' she asked him in a moment of weakness.

He put a hand on her shoulder and squeezed. 'Let 'er go. It is just an – 'ow you say – an explosion. She'll be 'appy again later. She is only looking for attention because it is a big moment for you now.'

'You're right,' Kate agreed, surprised at how perceptive this intriguing, moody man could be – and how kind. She shook her head as if to shake off her thoughts of how presentable and handsome Raimond *could* be. 'Let's go and see if anyone has arrived,' Kate said quickly. She should focus on the party, not wondering why Raimond was suddenly being nice and what it would be like if he had always been like this. After all, she reminded herself, he could be such a difficult and obnoxious man, too!

Glasses of champagne and canapes welcomed each guest as they arrived. Charlotte was the first one to arrive. Following the arrows' directions, she had parked her car around the back of the Château. Charlotte waved to Kate as she was handed a glass of champagne by the young waiter hired for the evening. She refused the offer of a canape from the tray held by another waitress as she threaded her way across the room to Kate.

'Kate, you look breathtaking!' Charlotte greeted her, clutching her glass of champagne. 'That red dress really shows off your tanned skin and beautiful dark hair,' she added, greeting her with a light kiss on her cheek. 'Where did you buy it?'

'Thank you, Charlotte,' Kate replied, feeling her cheeks beginning to flush. 'It was the one Mother wore on the night of her engagement to Maurice. I am also wearing her engagement ring. I thought wearing them would feel that Mother was part of the celebrations, too,' Kate explained. 'But I seem to have upset Isabelle in the process.'

'What a lovely idea, don't worry about Isabelle, she'll come around, I'm sure,' Charlotte nodded with agreement, patting Kate's hand.

Raimond interrupted. 'Yes. She'll get over it. She wants to be the centre of attention,' Kate had forgotten he was still by her side.

'You were right about the colour on the Winter Salon walls, by the way,' Charlotte said, drawing Kate into the centre of the room, away from Raimond. 'It does make the room look cosy and very inviting. Well done,' she added.

'I wonder if Mother would have approved?' Kate asked, noting that Raimond was still watching her from the other side of the room. She wasn't sure if she felt flattered or uncomfortable.

'Oh yes, definitely, I think she would. The colours, the furnishings and those beautiful curtains. She would have loved what you have done to this room,' Charlotte replied. 'Is that one of your paintings over there?' she asked.

'Ah, yes. It was one of my first experimental splodge paintings,' Kate chuckled.

'Your *splodge* paintings?' Charlotte asked, frowning.

'Yes. When I burnt my right hand in the fire, Phillipe persuaded me to be the new Michelangelo and paint left-handed. The style is more of a splodge than my usual fine detailed style paintings, hence the name,' Kate giggled. 'Ironically, it seems to have been more successful than my usual style – as you'll find out later,' she added, eyes twinkling with excitement.

Charlotte studied her with curiosity, and Kate giggled again. 'Well, splodge or not, I can see it's the view from the terrace here – right?' she asked.

'Yes, spot-on; it can't be that bad then,' Kate laughed.

'No, not at all. And the apple hasn't fallen far from the tree as far as the flair for design and colour goes; I say again, this room is exquisite,' she added, smiling and squeezing Kate's arm.

'Thank you, Charlotte. Of course, Stephen has been a great help with this project. It's been good having him here to bounce ideas off. I've really appreciated his input. He has such a wealth of knowledge and experience,' Kate enthused.

'Did I hear my name mentioned?' Stephen called to Kate, laughing as he strode into the Winter Salon, closely followed by Phillipe, his wife and Phillipe's parents. Kate was still conscious of Raimond on the other side of the room – his previously admiring expression had now turned to a scowl on Stephen's arrival.

'And don't you look stunning!' Stephen gushed, taking Kate by the hands and kissing her on the cheek. 'The dress and your hair down like that really becomes you!' he added with a broad grin. 'La plus belle dame!'

'You've certainly impressed someone!' Charlotte whispered in Kate's ear. 'More than someone, in fact. Some two…' she added with a slight tilt of her head towards where Raimond was still admiring Kate from afar.

Kate shook her head and greeted Stephen. 'Thank you, Stephen, but a piece of advice – you shouldn't eavesdrop. You might not like what you hear said about you!' Kate teased, lightly tapping him on the arm and chuckling.

Little did he know that after seeing him walk in with his glass of champagne, she'd deliberately dropped his name into the conversation with Charlotte for him to overhear. Raimond might be broodingly handsome, but there was no mistaking Stephen's tall, slim figure looking as sophisticated as ever and even more so tonight. He looked debonair in his light grey suit and pale blue open-necked shirt. Kate experienced the same strange fluttering sensation in her stomach that she'd felt the first time she'd seen him. It had taken her right back to where she'd been a few weeks ago, hoping that maybe?

On noticing Phillipe, his wife and his parents hanging back in the doorway. 'Stephen, you know Phillipe, of course, but have you been introduced to Phillipe's wife, Claudette?'

'Pleased to meet you, Claudette,' Stephen replied, smiling warmly and kissing her lightly on each cheek.

'Can I also introduce you to Phillipe's father, Géraud? He is our local celebrant; he officiated at my mother and Maurice's wedding.'

'I'm very pleased to meet you, Géraud,' Stephen replied, shaking Géraud's hand.

'And this is his lovely wife, Dominique, Phillipe's Mother,' Kate added.

'Dominique, ravi de vous connaître,' Stephen replied.

Kate smiled to herself – Stephen certainly had a way of charming everyone. She glanced around the room. Kate told herself it wasn't to see where Raimond had gone but to see who else had arrived. However, she noticed he was still looking miserable in the corner. A pang of conscience prompted her to go over to him just as more guests arrived, thrusting her into playing hostess once more. When she looked around for him again later, he'd disappeared. Kate wondered if she should look for him. Still, Florence's warning nod as she headed towards the exit reminded her that she should press on with the evening's programme. Kate stepped back into the centre of the room and took a deep breath.

'I think we are all here now,' she announced. 'If you'd like to follow me, I'll show you the way to the art exhibition. The Orangery is on the way, where you'll find drinks and light refreshments. Please help yourselves,' she added.

Chapter 24

Gathered outside the studio, ready to welcome the guests, were Florence and the art group. Kate was taken aback to see Florence had changed out of her usual uncoordinated paint-covered garments into an elegant long, cap-sleeved, sky-blue floral dress and the old leather sandals had been replaced by a stylish silver pair.

Florence greeted the guests with a radiant smile. 'Welcome to our exhibition,' she said, introducing herself and the rest of the group. 'Please do wander around at your leisure, and if you have any questions, please ask,' she added.

The studio had been brought to life with the collection of paintings hanging on the Old Coach House's cold, grey stone walls. Filling the vast space in the middle of the building were the temporary stands displaying further collections of paintings. Each picture portrayed colour, mood and atmosphere explosions, conveying the artists' vision.

After ensuring her guests were settled, Kate went to the Orangery to check on the refreshments. It was a beautiful evening. The sky was clear, the stars shining brightly – earlier, she had watched the sun go down behind the forest from the Winter Salon terrace. Inside the Orangery, long tables had been set up with selections of hot and cold dishes for the guests to help themselves. The caterers stood poised behind the tables to offer help when needed. Separate tables and chairs were scattered around the room for the guests to sit and eat. Kate saw Raimond in the corner – standing close to and whispering to Angeline.

She hesitated for a moment, then launched straight in. 'Ah, there you are,' she said, overly brightly. 'It looks wonderful in here, doesn't it? Thank you *so much* for all your help setting it up,' she gushed. She knew her tone was over the top and questioned why she felt the need for it. *Was it the sight of him chatting so intimately with Angeline that had prompted her?*

Was she jealous? Was she trying to draw Raimond's attention away from Angeline back to herself? After all, he'd said how beautiful she looked. But if she was trying to get his attention, she wasn't having any luck.

'I is just doing my job,' Raimond replied shortly, looking down superciliously at her. Angeline grinned up at him, and he returned her smile. The rejection it implied stung.

'Eventually!' Kate replied sharply before she could stop herself.

Raimond looked surprised, then scowled. 'I 'ave many jobs to do, and don't waste my time talking with that man Stephen or preening myself to look beautiful,' he retorted.

'Oh really!' Kate replied her anger building, ignoring the back-handed compliment that he had given. 'So, what's all this oily stuff in your hair, and why have you shaved? You had time to do that!' She took a step forward towards him, waggling her finger. 'And I shouldn't have to ask you more than once to do something!'

Angeline melted away, leaving Kate looking angry and flush-faced, facing Raimond.

'I do my best for you as I 'ave did it for the Marquis,' he said, stepping close to Kate and lightly batting her waggling finger aside. Kate could smell brandy on his breath and the faint scent of his vanilla aftershave. Her head started to spin and she forgot where she was for a moment.

'You deliberately try to upset me; that's what you do, whispering behind my back ...' Stephen's presence in the doorway stopped her in her tracks.

'Kate, I thought you would be in the studio,' Stephen called from the Orangery doorway, looking from her and then to Raimond with a curious expression.

Kate tried to compose herself. 'Oh, well... I leave that part mainly up to Florence; she's much better at showing the paintings than I,' Kate replied with an awkward laugh. 'Would you like a drink or something to eat?' Kate asked, stepping back from Raimond and taking a deep breath to steady herself. Her head still spun as she tried to control her anger at Raimond.

'Yes, please, come and show me what's on offer?' Stephen replied, eyeing up the dishes on the long table before him and holding a hand to her.

Kate hesitated, then turned to Raimond, who was now alone, staring belligerently at her and Stephen. 'I'm sorry, Raimond. Please forgive me. I'm just a bit tense about this evening. Why don't you come and join us?' she said, feeling guilty for what she'd just said to him.

'I 'ave something to do,' he replied gruffly, walking away.

'Can't it wait?' Kate called to him. 'Come and join us before it gets crowded in here.' She tried to sound cheery, as though they hadn't just exchanged hurtful words. Stephen picked up his plate.

'I'll find us a quiet seat in the corner,' Stephen announced, carrying his plate piled high with food. Kate had always marvelled at how slim he managed to stay despite all the food he consumed.

Raimond gave a slight nod and joined them, carrying his plate of food piled equally high as Stephen's, sitting at the table without a word. Kate kept up a lively conversation whilst they ate. She reminisced and relayed some of the funny stories, minor mishaps and near-miss disasters that had occurred over the past few months. She interjected these tales with praise to both Stephen and Raimond for their help and support since losing her parents.

'That's what we're here for,' Stephen had replied. Raimond nodded wordlessly.

'Nevertheless,' Kate continued. She took a deep breath – the first of her announcements … 'I've realised that I can't continue to run the Château single-handed. Raimond, it's not fair to expect you to cope with everything that needs doing. So, after taking advice, I have decided to appoint an Estate Manager,' Kate hesitated momentarily, then pressed on. 'Stephen, I would like to offer you the position,' she added.

Before Stephen could reply, Raimond slammed down his knife and fork. 'Why do you not offer me that job?' he yelled. '

Kate was taken aback and drew in her breath before she replied; she'd not expected such an outburst from Raimond. 'I feel that given Stephen's background and experience, he's better qualified for the role,' she explained. Nevertheless, she began to feel a little guilty offering the job to Stephen in front of Raimond. But, on the other hand, did he really believe for one minute that he'd be suitable for the role?

'After all the loyal years I 'ave given to the Marquis. So, you say I not good enough?' Raimond retorted.

'I'm not saying you're not good enough,' Kate replied steadily. 'I'm saying Stephen is better qualified. Not only with his knowledge of historic houses but also the administration, paperwork, managing staff and everything else involved with looking after these buildings,' Kate explained patiently. But Raimond's face showed that regardless of her explanations, they had fallen on deaf ears.

'Marquis say I always 'elpful and loyal. He would 'ave give me the job!' Raimond barked, pushing his chair back noisily and heading for the door.

'Tetchy…' Stephen commented as they both watched Raimond storming out of the Orangery, pushing past guests as they tried to enter. 'Surely he knows his place?'

Kate looked at Stephen, surprised at the arrogance of his remark and wondering if she'd made the right decision after all.

Chapter 25

Despite Kate's last words to her, '*Stay in your room,*' Isabelle had left the confines of her bedroom with Jacqueline, her doll, tucked under her arm. Isabelle could see through the railings from her vantage point on the stairs that everyone downstairs in the Winter Salon was dressed up. They, unlike her, were having a lovely time in the Winter Salon for the grand opening party. The ladies were wearing pretty dresses and beautiful jewellery. Watching them made Isabelle cross that she wasn't there, making her even more determined that *she* wouldn't be left out somehow. Although she wasn't dressed in an elegant dress, she was, however, wearing a pretty nightie Grandy had bought her. She settled down to watch and listen to the party downstairs, where no one could see her.

She had begged and begged Kate to be allowed to stay up and go to the party; she had even picked out a dress to wear, but Kate had said no. *This was for grown-ups*, Kate had told her, even though Isabelle had reminded Kate that she was almost nine years old. Still, Kate had said no, reminding her that it was Olivia's night off and that she would be far too busy entertaining her guests to keep an eye on her.

'Keep an eye on me? As if I'm a baby!' she muttered under her breath as she watched the guests laughing and chatting. 'She's being so mean. I helped her with the preparations, didn't I?' Isabelle said out loud to Jacqueline. Isabelle and Jacqueline had become inseparable since Isabelle had received the doll as a Christmas present from her Mama and Papa. Isabelle shared all her secrets with Jacqueline. 'And I did lots,' she continued to confide in her doll. 'I helped Raimond put the napkins on the tables in the Orangery and carried boxes of decorations for him to put up. I've not complained much that I've not been out anywhere for ages because Kate's been too busy organising this party. Even Grandy and Papi have been too busy to play with me because they've been helping her too.'

Isabelle stopped and thought momentarily, still holding Jaqueline out in front of her. 'I bet Kate's forgotten that I helped stick the stamps on the envelopes for the invitations, too, *and* I sat for hours in the car with her, delivering some of them by hand. I've done all that stuff, and I'm still not allowed at the party. It's not fair?' she cuddled the doll and stuck out her bottom lip. 'Why's it just for grown-ups, anyway? Why shouldn't I go? What's all this *fuss, fuss, fuss* for anyway?' Isabelle held Jacqueline out in front of her, then angled her to look down between the railings before turning the doll to face her again. She waited as though she was waiting to get an answer before continuing, 'I'm like that Cinderella in the storybook Grandy bought me – she wasn't allowed to go to the ball either.' Isabelle paused before adding, 'Although I already live in a castle. Still, I wonder if a handsome Prince will come and take me to the party like in the storybook?' she sighed.

'Ah, I thought I might find you here, petit,' Madame DuPont rustled up the stairs in her black taffeta dress and stood beside her. Isabelle jumped but, turning to look at her, soon noticed that Madame DuPont wasn't cross with her. Instead, she sat on the step beside her and stroked her hair. 'Look, I have something for you.'

Madame DuPont had sneaked her a plateful of yummy-looking food. She loved Madame DuPont – she understood. Sitting alongside each other, with Jacqueline in the middle, they peered between the railings onto the party below. In between mouthfuls of food, Isabelle remarked on the ladies' outfits. This was her favourite topic; she loved clothes and jewellery.

'I like Grandy's blue dress; she does look pretty in it, don't you think?' Isabelle asked.

'Oui. Trés bonne,' Madame DuPont agreed.

'I love her silver sandals, too,' Isabelle continued. 'See that lady in the stripes? I love her necklace and earrings. See how they sparkle when she moves around. I'd love some like that,' Isabelle exclaimed.

'Perhaps when you are growing up,' Madame DuPont replied, patting her on her arm.

Isabelle nodded enthusiastically. 'But I don't like that lady's blue dress. It doesn't suit her at all – ugh!' she added loudly, between mouthfuls.

'Shh, shh,' Madame DuPont hissed. 'She might be hearing you.'

Isabelle placed her hand over her mouth and giggled.

'Kate looks pretty in Mama's dress, doesn't she?' Isabelle remarked after a while. 'Red looks nice on her,' she added.

'Oui. Elle est magnifique!' Madame DuPont replied.

'That's what Raimond said when he saw her. He also said she was *de toute beauté*,' Isabelle told her. 'I think Raimond likes her. Sometimes he makes a soppy face when he thinks she's not looking,' she added, trying to mimic the face she had described.

Madame DuPont laughed. 'I don't know of such things,' she replied dryly. 'But Raimond is a good man.'

'I don't think she likes him that much, though. I've often heard her cross with him, especially if Angeline is around.' Madame DuPont huffed and puffed at the sound of Angeline's name. Isabelle paused momentarily, adding, 'I think she might like Stephen. She goes all soppy over him sometimes. And he went all soppy over her tonight when he saw her in that dress. He told her she looked stunning and kissed her on the cheek. Ugh,' Isabelle said, screwing up her face.

'I'm sure he a nice man too and helpful to Madame Kate,' Madame DuPont replied, but her lips were pursed together as if she'd just eaten something sour.

Encouraged by Madame DuPont's expression, Isabelle whispered, 'Actually, I don't like him much. I think he thinks I'm a nuisance and often ignores me. If I ask him a question, he always tells me he's too busy to answer and rushes away.'

'I think he just a busy man,' Madame DuPont said carefully. 'Madame Kate looks like your Mama in that dress,' she remarked, pointing to Kate as she stood talking to Stephen.

'Kate is also wearing Mama's ring. She won't let *me* wear her jewellery, though!' Isabelle moaned. 'Oh, why aren't I grown up?'

Madame DuPont put her arm around Isabelle's shoulder and squeezed it tight. 'You're just a petite fillette; plenty of time for growing up,' Madame DuPont replied softly. 'Here, have a piece of the gâteau; it's the only thing Angeline makes that is bien.'

'I suppose...' Isabelle said, her mouth full of a piece of the pink iced cake.

After Isabelle had finished the last petit fours, Madame DuPont took the empty plate from her.

'Time for sleep?' she asked.

'Oh, just a bit longer?' Isabelle begged her.

'Seulement un quart,' Madame DuPont cautioned, 'fifteen minutes!'

Isabelle nodded as Madame DuPont rustled back down the stairs, heading to the kitchen with the empty plate. Isabelle returned to peering through the railings. Kate was gathering everyone into the middle of the room and calling for their attention. She strained her ears to listen.

'I'm delighted to see you all here tonight, celebrating the grand opening of our lovely Winter Salon. Also, to enjoy the marvellous exhibition that our retreat painters have created for us. I also have something else to share with you too… I have been invited to hang some of my artwork in a gallery in the Montmartre district in Paris. I'll be travelling there shortly for the opening.'

There were gasps and a buzz of chatter. Some party-goers clapped and cheered; others thronged around Kate to congratulate her.

'Paris? That's where Raimond said the Folies Bergère is!' Isabelle whispered to Jacqueline. Her mind was racing, remembering the pictures of all the beautiful dresses she'd seen the dancers wearing in the magazine. Oh, she must go to Paris with Kate; she simply must! How could she get Kate to take her so that she could see the dancers at the Folies Bergère that she'd seen in Olivia's magazines? Isabelle only half-listened to the rest of Kate's speech as she told everyone how honoured she was, what a good opportunity it was, and so on. Her speech ended with everyone clapping again. Isabelle had switched off as she furiously thought of all the reasons she could give to persuade Kate to take her along with her.

The fifteen-minute grace Madame DuPont had granted was long over. Isabelle picked up Jacqueline and made her way back upstairs. Madame DuPont would be coming in search of her soon, plus she was getting bored watching the party below now. They were all just standing around talking. She couldn't make out what they were saying anyway. Madame DuPont was down there helping tidy away now, too. This gave Isabelle a great idea – if Madame DuPont was busy, Olivia was out, and everyone else at the party, she had the run of the Château! She would find her Mama's jewellery box in Kate's room and find something pretty that she could wear to make her look like one of the Folies Bergère dancers!

Tucking Jacqueline under her arm, Isabelle crept onto the landing and into Kate's room. She knew she wasn't allowed in there alone and half wondered what would happen if she was found out. Maybe Kate wasn't downstairs after all… Isabelle told herself not to be so silly. Kate *was* downstairs; she'd just seen her, so she wouldn't know anyway, would she?

'Anyway, it serves her right. Kate's enjoying herself and I'm not!' she said out loud to Jacqueline.

Isabelle searched Kate's room for the jewellery box – in her drawers, cupboards and wardrobe. She even looked under her bed. No jewellery box! She threw Jacqueline hard onto the bed in frustration.

'It's not here,' she told Jacqueline. She flung herself onto the bed next to Jacqueline. She lay looking up at the ceiling, puzzling over where the jewellery box could be. Kate must have hidden it somewhere else – or worse… 'Kate has stolen Mama's jewellery,' she announced to Jacqueline. 'She must have! I hate her!' she yelled out loud and burst into tears.

Chapter 26

Isabelle felt so alone; she missed her Mama and Papa. And now, Kate was being mean to her and had taken her Mama's jewellery box. She pulled Jacqueline tightly to her, buried her face into its soft body and sobbed. After a time, Jacqueline's softness began to have the desired comfort. Isabelle's crying eased, and she began to feel better as she wiped her eyes with her nightie. If Madame DuPont came looking for her and heard her in here, she'd be in trouble. Straightening the bedclothes on Kate's bed, Isabelle crept out of the room and returned to her vantage point. The party downstairs had moved on, *probably to the art exhibition,* Isabelle thought. 'Now is our chance to really explore,' Isabelle said aloud to Jacqueline, 'and Kate isn't here to stop us!'

Returning to the first-floor landing, Isabelle opened each of the Chambre doors. Most hadn't been occupied over the summer, so she discovered there wasn't much to see except one room. It had a long mirror on the wall directly in front of her behind one of the doors. Isabelle stood in front of it and gazed at herself. Grandy had said how pretty she looked in her pink rosebud nightie. Isabelle stood with one hand on her hip and posed, just like the models in Olivia's magazines do. She also pouted and tilted her head upwards slightly, then laughed at her reflection.

'Hmmm… looking okay… but' Isabelle said with a smile. 'What we need is a pretty necklace,' she added, picking Jacqueline up from the bed where she'd left her, 'and I know where we might find one.'

The house was utterly still. The only sound to be heard was the loud ticking of the giant clock in the grand entrance hall. Isabelle crept along the corridor to her Grandy and Papi's room. She felt a mixture of trepidation and excitement. On reaching the room, she hesitated before gingerly turning the door handle.

'Shh,' Isabelle whispered to Jacqueline, 'we must be very quiet.' Isabelle closed the door carefully behind her and listened again to ensure no one approached outside in the corridor. All was still silent. She made her way to the dressing table and switched on the small glass lamp in front of the mirror on the dressing tabletop.

She had seen her Grandy's jewellery box lots of times. Grandy, like her Mama, had lots of beautiful jewellery. She had often played with the pretty pieces in her box whilst listening to Grandy's beautiful stories about each of them. Still, she mostly wore her favourite jewellery –earrings, a matching chain and locket, and a silver bracelet. These everyday pieces had been left on the dressing table to one side of her jewellery box.

'Grandy must have her bestest jewellery on tonight,' Isabelle told Jacqueline on seeing them. She picked up the locket and opened it. Inside was a picture of a handsome man in uniform. She had seen the picture before; it was of Grandy's first husband the day he went to war, Grandy had told her. Isabelle ran her fingers over the shiny raised silver knots that intertwined, forming a circle. She remembered the story Grandy had told her about the locket. Her husband made it for her as a present when he left for the war. The silver knots were made from loops that had no start or finish. Grandy's husband had told her that she shouldn't be sad that he was going to war, that their love for each other was like those knots – there was no end, and the locket would get him back safe to her. And he was right; Grandy had told her it brought him home safe.

Isabelle loved that story. She tried on the locket and looked at herself in the mirror, twisting her head this way and that as she admired the way the light glistened on the raised silver knots as it hung around her neck. It was so pretty… it made her feel pretty… and special, too. Isabelle smiled to herself. *Prettier than Kate*, she reckoned! She was just about to tell Jacqueline this when she heard voices in the corridor.

'I think it's this room,' a woman said. Isabelle gasped and quickly flicked the lamp off before ducking underneath the dressing table. The door flung open.

'Told you. It's *not* this room!' the other voice said as the door closed loudly. Isabelle remained under the dressing table, her heart pounding until it had gone quiet outside again. Grabbing Jacqueline, she made a dash back to the safety of her bedroom after making sure the coast was clear. Fully clothed and still hanging onto Jaqueline, Isabelle jumped into bed, pulling the covers up high over them, laying perfectly still and squeezing her eyes tight as if she were fast asleep in case anyone came to check on her. Although she'd not been invited to the party, she had enjoyed the evening. The ladies' dresses, jewellery, and learning about Kate's announcement on going to Paris…

When she next opened her eyes, she found it was morning and her Grandy's necklace was still fastened around her neck.

Chapter 27

'Ah, there you are,' Stephen greeted Kate, finding her sitting at one of the tables in the Orangery. On the table before her were plates of congealed leftover food and half-finished glasses of wine – remnants from the previous night's party. 'Madame DuPont said she'd not seen you this morning, so I thought I'd come and look for you. What are you doing here?' he quizzed.

'I couldn't sleep, so I thought I'd have a walk around the grounds; I often go for a walk when I can't sleep. It's so lovely this time of the day. The air is so fresh and crisp this time of the year. And apart from the bird song, there's a special quietness everywhere,' Kate replied.

'I love early mornings, too. I often sit in my bedroom window and watch the sunrise. I must have the best view of it out of my Château window,' Stephen remarked.

'I agree. You have the best view from that window in your room. I was on my way down to the forest. If I'm lucky, I often see deer down there. However, this morning, I somehow ended up here amongst remains of last night's party,' Kate laughed, pointing to the array of plates and glasses strewn across the tables.

'It is a bit of a mess, isn't it?' Stephen replied. 'Do you need some help to clear it up?'

'No, thank you, it's fine. Between the caterers, Angeline and Madame DuPont, they will soon get this cleared,' Kate replied. 'Let's leave this mess and go and see if we can find some deer in the forest, shall we?' she added brightly.

'Yes, why not! Now we're back in our casual gear, unlike last night's fine clothes; we're both dressed for the part, so let's go!' Stephen replied, heading out of the door.

'Did you enjoy last night, Stephen?' Kate asked as they descended the steep, grassy slope towards the forest.

'Yes, I did. I met some fascinating people. Everyone admired the restoration in the Winter Salon. I felt a bit of a fraud at times taking all the compliments when it was really you who did the marvellous job choosing the decorations, furnishings and furniture,' Stephen answered.

'I can't take all the credit. It was you who interpreted my sketchy notes and ideas and accompanied me to the local brocantes. We found some wonderful mismatched furniture and objects to dress the room, didn't we?' Kate replied with a smile, remembering their many outings driving around to the brocantes, often stopping off for refreshments along the way.

'Yes, I think we made a good team. I've loved every minute of it,' Stephen agreed.

'I have, too. I'm almost sorry the room is finished,' Kate laughed, then bit her lip and flushed pink as Stephen remained silent, not echoing her sentiment. He still hadn't declared himself to her all those special times together. She stifled a sigh.

They had reached the opening into the woods. With their eyes quickly accustomed to the dappled shade from the bright sunlight, they followed the path as it weaved into the forest. The forest was still except for the bird song, the crunching of the leaves underfoot, and the leaves rustling on the trees overhead.

'We need to be quiet if we are to see the deer,' Kate warned in a low voice.

Stephen nodded. 'But while we have a quiet moment,' he whispered, 'we didn't get the chance to discuss your offer of the Estate Manager job you made me last night?'

'That's right, I'm sorry,' Kate interjected. 'It probably wasn't the best moment to pick to offer you the post. I did rather drop it into the conversation without any warning or explanations, didn't I?'

'That's okay. I understand,' Stephen replied.

'And then I got side-tracked for the rest of the evening,' Kate added.

'But tell me, was your offer a serious one? Only I got the feeling that you offered it to me because you were getting back at Raimond?' Stephen replied.

'Oh no, absolutely not! I can assure you that wasn't the case. I admit it was totally unprofessional of me to announce my intentions of appointing an Estate Manager and then offer you the position in front of Raimond. I can assure you, though, I didn't offer you the job to get back at Raimond.

As I said then, I firmly believe that with your background and from working with you over the past few months, you are just the person I need to help me run things here at the Château. What do you think?'

'I can't deny that I have enjoyed working here and being in one place for a change instead of moving from job to job all over the world,' Stephen admitted. He hesitated. Kate stopped, and he stopped alongside her, waiting.

'I still need to work out the finer details with you: salary package and the role. If we could come to an agreement on this, would you be interested in principle?' Kate asked.

'I may well be interested. As I said earlier, maybe it is time for me to settle in one place, cease being a nomad living out of a suitcase,' Stephen replied. He hesitated again before adding, 'Stop running away...'

'Running away? Running away from what?' Kate probed.

'Life... situations... reality, I guess. I've always thrown myself into work to avoid facing difficult situations, even more since my divorce. Being here, I've had time to reflect on the past year. My addiction to work put a strain on my marriage. I was rarely home; we grew apart, and we lost the closeness and the warmth in our relationship. So really, the divorce was my fault and I'm still feeling guilty that I was the cause of the failure of my marriage,' Stephen answered.

'Do you not have a circle of friends or one particular friend you can talk to?' Kate asked, wondering if Stephen was still feeling like a lost soul. If so, maybe she could now understand why he was keeping his distance from her.

'Because I move around so much, building a network of friends isn't easy. I've lost touch with most of my friends over the years,' he replied quietly.

Kate nodded. 'I moved here after my marriage break up, so I think I know some of what you are feeling. However, I was luckier than you; I have – or did have – a family to lean on here and I've made some good friends since. Do you think this place is where you *could* feel comfortable putting down roots?' Kate asked.

'Are you angling after an answer as to whether I want the job or something else?' Stephen asked, laughing.

'No... well... yes, perhaps I am. I'd love you to say yes to the job, of course,' Kate replied, blushing.

'Part of me would love to say yes to that, too,' Stephen replied cautiously, 'but....'

'But? Why the hesitation? Not keen on having a woman as your boss?' Kate laughed.

'Not at all. I've worked with you all these months, so I know what a hard taskmaster you are!' Stephen teased. 'In all seriousness, though, I like being around you. The first time we went out together to the gallery, we bonded. I felt that we might be kindred spirits. Not just as two friends and work colleagues but a bit more than that. But there was a spark, a magnetic chemistry between us. All those things I'd not felt for anyone in a long time. Although I believe it's important for two people to be friends before becoming lovers. I've not revealed these feelings to you before because I'm not sure I'm ready for another relationship. Maybe it's too soon for you, too. After all, you have only just lost your mother and stepfather?' Stephen added.

Kate sighed. So, there it was; he was interested but not ready for a relationship. 'I felt the same way about you that first day, too,' she admitted, looking up at Stephen and blushing before quickly lowering her eyes. 'But like you, I didn't want to push anything for either of us if we're not ready....'

Suddenly, Stephen stopped and took both of Kate's hands, pulling her towards him and holding her close. 'Oh, I'm ready – and I've wanted to hold you like this for a long time,' Stephen said in a hushed tone. 'I just wasn't sure how you felt – you are always so busy – and a little enigmatic too,' he added.

'Me, enigmatic? I'm as clear as a pane of glass, aren't I?' she replied, surprised.

'You are now,' he grinned, then drew her back from him; he gently held her head between his two hands, lightly brushing each of her eyes with his lips before kissing her softly on her mouth. In the moment of that kiss, Kate realised how much pent-up passion was inside her. Her head swam and her heart pounded. They stayed locked in that embrace for what seemed an eternity. *At last, at last…* Kate signed inwardly.

Chapter 28

Leaving Stephen to look at a missing panel in the workshop next to the gallery, Kate walked alone through the rose garden on her way back to the Château. She was deep in thought, thinking of Stephen's revelation of how he felt had been like a bombshell, and their first kiss had made her tingle just thinking about it.

However, Kate's pleasant state of excitement was jarred back to reality on spotting Raimond out of the corner of her eye, talking earnestly to Angeline on the far side of the rose garden. Her steps slowed as she watched the two of them together. The pleasant feeling of excitement she had felt earlier was now transforming first into unease and then into downright irritation. Why did seeing Raimond and Angeline together make her so angry – like she'd been betrayed? Raimond was nothing to her, she reasoned with herself. He was an irritating thorn in her side, she reminded herself. Hadn't she and Stephen shared intimate feelings they felt for each other just a few moments ago? She didn't feel that way about Raimond, so why would she be … *jealous* of Angeline being with Raimond? Kate stopped as the shock of the word she'd just used to describe her feelings sunk in. Jealous! Was she really jealous? If so, then what *were* her feelings for Raimond? She could feel the blood rushing to her cheeks and her head spinning with confusion.

Kate quickened her steps to get out of the rose garden before being spotted. Until she'd worked out what on earth was going on with her, she desperately needed to get as far away from Raimond as quickly as possible.

Kate buried herself in her office, ploughing through a mound of paperwork, hoping no one would find her there. Later that morning, she heard raised voices between Stephen and Raimond in the corridor outside her office, leaving her no choice but to investigate. Raimond was waving a fistful of papers at Stephen.

'I look at these bills for work on cornices in Winter Salon. You over-charge Madame, see?' Raimond was saying, thrusting the invoices in his hand into Stephen's face.

'As I've told you before. All the quotes for work done have been discussed and passed by Kate before starting any work. Kate is well aware of the cost of the repairs to the cornices. It's a specialist job; that's why it's expensive,' Stephen replied in a firm but controlled voice.

'That's what you say. I say, Madame, do not understand what you say. She a woman and you put the wool on her eyes to make her believe you,' Raimond retorted.

Kate could sense that this could get beyond a heated argument. The reference to her being fooled because she was a woman angered her. Did Raimond think her so useless? Taking a deep breath, she emerged from the office and stepped in.

'All Stephen has said is true, Raimond. I have been consulted on the matter of costs throughout this project,' Kate told him, stepping in between the two men. 'And I fully understand all of them, whether I'm a woman or a… a … Martian!' she exclaimed irritably.

'Pah! He tells you only some, not all, of what is happening. I know the truths!' Raimond replied haughtily.

'Raimond, that's not true. I trust Stephen,'

'Pah!' Raimond retorted.

Kate turned and smiled at Stephen. 'It's okay, I'll deal with this.' Stephen nodded and strolled down the corridor back to his office, glancing over his shoulder with a pitying look at Raimond as he went.

'Since Marquis went, I here to protect you as he protected you,' Raimond declared, deliberately loud enough for Stephen to hear even at a distance.

'I don't need protecting and I don't need your help. Now get back to your work!' Kate snapped, her head pounding and her ears ringing. Despite being left feeling angry, there was still that underlying pull towards Raimond that she'd felt as she watched him in the rose garden with Angeline.

Raimond turned on his heels and stomped off, his heavy boots echoing along the corridor and the grand entrance hall floor. He slammed the heavy oak front door behind him. Kate was left standing awkwardly with Stephen peering out of his office door, the silence ringing in her ears as loudly as Raimond's footsteps had. Stephen shrugged ruefully and retreated into his office. She let out a loud sigh and returned to her desk. *Now what?*

Lunchtime was a frosty affair – Raimond glared at Stephen repeatedly throughout lunch and said nothing. He avoided eye contact and conversation with Kate. Olivia shared her latest magazine with Angeline at the end of the long kitchen table. They were oblivious to the strained and cold atmosphere at the other end of the table. They were discussing an article on room makeovers that they both liked.

'I love all the bright colours they've chosen in this picture,' Olivia said, pointing to one page. 'When I have my own room, I'm going to decorate it like this,' she added.

'You have an ugly taste!' Angeline quipped, taking the magazine from her and flicking over the pages. 'This much nicer – shaggy sheep – much better,' Angeline added.

Olivia burst out laughing. 'Don't you mean shabby chic?'

'That's what I say, shaggy sheep!' Angeline retorted, throwing the magazine back at Olivia.

'Thank you for organising clearing up the Orangery, Madame DuPont,' Kate interjected before World War Three could break out between Angeline and Olivia.

'It is done except for tables and chairs,' Madame DuPont replied.

Kate nodded and took her cue. She took a deep breath and said, 'Raimond, would you get Sébastien to help you pack up the tables and chairs and take them back to the attic this afternoon, please? I want to get the Orangery back to some sort of normality as soon as possible,' she added.

'I 'ave my work to do this afternoon,' he answered gruffly. 'Use your Estate Manager to 'elp as he 'as nothing much to do, except makeup costs.'

Kate saw Stephen's jaw set and a little tic flicker under his left eye. She hoped he didn't think she believed what Raimond accused him of, but what could she say without starting an all-out argument again? Gritting her teeth, she replied firmly, 'Getting Sébastien to help you pack up the tables and chairs and take them back to the attic is *your* job.'

'Pah!' Raimond answered contemptuously, noisily scraping his chair across the stone floor as he got up from the table and stomped out of the kitchen.

Everyone stared – first at Raimond's departing back and then at Kate, waiting for her reaction. Kate just shook her head; she had as much idea as them as how to deal with Raimond!

Stephen got up and exited quietly as Kate sat, paralysed by indecision. In response, she quietly got up and went outside to find Isabelle and clear her head. Stephen's appointment as Estate Manager and the declaration of his feelings towards her earlier today were rapidly becoming more complicated.

It was hard enough that she was caught in the crossfire between Raimond and Stephen. But Kate also felt guilty that she'd been unable to spend time with Isabelle the previous evening during the party. Each time she planned to see if Isabelle was alright, she'd been side-tracked by one of the guests or had to deal with the caterers. It was not until the end of the evening when Kate looked in on her and found her fast asleep, that she realised she'd not seen Isabelle all evening after sending her away at the start of it. She found Isabelle, who had followed Stephen to the back of the Château. He was measuring the patio leading out from the Winter Salon doors.

'What are you doing?' Kate heard Isabelle ask Stephen as she approached.

'Measuring,' Stephen replied indifferently.

'Why?' Isabelle asked.

'I need to know how big this area is,' Stephen replied curtly, readjusting the tape measure.

'Why?' Isabelle asked again.

He straightened up and sighed. 'Can't you go and find something to do instead of getting under my feet?' he snapped, looking up at Isabelle as Kate rounded the corner. As she came into view, Stephen adjusted his scowl to a smile. 'Oh, hi. I thought it would be a better atmosphere out here,' he said apologetically.

Kate hadn't seen this impatient side of Stephen before and she was taken aback. If he were to stay and take on the Estate Manager's role, he needed to get along with everyone, including Isabelle – and Raimond. The little imp in her head nudged at her. However, she pretended not to have noticed Stephen's bad temper; after all, they had both just come from a particularly toxic lunchtime. No wonder he was irritable. She was, too.

Plastering a smile on her face and holding her hand out to Isabelle, she beckoned, 'Come along, Isabelle. Let's leave Stephen to finish his work and find something else to do.'

Stephen, looking somewhat awkward, nodded his thanks. She gave him a wry smile in return.

'I'm bored, Kate,' Isabelle moaned as they walked away hand in hand.

'So, what would you like to do this afternoon? I've just got one little job to do, then I'm all yours,' Kate replied.

'You said I could look at Mama's jewellery sometime. Can we do that this afternoon?' Isabelle implored.

'Yes, of course. It's going to rain this afternoon, so we need an indoor activity anyway. Going through Mama's jewellery will be a perfect activity. Still, first, I must check that Raimond and Sébastien are clearing the Orangery. Then we will go back to the Château and I'll fetch Mama's jewellery box. Maybe we could find a corner to sit in the Garden Room and get some snacks from Angeline to munch on while we go through Mama's jewellery box. What do you think?' Kate replied.

'Oh, yes. I love that idea,' Isabelle replied, skipping alongside Kate, her face wreathed in smiles.

As they approached the Orangery, they met up with Florence. Isabelle raced on ahead and flung her arms around her.

'*Grandy! Grandy!*' Isabelle cried.

'Whoa! Steady child. ' Florence replied with one of her tinkling laughs, 'You nearly knocked me over.'

'Where are you off to?' Kate asked Florence.

'I'm heading back to the Château. I've checked the gallery to ensure the paintings are still hanging up, and none have fallen. I was slightly concerned about one of the temporary stands being a bit wonky last night.'

'I've not had a chance to go into the gallery this morning. Was everything okay in there?' Kate asked.

'Yes, everything is fine. So, we're all set for the local newspaper photographer tomorrow to get some photographs for the paper,' Florence told Kate.

'Thank you for taking care of that and your help last night. I didn't get a chance to see you before you and Don went to bed. It went off very well, didn't it? I needn't have been so nervous,' Kate said, laughing.

'Yes, the art we chose to display in the gallery went down well. We've had lots of interest for sales of the paintings and possible commissions,' Florence replied.

'Did the ladies from the art retreat have a good time? I must catch up with them before they leave tomorrow,' Kate asked.

'Yes, they really enjoyed it. And the group were very excited listening to the lovely comments about their paintings,' Florence replied, smiling.

'Last night has been a good experience for me too, especially with the Paris exhibition coming up in a few weeks. I'm getting a little nervous though about whether they will like my art,' Kate confessed.

'Of course, they will like your paintings,' Florence replied, giving Kate's arm a playful nudge.

'Thanks for your vote of confidence, Florence,' Kate giggled.

'So, what are you two ladies up to this afternoon?' Florence enquired, pulling Isabelle into a tight hug. Isabelle giggled and wriggled free.

''You're squashing me, Grandy!' she protested. 'We are going to get some food from Angeline and then after finding Mama's jewellery box, find a corner in the Garden Room to try it on.' Isabelle gushed.

'Ah! While you are looking for your Mama's jewellery, perhaps you'd also look for my special locket then?' Florence replied.

'That silver locket you wear every day? Is it missing then?' Kate asked, looking concerned.

'Yes. I took it off last night to wear a different necklace with my dress. I was sure I left it on top of the dressing table along with the earrings and bracelet I usually wear that match the locket. When I came to put them on this morning, the earrings and bracelet were there, but the locket was missing,' Florence replied.

'Did you look to see if it had slipped down behind the dressing table, perhaps?' Kate asked.

'Oh yes. Don even pulled it out from the wall and lifted the carpet. Sadly, it was nowhere to be seen,' Florence replied, shaking her head.

'Oh dear, I know how much that locket means to you. I hope you find it,' Kate said, reassuringly squeezing Florence's arm. Isabelle stood by, looking uncomfortable and scraping her feet in the gravel.

Kate and Isabelle continued over to the Orangery in silence. They found Sébastien on his own, loading the trailer with the remains of the tables.

'Where's Raimond?' Kate asked.

'He 'ad a job to do,' Sébastien replied.

'Has he left you to do this all on your own?' Kate queried.

'He 'elped for some moments but was called away by Angeline,' Sébastien replied.

On hearing this, Kate could feel anger building up inside her. She barely managed a polite 'Thank you, Sébastien,' before grabbing Isabelle's hand and hurrying back to the Château.

'Slow down; my legs hurt!' Kate was eventually aware of Isabelle's complaint.

'I'm sorry. We're nearly there, look,' Kate replied, pointing to the front steps. Kate realised she'd been so wrapped up in her thoughts of learning that Raimond and Angeline were together that she'd forgotten that poor Isabelle was tagging along. 'Let's go and see what Angeline has been baking today,' Kate added as they entered the grand entrance hall. But on entering the kitchen, there was no sign of Angeline, only Madame DuPont tidying away some crockery.

'Where is Angeline?' Kate asked Madame DuPont.

'I not know. I have not seen Angeline for a few moments,' Madame DuPont replied. 'Can I help you with anything?' she added.

'Isabelle and I thought we'd had a little picnic in the Garden Room this afternoon while we look through Mother's jewellery box. I know you are probably busy, but could you make up a little box of goodies for us, please?' Kate replied.

'Maybe some madeleines and some chocolate eclairs and….' Isabelle interrupted.

'Let's leave it up to Madame DuPont, shall we?' Kate said, putting a playful hand over Isabelle's mouth to stop her from giving out her list of wants.

'Oh, okay,' Isabelle peeled Kate's hand away and sighed, slumping in the chair.

'I'm just going to get Mama's jewellery box. Wait for me here, please,' Kate added.

Kate ascended the stairs to the Marquis Suite to retrieve the jewellery box from the secret panel in her mother's bedroom where she had hidden it. As she rounded the second flight of stairs, she stopped abruptly and drew in a sharp intake of breath. Through the railings, Kate could clearly see Angeline coming out of the Marquis Suite. She was giggling and looking coyly back over her shoulder at Raimond, who was close behind her and teasingly prodding her onwards.

Chapter 29

28th August 1981 was ringed in red on the calendar in the kitchen. Today was Isabelle's ninth birthday. Kate watched as her little sister, all dressed up for her party, gracefully descended the stairs.

'Happy Birthday, Isabelle!' Kate called up to her. It was the first glimpse Kate had caught of Isabelle in the new dress Olivia had been put in charge of buying for her party. 'You look lovely.' Kate added.

Isabelle smiled and continued her descent, nose in the air; *the image of a budding Chatelaine herself*, Kate thought. She couldn't help but notice how grown-up Isabelle looked. She'd grown so tall and willowy, just like her Papa. Kate also observed that Isabelle was wearing pale pink lipstick and a hint of blue eyeshadow, matching her pale cornflower blue dress. Olivia's doing, no doubt! She reflected how lucky Isabelle was that her childhood was much more easy-going than hers, albeit unusual in its own way. Kate's strict religious upbringing by her adoptive parents had been far from easygoing. *She* hadn't been allowed to touch makeup until she left school. Kate remembered when she'd experimented with makeup at her friend's house and had gone home wearing it. When her mother saw her, she'd flown at her, telling her she looked like a Jezebel!

'Come and join your guests, Isabelle. They're waiting for you,' Kate said, placing an arm around Isabelle's shoulders as she reached the bottom of the long staircase. Kate kissed her cheek before steering her towards the corridor leading to the Winter Salon.

'Happy Birthday!' chorused the assembled group as Isabelle entered the room. Isabelle blushed and momentarily, her grown-up air deserted her.

'Joyeux Anniversaire!' Isabelle's best friend, Stephanie, gushed as she rushed up to her and thrust a brightly coloured, wrapped present into her hands.

'*Merci!*' Isabelle replied excitedly. The now would-be grown-up was replaced by an excited nine-year-old, ripping off the paper around the package to reveal a display box with a cloth doll inside. It had a chubby face, arms, and legs; its thick mass of blonde woollen hair was tied into two bunches by lilac ribbons on either side of its head. She was dressed in a lilac gingham smocked dress and white shoes. 'A Cabbage Patch Kid!' Isabelle cried, 'just what I wanted! How magnifique!' she added. She read the enclosed adoption papers and announced, 'Her name is Julie.'

Kate was in charge of photographs. She snapped away at the excited group clamouring around Isabelle. It was a joyous scene, seeing everyone happy and smiling for once – even Raimond!

'She is magnifique, ma chérie,' Madame DuPont agreed, smiling down at Isabelle. 'Here is my cadeau, but open it later with the other cadeaux,' she added.

'Thank you,' Isabelle replied, flinging her arms around Madame DuPont's neck while holding her present tightly.

'And here's mine and Papi's present,' Florence said, handing her a small, prettily wrapped package. Seeing Isabelle's hands were full, she suggested, 'Perhaps I'll pop it with the rest of your presents for you to open later.'

'Thank you, Grandy,' Isabelle replied, giving her a beaming smile.

'You do look so grown up in your new dress. It's charming. Are you sure you're only nine years old today and not a teenager?' Florence added with a chuckle.

'No, I'm nine today, *silly*,' Isabelle replied with a frown.

'I know, I was only teasing. But you have grown up suddenly!' Florence replied.

'Olivia and I chose the dress without Kate, didn't we?' she said, turning to Olivia.

'Yes, we had a lovely girly shopping day looking at lots of dresses,' Olivia replied.

'Yes, lots and lots of dresses….' Isabelle added, pulling a face. Olivia pulled a look back. 'But I do like this one,' Isabelle admitted, and Olivia beamed at her.

'I love your necklace, Florence. Is it new?' Olivia asked, peering closely at the heart-shaped silver necklace Florence was wearing.

'No, I've had this one for a while. It has a moonstone in the middle of the heart. See how it reflects colour around it? It's a good luck gem and my birthstone,' Florence replied.

'It *is* beautiful,' Olivia cooed. 'But where is the locket you usually wear? I loved that one.'

'Sadly, I've misplaced it,' Florence replied, shaking her head.

'Oh, that's awful. I hope you find it!' Olivia responded.

'Thank you. I do, too. It's a special necklace and one very dear to my heart,' Florence replied.

Isabelle shuffled her feet before interrupting, 'Olivia, let's go and put these presents on the table with the others and dive into the food. I'm starving!'

Kate laughed and abandoned her role as the official photographer to help carry the mound of presents over to the table where the birthday feast awaited.

Madame DuPont and Angeline had been baking all week and, for once, had worked well together. It really did look like a feast. Isabelle, who had been distracted and had skipped off with Stephanie, soon came running when called, making a beeline for the long table on the terrace piled high with food. Diving into the assortment of food on offer, they knocked over a jug of brightly coloured juice, which formed a puddle on the paper tablecloth. Undeterred, the bunch of hungry children continued to grab sandwiches and other savoury foods and, when done, filled their mouths with petite fours and sweets. Kate smiled ruefully – Isabelle might look older than nine, all dressed up, but she was clearly still a child. Kate sighed with a sense of relief. She feared losing her parents would have a lasting effect on Isabelle, forcing her to grow up too fast. At least today, that didn't seem to be the case!

Angeline had made an enormous birthday cake. It was covered in thick white icing and decorated with tiny pink roses in the shape of a number nine, along with nine pink candles. This took pride in place in the centre of the table, amongst the vibrant plates overflowing with food and the steadily growing puddles of spilt juice.

'Better get the cake cut and distributed soon before it floats away,' Kate joked to Madame DuPont. Madame DuPont nodded, chuckling.

'I think the icing will protect it for a while,' she laughed. 'Angeline has plastered it on since Mademoiselle Isabelle has such a sweet tooth.'

After the candles were lit and blown out several times and several choruses of *Joyeux Anniversaire* had been sung, Kate organised games to keep the children occupied for the rest of the afternoon. These included blowing soapy bubbles, which saw the excited children squealing with delight as they chased the bubbles around the terrace and onto the lawn. This was followed by hide and seek and the final game took the form of charades to calm them all down.

As the party ended, parents picked up their tired and dishevelled children one by one and Isabelle and Kate waved them off.

'Thank you, Kate,' Isabelle exclaimed when the last guest had departed. 'I had so much fun – and now I'm going to play with my presents.' She grinned and ran off towards the pile of opened presents on the now tidied and cleaned feast table. Kate laughed as she watched her leave. Her laughter stopped as she sensed someone behind her; she turned around.

'Have you seen what they've done to the Winter Salon?' Stephen asked Kate, frowning. He solemnly took her hand and led her to the Winter Salon.

'Ah…' she said as they surveyed the mess in the doorway.

It resembled an assault course with balloons drifting aimlessly on the floor amongst the discarded wrapping paper, making it difficult to walk around or through the room out to the terrace.

'It's fine. We can easily tidy it up,' Kate replied brightly.

'But do you think hanging those Happy Birthday banners all over the doors and fireplace was a good idea? They may have damaged the freshly painted walls,' Stephen continued, frowning and pointing to where the brightly coloured banners adorned the room.

'No, they should be fine; we used some special fixing stuff. Maybe you would help us take the banners down?' Kate asked.

'No, sorry, I can't. I have to go through some estimates,' Stephen replied stiffly. His expression, rather than the refusal, annoyed Kate – a mix of disgust and disdain.

'At this time of night?' Kate questioned with an edge to her voice. Sensing someone else had joined them, Kate turned around sharply.

'I'll 'elp you, Madame,' Raimond chipped in, giving Stephen a sideways look. 'It was wonderful seeing the children 'ave so much fun. It 'asn't been an easy time for la petite fille.'

Despite her annoyance with Stephen, Kate relaxed in the warmth of Raimond's smile and the sentiments he'd expressed – at least *he* understood! She looked at Stephen again; he was still staring at the mess and Kate realised she'd not considered how he must have felt seeing all his hard work swamped with messy, noisy children. On this one, she couldn't win.

'Thank you, Raimond. But maybe we'll leave it until the morning; it's getting late and there is a lot of mess to clear up, isn't there?' Kate replied with an overly bright smile, hoping it would mollify both, particularly Stephen. 'Maybe we'll have parties outside in the future.'

With that, Kate made a quick getaway to ensure that Isabelle, the reason for all the mess, was safely out of the way of making any more. Kate found her in the kitchen, regaling Angeline and Madame DuPont with what she'd thought were the *best-ever* moments of the party.

'Come on, bedtime, young lady,' Kate stood in the doorway, beckoning her.

As Kate tucked her into bed, Isabelle hugged her tightly and told her she'd had *'the bestest time'*. As Kate was exhausted and didn't want to risk facing either Raimond or Stephen again, she made her way to her bedroom. She kicked off her shoes, flopped onto her bed and let out a satisfied sigh. Lying on her bed, Kate reflected on how perfect, much to her relief, the day had been – most of it anyway.

Kate was cross with herself the following morning, finding she'd slept in late; there was so much to do. Clearing up after the party, packing up her paintings ready to take to the gallery the next day in preparation for the exhibition, and, as always, navigating between Stephen and Raimond.

'Good morning, Madame Kate,' Angeline greeted her as she entered the kitchen. 'You want some eggs for breakfast?' she asked.

'No time today, thank you. Just toast and coffee, please,' Kate replied. 'I have to start clearing up from the party,' she added, spotting that Raimond and Stephen were already seated at the table. She smiled at them, hoping neither had taken offence to anything she'd said the night before.

'That's all done, Madame,' Raimond announced.

'All done?' Kate asked.

'Sébastien and me 'ad an early start, and all is back together now,' Raimond replied, looking pleased and glancing at Stephen.

'Oh! I don't know what to say other than thank you, Raimond. I really appreciate it. I still have to pack up my paintings for the trip to Paris tomorrow, so clearing up after the party is a great help.'

Raimond looked smug. 'I can 'elp you with your paintings too if you like?' he offered.

Kate was taken aback by Raimond's sudden *helpfulness* and wondered what was behind it all. 'Thank you. I might need some help loading them into the van later. I'll give you a shout if I do,' Kate replied. She looked across at Stephen, surprised at his silence; Stephen avoided her gaze and poured himself another cup of coffee.

'What are you loading in the van? Where are you going?' Isabelle asked as she blundered into the kitchen, still in her pyjamas and looking half asleep.

'It's the art exhibition in Paris this weekend, remember?' Kate replied.

'Oh yes! Can I come?' Isabelle pleaded, cuddling up to Kate.

'No, not this time. I will be too busy to look after you. Maybe another time,' Kate answered, patting her hand.

'But Olivia could come and look after me? *Pleeeease*, let me come?' Isabelle begged.

'I'm happy to go with you and look after Isabelle,' Olivia chipped in with a big smile. 'Paris is such a lovely city. I would be happy to spend the weekend there.'

'See, Olivia doesn't mind coming to look after me! So... can I come? *Pleeeease*, pretty *pleeeease*?' Isabelle pleaded, placing both arms around Kate and hugging her tightly.

'Hmmm...' Kate looked from Isabelle to Olivia, then over to Madame DuPont, smiling indulgently at Isabelle and encouragingly at her. Kate wondered how she would get out of taking Isabelle with her.

'If it had been Mama going, she would have taken me,' Isabelle added slyly.

'Oh, okay, okay, you can come. On one condition, though....'

'What? Anything! I promise, anything!' Isabelle replied wide-eyed.

'I'll let you come as long as you promise to behave yourself and do whatever Olivia or I tell you to do. And not to get in the way while I'm setting up the exhibition. Do you promise?' Kate asked.

'I promise, cross my heart and....'

'There's no need to say that,' Kate interrupted. 'Just do as I ask,' she added, laughing and returning Isabelle's hug.

Chapter 30

As they neared Paris, they could see the white-domed Basilica of the Sacré-Cœur on the hill's summit ahead of them. Its majestic dome gleamed in the morning sunshine.

'Look at that big church!' Isabelle marvelled.

'Yes, it's magnificent, isn't it? There are lots to see in and around here. I wonder...'

'Wonder what, Kate?' Isabelle asked.

'I wonder if there's a bus tour or the like that you and Olivia could do while I'm setting up the exhibition? It could be a good educational opportunity for you to learn something about the city's history,' Kate responded.

'Educational? Ugh! I'm still on holiday, remember?' Isabelle replied, looking horrified.

'No matter. There are always new things we can learn every day and there's so much history here,' Kate answered.

'History! Ugh!'

Ignoring Isabelle's response to her idea of a bus tour and before Isabelle could list her reasons why going on a bus tour was a bad idea, Kate quickly added. 'I will ask Madame Schmidt if she knows of any tours you and Olivia could do.'

Marie Schmidt's gallery was on one of the side streets in the vibrant Montmartre district. Madame Schmidt greeted them warmly as they drove into the courtyard at the back of the gallery. She signalled for two young men to come and help Kate unload her paintings.

'Welcome! Did you have a good journey?' she asked.

'Yes, thank you, we did. We set out early and missed most of the heavy traffic, it seems,' Kate responded.

'Very early!' Isabelle grumbled.

'Come and have some refreshments before I show you where you can hang your paintings,' Madame Schmidt said, showing them into the gallery.

'Is there a tour that Isabelle and Olivia could take this morning while I set up my paintings?' Kate asked over coffee and pastries, which had already been laid out on the table in the staff restroom.

'And somewhere we could do some shopping?' Olivia added, smiling innocently.

'Yes, you can do both,' Madame Schmidt replied, shuffling through the paperwork in a large metal filing cabinet and handing Olivia a leaflet. 'Here you are. There is an open-top bus tour; it leaves roughly every thirty minutes from the corner. You can also 'hop on and off' and visit the shops along the way,' she added.

'Thank you, that's marvellous!' Olivia turned to Isabelle. 'Hurry up and finish your orange juice, Isabelle, and we'll get going.'

'Okay… if we must,' Isabelle complained. 'But not trying on hundreds of dresses again, please….'

'Remember your promise, Isabelle? Do as Olivia tells you to, and no running off, okay?' Kate said, wagging her finger at Isabelle.

'Yes, I know, I know….' Isabelle muttered.

***

The trip was not turning out to be as exciting as Isabelle hoped it would be. Kate had continually nagged her all the way in the car to Paris about what she could and couldn't do and reminded her to be on her best behaviour. Wasn't she always? And now she was stuck with soppy Olivia for the rest of the morning, doing a stupid bus tour and endless hours of dress shopping, no doubt!

'Come on, slowcoach,' Olivia called. 'The bus will be going soon and we'll miss it if we're not careful.'

Good, cos I don't care, Isabelle thought sullenly, wishing she'd brought Jacqueline along for company. She followed Olivia onto the open-top tour bus and waited while she bought the tickets from the driver.

'Do you want to hold onto them?' Olivia asked Isabelle before adding, 'I put you in charge of bus tickets!' smiling ingratiatingly at Isabelle without waiting for a reply.

'Alright,' Isabelle replied sullenly, taking them from Olivia and stuffing them into her bag but wondering why Olivia thought she would want them. Being in charge of the bus tickets didn't make her look forward to the bus trip any more than it had before. Nevertheless, Isabelle was the first to clamber up the steep spiral staircase to the top deck. She hurried down the narrow aisle in the middle of the bus between the rows of red leather seats on either side before plonking herself down on an empty seat at the front of the bus. If she was to be stuck on this boring bus, she might as well get the best view!

'Here. I've saved us a seat!' Isabelle yelled down the bus to Olivia, who was still struggling up the stairs.

'Well done! You've chosen some good seats. We'll get a bit of shelter with that half window in front of us,' Olivia replied.

Isabelle sat hugging herself, smug she'd done the right thing for a change instead of Olivia grumbling at her as usual.

The conductor rang his bell and the bus slowly pulled out into the traffic. A recorded voice came over the loudspeaker and began a commentary in French. Olivia pulled a face. 'I've no idea what he's saying. I'll need you to translate,' she said, laughing.

'He's just saying where we're going, and he will be pointing out places of interest. You know, all that boring stuff,' Isabelle explained.

Isabelle slumped back in her seat. She folded her arms in front of her, putting her feet up on the window ledge. Olivia tapped her legs, 'Down, please! Remember what Kate said about behaving yourself.'

Isabelle sighed as she put down her legs as instructed. This bus trip was going to be awful – she could tell!

The bus rocked side to side as they travelled along the road, the commentator pointing out various places of interest. Isabelle was bored and getting very hot and sweaty sitting in the full sun. The bus pulled up at a set of traffic lights; Isabelle gazed absent-mindedly at the shop window alongside her. In the shop window, she saw a poster, *Folies Bergère*, with a picture of a beautiful-looking lady in a white and gold sparkling costume and wearing a large feather headdress. Isabelle sat up straight in her seat. She peered through the dusty window before her to get a closer look.

'Do you know where the *Folies Bergère* is?' Isabelle asked Olivia excitedly.

'You're asking me? I've no idea,' Olivia shrugged.

'Can I have that bus tour leaflet Madame Schmidt gave you, please? I think there's a map on it,' Isabelle asked.

'Be my guest, but I couldn't make sense of it – it's all in French,' Olivia replied, handing her the leaflet from inside her bag.

Isabelle studied the map. 'Can we get off at the next stop, please?' Isabelle asked.

'Why?' Olivia replied.

'Cos, I'm hot, and I need the bathroom.'

'Okay, I wouldn't mind getting a drink and using the bathroom. Maybe we could also look around the shops before continuing the tour,' Olivia replied, peering out the window at the gigantic department store they were passing.

Shops! Isabelle inwardly groaned at the thought, but she had a plan!

Luckily, the bus stop was some way from the department store, but Olivia had a plan to make her way back to it! Isabelle trailed behind Olivia. They explored the narrow, winding, cobbled streets jam-packed with sidewalk cafés, pavement artists and shops until they came across an outdoor market. Its fresh produce was set out on tables under a sea of red and white canvas awnings – plump fruit and vegetables, cheeses, loaves of bread of all shapes and sizes, jet-black shiny mussels and containers full of flowers for sale. They wandered around it for hours before Isabelle pointed to the sidewalk café. 'Can we stop here for a drink? I'm tired,' Isabelle moaned.

'Okay, but let's pop into the boutique next door first,' Olivia answered. "I don't think we're going to find that big shop again, so we'll just have to look in all the little ones instead.'

'Do we have to?' Isabelle whined.

Olivia ignored the question and entered the shop. Isabelle followed, dragging her feet. *At least they were out of the sun*, she thought as they made their way through the narrow aisles that snaked around the shop. Isabelle slumped down onto the floor in a corner out of the way. She'd never seen so many tee shirts, sweatshirts, bags and belts hanging from racks packed between the floor and ceiling. Isabelle searched through her bag for her handkerchief. As she pulled it out, something shiny fell out and caught her eye. She reached out to retrieve it. It was Grandy's locket!

Isabelle had tried to return it to Grandy's room several times, but she'd not found an opportunity to slip into her room without being seen. So, in the meantime, she had dropped it into her bag to keep it safe. As she sat slumped in the corner, Isabelle opened the locket and looked at the photograph of Grandy's husband inside. She was lost in dreamy imaginings of her Grandy's story behind the locket and how romantic it was when, right by her ear, Olivia's voice made her jump.

'What have you got there?' Olivia shouted.

'Er. Ummm…' Isabelle dropped the locket back into the open bag and clutched it to her.

'That's Florence's locket. Give it to me!' Olivia yelled, reaching for Isabelle's bag.

Isabelle scrambled to her feet and pushed Olivia away, holding her bag tightly against her. Olivia went sprawling on the floor, legs waving in the air like a beetle stuck on its back. Isabelle stopped long enough to laugh aloud before running towards the front of the shop. She weaved in and out of the clothing racks, ran out onto the street, and disappeared into the crowds outside.

Isabelle ran until she could run no further and flopped down on a bench to catch her breath. Isabelle smiled to herself; Olivia would never have been able to catch up with her in those silly high-heel shoes she insisted on wearing. She was safe here for a while – but where was here? Isabelle took out the bus tour leaflet and studied the map to see if she could work out where she was and where she would find the *Folies Bergère*. She would run away and go there, and then they would all be sorry that they'd been ignoring her! She turned the map this way, but the map made no sense.

'Are you lost?' Isabelle heard someone ask.

She turned to see that a girl of Olivia's age had sat down on the bench beside her.

'Yes, sort of,' Isabelle replied sheepishly. Kate and her mother had warned her about speaking to strangers, but this was a lady Olivia's age, so she felt sure it was okay.

'Where do you need to get to?' the stranger continued.

'I was on a bus tour with my sister and we got split up. See, here are the tickets,' Isabelle replied, holding out the bus tickets.

'Where were you heading?' she asked.

'*Folies Bergère*. Do you know where that is?' Isabelle asked, hopefully.

'Yes, that's easy. You can hop back on the bus from that bus stop over there and ask the driver to let you off there,' she replied, pointing to a stop marked on the map. There was the *Folies Bergère!* Isabelle breathed a sigh of relief and thanked the stranger before heading to the bus stop to wait for the next bus.

Her tummy jumped around and gurgled as she stood at the bus stop, waiting. It felt like a butterfly trapped in there, a strange mix of fear and excitement – she wasn't used to traffic or hordes of people. A motorbike roared past so close to her that it made her jump back. She watched anxiously as the traffic whizzed non-stop and at speed in both directions. She struggled to keep her place in the bus queue and on the pavement as she was jostled by shoppers and passers-by. They squeezed past her on the narrow pavement, almost knocking her into the road several times. She didn't like this. She didn't like this at all, but it would all be alright once she found the *Folies Bergère* and the beautiful ladies she'd seen in Angeline's magazine. She was sure it would be okay then, *wouldn't it?*

Chapter 31

Kate wasn't sure what she had expected as she stood alongside Madame Schmidt in the middle of the Art Gallery. Still, she'd certainly not expected such a remarkable place. It was a bright, cavernous space with a vast vaulted oak ceiling; a wooden staircase at the back of the Gallery led to the mezzanine floor above.

Turning around slowly on the spot, Kate gazed at the artwork hanging on the walls. There was an array of still-life, abstracts, portraits and landscapes; some dramatic, others delicate and simple in their style with mixtures of vibrant, warm, subtle and earthy colours. Each piece highlighted its own individual focal points.

'This place is astonishing!' she exclaimed.

Madame Schmidt smiled. 'Come, let me show you your space. Marc has unpacked and placed your paintings in there for you. Once you have decided where you want them, he will hang them for you, too,' she informed Kate.

'Thank you,' Kate replied, returning the smile and trying not to show she was a little overwhelmed. Kate had come prepared to hang the paintings herself. She had brought her trusty little toolbox containing bits and bobs, her hammer, and other essential tools. Kate acknowledged Marc with a grateful smile and nod as they followed Madame Schmidt to a small, three-sided, white-walled, cuboid area to the left of the main room.

'Here we are!' Madame Schmidt declared, gesturing to the empty space in front of them. 'Anything you need, let Marc know; he's at your disposal,' she added with a smile.

Kate's footsteps echoed as she walked around her allocated area. It looked so big. *Had she brought along enough artwork to fill it?* She wondered. Of course, she had! Hadn't Madame Schmidt been given the measurements? *How will my paintings compare with the others hanging here?* She worried. Oh well, it is too late to be concerned about that now. She was here now and there was no turning back, she told herself.

Conscious that Madame Schmidt was still standing alongside her, Kate turned to her. 'Thank you, Madame Schmidt. I'm sure we will manage just fine,' she responded, trying to look confident despite her churning insides.

After Madame Schmidt had gone, Kate turned to the young man standing awkwardly to one side. 'We haven't been formally introduced, have we?' she asked. 'I'm Kate Sinclair,' then wondering if it was the right thing to kiss his cheeks or whether to be more formal. Ultimately, she plumped for the latter and thrust her hand out to him.

'Hello, I'm Marc Boucher,' he replied in a polite British accent, grasping Kate's hand and shaking it firmly.

'You're not French then?' Kate remarked.

'Only partly; my father is, but my mother is English,' he replied. 'I don't actually live here; I live in the West Country in England.'

'How did you end up working here in this gallery, if you don't mind me asking?'

'I'm a work-away volunteer. I'm currently studying art and working here during the university holidays to get some experience.'

'Well, thank you for helping me today. I see you've already removed the reams of protective wrap I used around the paintings,' Kate said, laughing. 'It appears my caution has paid off, though, as I can't see any damage so far,' she added, inspecting her artwork resting up against the walls.

'I have had a quick look, too, and I think they are all fine,' Marc agreed. 'I love your work, by the way. My particular favourite is the field of sunflowers,' he added, pointing to the painting nearest to them, which was catching the sunlight as it streamed through the doorway into the display area.

'Thank you. I think that is one of my favourites, too,' Kate replied, nodding in agreement. 'Sunflowers are one of my favourite flowers; they bring so much joy; they're such happy flowers, aren't they?' she added.

Kate's thoughts returned to when she painted the picture; it was before her mother died. The flowers captured some of the carefree joy she'd felt that summer's day – joy that had been in somewhat short supply recently. Although this trip to Paris was a bright spot amongst the pressures of keeping everything going at the Château... Kate stopped her maudlin thoughts as she didn't want to think about that right now – she *wouldn't* think about that right now. Everything was in hand with Stephen as Estate

Manager; Isabelle was appeased by coming to Paris with her and under Olivia's supervision and Raimond… Well, Raimond, she would leave to think about until much later!

'I agree. The flowers are striking. I guess that's why Van Gogh painted them – to capture some of their joy for himself,' Marc replied with a smile.

'Yes, maybe,' Kate compared Van Gogh to herself – not for her ability, but in their respective emotional states. She'd already recognised that need for some joy as well. 'I love how they stand so tall, and their brilliant yellow flowerheads really do turn and face the sun. They are, indeed, a joy to grow and paint,' Kate replied, smiling wistfully.

'I'm no gardener, I'm afraid. I leave that to my mother, but I can appreciate your painting,' Marc replied, smiling. 'And I might even try painting some sunflowers myself now.'

'Thank you! There are masses of sunflower fields all over France for you to paint. They flower from early June to mid-August. The best places to see them are in Provence. I painted this picture there last year. It's also a good place to see and paint the lavender fields. That's if you get the chance one day,' Kate added, slipping into teacher mode without realising.

'Well, I'm not a painter either – I'm more of a sculptor. But thank you for the tip. I wish my tutors at the art school were more encouraging of us to try other media. We do tend to get stuck in a rut sometimes.'

'Oh,' Kate blushed. 'I didn't mean to preach, but I'm glad if my idea helps.'

'It does,' Marc beamed at her. 'Maybe I'll even become a painter one day! By the way, putting in my own two pennorth, have you seen the sculptures in the exhibition upstairs? They are brilliant,' Marc replied.

'Oh? Perhaps you could show me up there after we've finished here?' Kate asked. Marc smiled and nodded delightedly.

'Madame Schmidt was even gracious enough to include one of mine,' he whispered. 'A tiny one…' he beamed.

'How exciting!' Kate grinned back. Kate was confident that she and Marc would get along well and he would do a much better – and easier – job of hanging her work than she would. Maybe this exhibition trip wouldn't be as demanding as she'd feared after all.

Kate had already done a rough sketch of how she wanted her artwork grouped and displayed. With Marc's help and following the plan she had drawn up, they carefully handled the paintings, standing each one up against the wall where they would be hung. One by one, Kate passed each picture for Marc to hang at eye level, standing back to check how the arrangement worked.

'Yes, I'm happy with that,' Kate nodded. 'Let's hang the ones above them now.' Kate passed the first picture to Marc, who had climbed up the ladder and waited to receive it. 'I'm so grateful to have your help today, Marc,' Kate said. 'I hate heights. Even at that height, it would worry me!' she said nervously.

'It doesn't bother me, and I'm only too happy to help,' he replied, smiling.

The paintings were all hung in their final positions, straightened and secured. The spotlights were adjusted to ensure the artwork was lit to its optimum. Marc climbed up the ladder once more; this time, he placed cards under the paintings, showing each one's details and price.

'Time to put the kettle on and make a cup of tea, I think!' Kate announced as she stood back to admire her exhibition. It had been months of planning and now her first exhibition was ready to be received by the public! But Kate's moment of personal satisfaction was shattered as Olivia burst through the door of the Gallery, howling like a banshee.

'I've… I've… lost Isabelle!' she wailed, coming to a halt in front of Kate and standing there wringing her hands melodramatically.

Chapter 32

'Sit down and calmly tell me about it from the beginning,' Kate said, guiding Olivia to a chair. Kate attempted to quieten her hysterical outpourings despite feeling her own anxiety reaching a crescendo. 'What do you mean you've *lost Isabelle*?'

'We were in a shop and she ran away!' Olivia replied in between sobs.

'I don't understand. Why would Isabelle run away?' Kate asked, outwardly trying to stay calm, but a feeling of panic was rising inside her.

'I saw her with Florence's locket and questioned her about it and she ran away,' Olivia replied, biting her lip.

'How long ago was this? Where were you? Is there anything you can think of to help us find her?' Kate's questions came tumbling out as she felt her stomach twisting in knots.

She listened intently to Olivia's account of their movements that morning whilst at the same time trying to keep a clear head.

Olivia explained they had left the tour bus and walked around the shops and a market, but she didn't know where. It had all looked so alike to her. Then they'd gone into a shop – but she couldn't remember the name of it – she'd turned her back just for a moment and…

'There she was, sitting on the floor, playing with Florence's locket and being absolutely brazen about it!' Olivia's hysteria had now morphed into indignation.

Kate listened patiently, trying to contain her fury at Olivia for being so irresponsible to lose a nine-year-old child. She obviously had not been paying Isabelle enough attention. Her head was no doubt in the clouds, as usual. However, it did seem that there was a simple explanation for Isabelle running off – the appearance of Florence's locket. Kate bit her lip as she debated how to deal with the situation.

'There's nothing for it,' she announced eventually. 'We will have to call in the gendarmes,' she told Olivia. 'Although what they have to go on, given the account you've given me on your whereabouts, goodness knows how they will know where to start!' she retorted.

'I'm sorry, Kate,' Olivia replied, snivelling. 'Don't call the gendarmes just yet. Let's call Raimond and see what he suggests first.'

'Raimond? And how can Raimond help?' Kate replied crossly.

'He used to live here, remember? He knows the city like the back of his hand. Maybe if I told him the places I remembered seeing, he might recognise the landmarks and work out where Isabelle might be?' she replied. 'And Isabelle is close to him. It's worth a try, isn't it?' Olivia pleaded.

Kate thought for a moment. 'I don't know….' She didn't relish calling in the gendarmes either. Yet, Isabelle was only nine and Paris was a big city – potentially dangerous for a child.

'Please, let's try. Let's ring Raimond?' Olivia begged. 'I am so sorry. I know I should have paid more attention to what she was doing, but I got caught up; I've never been to Paris before. Anyway, you know Isabelle, she's always complaining to get her own way … if the gendarmes get involved, this might go on my records. How would I ever get another job working with children?' Olivia howled.

Taking pity on Olivia, who looked dejected and repentant, Kate gave in and agreed to ring Raimond. 'But you have to think about everything you can remember, too,' she cautioned Olivia. The latter nodded emphatically as Kate dialled Raimond's number. Kate listened to his surprised, yet clearly pleased she'd asked for his help after she'd told him why she was ringing.

'I'm on my way, don't worry, Madame. I'll be there as soon as possible,' Raimond assured her.

'Thank you, Raimond,' Kate replied, her voice quivering as she tried not to cry with relief. For all their differences, she instinctively felt she could rely on him. Kate didn't want to involve the gendarmes unless she had to – what would it say about her? She was more interested in her exhibition than her little sister.

Raimond arrived some three hours later and found Kate looking worried and ashen-faced. Olivia was sitting in the corner, her eyes puffy and swollen, her face red and blotchy.

'Thank goodness you're here,' Kate ran to Raimond on seeing him. 'I'm so worried. Isabelle's been missing for hours now,' she added, trying to hold back the tears that were pricking the back of her eyes.

'I'm 'ere now, I will find 'er. Don't worry,' Raimond replied gently, placing his hand reassuringly on her shoulder. 'Now,' he said in a more business-like tone, turning to Olivia, 'What do you remember about where you were when she ran off?' He listened intently to Olivia's account of their movements, nodding in places and asking questions in others.

Raimond rose from his seat. 'Eh bien, I go now. I think I know where you were, so it'll be a case of asking around to begin with and see if anyone saw 'er. I hope to be back with Mademoiselle Isabelle very soon,' Raimond announced. He gave Kate a gentle hug. 'Don't worry,' he said softly as he left the Gallery to look for Isabelle. 'Les Parisiennes are good people. We will find 'er safe and sound – but maybe a little sorry for 'erself. Olivia, you go back to the hotel, and Kate, you stay 'ere; if Isabelle finds 'er own way back, then at least there will be someone at either place.'

As Kate watched him leave, she felt overwhelming relief that Raimond was here and taking charge. Kate also couldn't help thinking about the reassuring hug he'd given her before he left. She'd not treated him very well in the past, so maybe his surliness had been her own fault because of this. He certainly didn't seem surly or churlish now – quite the reverse. She'd also not forgotten that he'd told her how beautiful she'd looked at the Winter Salon soiree. *Had she been wrong about him all this time?*

Kate sent Olivia back to the hotel, as Raimond had suggested. She was tired of her constant crying anyway; Kate welcomed being left alone to her thoughts for a while. As she sat back into the chair by the reception desk and waited, the bright afternoon light started to dull. Kate acknowledged that the emotions of the day had exhausted her. Her thoughts drifted over the day's events as she closed her eyes against her nagging headache. She floated off to sleep. The high-pitched shrill of the telephone made her jump.

'Hello?' she answered anxiously.

'Oh, hello, Kate. It's Stephen here. I wondered if there was any news?'

Her heart bumped disconsolately against her ribs that it wasn't Raimond on the other end of the telephone. 'No, nothing yet,' she replied dolefully but nevertheless appreciative that Stephen was showing some concern. 'Raimond is out looking for Isabelle now. He's confident he will find her,' she replied, realising, much to her surprise, that she was smiling despite herself as she mentioned Raimond's name.

'That's good news. You must be relieved Raimond is there looking for her?' Stephen replied.

'Yes, I am, very! How are things back at the Château? Anything new there?' she asked.

'Umm… no, not really,' Stephen hesitated.

'You don't sound too sure, Stephen. Is everything okay?'

'Yes… and no….' Stephen paused again, then added, 'This probably isn't the time to discuss it.'

'Discuss what?' Kate asked apprehensively. *Now, what had been going on in the last few hours?* She wondered. Not Madame DuPont and Angeline at it again? Or another run-in with Raimond before Raimond had left for Paris? No, it couldn't be that. Raimond hadn't said anything when he arrived. Nevertheless, she waited nervously for Stephen's reply.

'I've been offered another job,' Stephen announced.

His words hit her like a bombshell. 'But… but I thought you'd agreed to take the role of Estate Manager at the Château?' Kate cried.

'Well, yes, I know I did. But things have changed since then,' Stephen replied.

'What's changed?' Kate asked quickly.

'Look, perhaps this is the wrong time to discuss this. Let's leave it for now and talk it over face-to-face when you return.'

'No!' Kate's response was sharper than she'd intended, but she felt no inclination to be fobbed off right now. 'This conversation is not well-timed, you're right, but now you've brought it up, please continue!' she replied curtly.

'Well, I have just been offered a long-term contract in the UK. It's restoring a mansion house that has had extensive fire damage. It's a big project and a very prestigious one. The project is perfect for me – using all my skills and experience – and it's the sort of work I enjoy. They need someone urgently,' Stephen explained. 'And…'

'And what about my Château? You said you loved its history and enjoyed working on it?' Kate reminded him.

'I do love the Château; it's a lovely home. And that's exactly what it is – a home, your home. It's not a historical monument, something to restore and preserve to hand down to future generations. That's the kind of work I love doing – conserving historical buildings to prolong their life. That's why I was shocked when I found the Winter Salon looking trashed after Isabelle's party.'

'Yes, I realised afterwards that holding Isabelle's party in there and making a mess had upset you. I am really sorry about that. But you're right;

the Château is a living home to live in and enjoy. Even to make the occasional mess in. It's not one of your stuffy museums,' Kate acknowledged.

'No, please don't be sorry, I do understand. Your vision for that room was for it to be used. I see it only as something to look at and admire. So, you see, clearly, we're not on the same page,' Stephen added.

'Does that go for our relationship, too?' Kate asked after a moment's silence.

'Sadly, I think that may be the case. I can't see we can have one without the other....' Stephen's voice trailed off.

'So, you're running away again then?' Kate asked sarcastically.

'It may appear that way, but there's one thing you have taught me over the last few months – to face my feelings and not run away from them. That is what I am doing now by being upfront with you. I feel I *can* tell you what has been weighing heavily on my mind for the past few weeks and not run away from it.'

'Really? Go on...' Kate said caustically.

'I still feel there is something special between us, but I've realised we have different goals. Yours for the next few years is to be the guardian of Isabelle and the Château. I don't see myself settling down in one place with a wife or family; rather, to move around and have a career. I don't think I'm ready to commit to your goals or a long-term relationship with you right now. The last thing I would want to do is hurt you if we entered a relationship and it didn't work out. You mean too much to me for that to happen,' Stephen explained. 'I'm so sorry, Kate. I do hope you find Isabelle and things work out for you. I'll get things sorted here and packed, so I'm gone before you get back to save any more upset.'

The telephone clicked softly at the other end and Kate was left transfixed, still holding the receiver to her ear. Her heart was beating fast, her breathing was irregular and tears had begun to fill her eyes. Isabelle was lost, and now Stephen was about to be lost to her, too. She had followed Elisabeth's advice. *Follow your heart, decide what you want to do and go for it....* She'd given her heart and hopes to someone she believed was ready to build something special with her. Now, he was walking out of her life for a better job! It felt like her whole life was falling apart again – oh, when would she ever get it right?

Chapter 33

'Folies Bergère!' The bus tour driver shouted. Isabelle grabbed her bag and hurried down the bus aisle to the exit door.

'Merci beaucoup,' Isabelle sang out to the driver as she jumped off the bus.

Watching the bus drive off, Isabelle stood momentarily to get her bearings. Across the road, right in front of her, was what she'd been looking for. In shiny golden letters, emblazoned across the top of the white façade of the building, right above a golden plaque of a silhouetted dancing figure, were the words *Folies Bergère.* Isabelle clapped her hands in glee. 'I've found it!' she announced to no one in particular.

Isabelle carefully crossed the busy road to get a closer look at the building. After walking up the short flight of steps, she tried each double glass door. They were all firmly shut. She peered through one of the doors to see that the foyer was in darkness. Isabelle slumped down on the top step, despondent, resting her head in her hands. *What now?* She sighed as she watched the passers-by hurrying past and ignoring her. Everyone seemed to have somewhere to go except her. The place *she'd* wanted to go to was shut.

'Are you okay?' a voice asked.

Isabelle looked up, squinting, as the sun shone directly into her eyes. She could make out the silhouette of someone standing over her. Isabelle jumped up. Standing before her was a girl of Olivia's age, dressed casually in jeans and a tee shirt. Her blonde hair was scraped in a high ponytail, swinging jauntily around her head.

'I'm… I'm fine,' Isabelle stammered nervously, fumbling with her bag and feeling a little timorous. She was beginning to wish she was back at the Gallery with Kate. Or even with Olivia!

'What are you doing here all alone?' the girl asked.

'I'm waiting for my sister; she will be here in a minute,' Isabelle lied, trying to put on a brave face.

'I've got a little sister your age, and I wouldn't feel comfortable leaving her here alone,' the girl replied. 'Are you sure you're okay?' she added softly, peering into Isabelle's face.

Isabelle's face crumpled, and she burst into tears. 'I am lost. I don't know how to get back to my sister,' she wailed.

'There, there,' the girl replied, squatting beside Isabelle and putting her arm around her. 'Let's go inside and see what we can do to find your sister.'

'Inside?' Isabelle's bawling stopped. 'But it's all closed up.'

'Yes, until I open it,' the girl laughed, waving a bunch of keys at her. 'Ta-dah! Come on, not the front door, though, or everyone will want to come in.'

The girl led Isabelle around to a side door, which she unlocked and signalled for Isabelle to follow her inside. She switched on the lights. Beams of gold flooded the theatre foyer from the massive chandeliers hanging overhead. Isabelle was transfixed. Momentarily, her anxiety melted away as she studied the lavishly decorated blue and gold lobby walls and the spectacular grand staircase directly in front.

'This is the most beautiful room I have ever seen,' Isabelle marvelled, her mouth hanging open and eyes wide with amazement.

'I'm Claudia, by the way. What's your name?' the girl asked, standing alongside her.

'Isabelle,' she replied shyly, shutting her mouth belatedly and swallowing.

'Right, Mademoiselle Isabelle, what will we do with you?' Claudia asked.

'I don't know....' Isabelle answered sheepishly.

'First question. Why did you come here of all places?' Claudia asked.

'I... I wanted to see the pretty dancing ladies from Olivia's magazine, that's all....' Isabelle answered quickly.

Claudia smiled. 'Oh, I see. I'm sorry to disappoint you, but we're not open today. I am the only one here and I'm only here to get things ready for the show tomorrow.'

'Oh!' Isabelle replied, casting her eyes down to the floor.

'But first things first. We need to find your sister. Do you know where you last saw her?'

Isabelle relayed how she had visited Paris with her sister for an art exhibition. Then, she split up from Olivia, who was looking after her while they were on the bus tour, which her sister had arranged while she set up her art exhibition.

'Do you know where the art exhibition is?' Claudia asked.

'It's down a bumpy stone street?' Isabelle replied, hopefully.

'I see. Do you know the name of the person who owns the Gallery?'

'Yes! It's a Madame… Madame… something,' Isabelle replied, giggling.

Claudia pulled a face. 'Okay. There is not much to go on. Let's go to the back of the theatre and see what we can find in the tourist directory.'

Isabelle followed Claudia through the double wooden doors at the end of the lobby. A musty odour hit her as she entered the auditorium. Stretched before her, Isabelle saw rows of wooden seats upholstered in red velvet edged with gold-coloured studs running down to the stage that was in darkness. A tiered, gold-fronted balcony encircled the theatre above. Isabelle's eyes widened as she followed Claudia out of the auditorium through a side door alongside the stage and down a long, dark corridor. The corridor opened up into a large wooden floor area filled with racks of costumes encrusted with crystals, sequins and feathers, all in different designs and colours. Isabelle paused in front of them, totally mesmerised by what she saw.

'These are just like the ones in Olivia's magazines,' Isabelle whispered. 'Are these your dance costumes?' Isabelle enquired aloud to Claudia.

'Oh, my goodness. No!' Claudia replied, laughing. 'I'm one of the couturière,' she added.

'You made these? They are *so* beautiful,' Isabelle replied in wonder.

'Thank you,' she replied, smiling. 'Now, let's see if we can find your sister,' she added, thumbing through a street directory. After pouring over the directory and a local map, Claudia sat back in her seat and scratched her head. 'Have you no idea of the name of the Gallery?'

Isabelle shook her head. 'No, it was a bit boring there, so I didn't take much notice.'

'Hmm… how about the name of the place where you're staying?'

Isabelle shook her head. 'It's big,' she offered. 'A hotel?'

Claudia laughed. 'Oh dear, we'd better be more imaginative than that, hadn't we? Home phone number?'

Isabelle shook her head. 'Kate and Olivia know all that kind of stuff. I don't need to.'

'Everyone needs to know their home phone number. Every young girl must learn *not* to rely on someone else to keep her safe. You remember that for the future, young lady,' Claudia wagged her finger at Isabelle with mock anger. Isabelle hung her head in shame.

Chapter 34

Raimond did a second circuit of the shops in the vicinity that Olivia had described, enquiring about Isabelle's whereabouts along the way. No one, it appeared, had seen a taller-than-average nine-year-old with long, blonde curly hair. But as so many people would have passed through this part of the city, shopping and browsing, he wasn't surprised he'd drawn a blank. Whoever had been there four hours ago would, no doubt, have long since moved on to somewhere else.

Raimond sat on a park bench and pulled out Madame Schmidt's spare bus tour map after learning Isabelle had the one Madame Schmidt had given Olivia. Using the map as a fan to cool himself down, an idea came to him as he sat there. Isabelle had the tickets, didn't she? So, what could have been easier for Isabelle to escape from Olivia than hop back on the bus? In which case, where did the bus go from here?

He unfolded the map and spread it across his knees.

'You require assistance, Monsieur?' A young girl called out from a bench opposite him. She had been tuning up her guitar by playing the first few bars of a popular pop song. 'I can help for a few cents,' she continued.

Raimond looked up sternly. 'Ah, non merci.'

He paused as another idea followed the first and smiled at the young busker. She was only young, but she had the streetwise look of someone used to making their living from their wits. It would be hard making an honest living on the streets of Paris, especially when you weren't a native, he thought.

'Mais, peut-etre… 'ave you seen a young girl – blonde, nine or so but quite tall? She would 'ave been on 'er own and maybe looking for the bus?'

The girl rested her guitar on her knee. 'Yes,' she said, eyebrows lifting in surprise. 'I have, a few hours ago now, though. She was looking for the tour bus stop. She wanted to go somewhere quite particular.'

Raimond grinned. *And I'll bet I know where that was! he thought.* His index finger slowly traced the tour bus's looping journey until it arrived near an advert placed along the side of the page. *Folies Bergère!* Returning to the bus route on the map, Raimond followed the journey shown on the map from the bus stop across the road. His finger stopped at the place that he knew Isabelle had been heading for.

He held it up to the girl and pointed to the advert. 'Is this where she wanted to go?'

'Yes! That's it!' she nodded, laughing.

He could even hear her now – her high, fluting voice announcing, *'I'm going to be a dancing girl like them when I grow up!'*

Dancing girl, is it, young mademoiselle? He laughed. *Well, let's see if we can get you to dance back home,* he chuckled as he handed the busker a crisp new ten franc note.

Chapter 35

Claudia pushed the street directory and the local map she had been studying away from her and sat back in her chair. 'I'm not having much luck finding this Art Gallery. Are you sure you don't know the name of it or the name of the hotel you are staying at?' Claudia asked.

'No idea,' Isabelle replied carelessly, still totally engrossed in looking through the racks of extravagant costumes in front of her.

'Oh, dear!' Claudia sighed. 'Where do we go from here?'

'Dunno,' Isabelle replied offhandedly. 'Can I try on one of these costumes?' she asked, her offhanded tone replaced with one of excitement.

'No! They won't fit you; anyway, we don't want your grubby hands on them!' Claudia snapped.

'Sorry,' Isabelle replied sheepishly, somewhat taken aback by Claudia's sudden abruptness. Her lower lip started to tremble.

Claudia sighed. 'No, I'm sorry. I didn't mean to snap. I'm just worried about how I will get you back to your sister,' she added. 'And she'll be worried by now, won't she?'

'I suppose so,' Isabelle replied with a grimace. 'If Olivia's told her.'

'Olivia?' Claudia asked, frowning.

'My...' Isabelle didn't want to say *nursemaid* – that made her sound like a baby. Still, she supposed Oliva was her nursemaid somehow, which *did* make her a bit of a baby. And Kate *would* be worried... 'Someone my sister had asked to keep an eye on me whilst she set up her exhibition,' Isabelle explained, eventually.

'So, two people will be worried about you, then?'

'I suppose so...' Isabelle thought about Olivia. *Would Kate be worried?* Isabelle grimaced again. *Yes, she would, probably,* she had to concede. But for now, she *wished* Claudia would let her try on just one of the costumes first.

'Okay, I have an idea,' Claudia said after a while. 'I'll get in touch with an artist friend of mine. He knows most of the galleries here in Paris, so he may know which one your sister is exhibiting in. I'll go and call him. Wait here, and don't touch anything,' she directed, wagging her finger and grinning.

'Okay,' Isabelle replied, quickly tucking her hands behind her back and looking back innocently at Claudia.

Isabelle carefully parted the tightly packed costumes as soon as Claudia had gone. Examining each one with delight, Isabelle imagined herself dressed in them. She was standing in the spotlight, centre stage; a towering feather and jewel-encrusted headdress on her head made her look – and feel – ten feet tall. Her feet were gliding over the wooden floor, dancing in time to the music. On coming to the end of the dance, the music reached a crescendo and then faded. Isabelle took a deep curtsy, then another – and another – standing ovation. She was too engrossed to notice how long Claudia had been gone or when she returned.

'I thought I said no touching?' a voice hissed behind her. Isabelle returned to earth with a bump as she whirled around to find Claudia behind her, eyebrows raised disapprovingly. 'No wonder you got lost. You need to pay more attention,' Claudia was smiling, but her tone also had an underlying sternness.

'I'm sorry,' Isabelle pushed the costumes back together and looked contrite – or at least she hoped she did.

'Well,' Claudia looked less stern. 'We might be in luck,' she added, looking triumphant. 'My friend has a good idea at which gallery your sister maybe. He's going to make some enquiries and get back to me.'

'Oh,' Isabelle's face fell, realising her magical time in the theatre was coming to an end and she'd shortly have an angry Olivia and Kate to deal with instead. 'Can I perhaps look around the theatre while we wait?' she pleaded.

Claudia hesitated momentarily, and then her expression changed to a broad grin. 'Okay, sure, why not. Follow me; let's start with backstage and the dressing rooms as we're here,' Claudia replied, linking arms with Isabelle as they left the wardrobe area. 'This way!'

Isabelle followed Claudia down the narrow, dimly lit corridor. 'Down here are the dressing rooms,' Claudia said, pointing to the doors on either side of the passage. The first door had a large golden star on it. Claudia opened the door and switched on the lights.

Isabelle was almost blinded by the brilliance of the illuminations surrounding a large mirror on the wall straight ahead. It took a moment for her eyes to adjust and focus on the rest of the room: a sorry-looking, well-worn, green upholstered chaise lounge sat against the wall on the left, overflowing with various coats, hats and several umbrellas, was a wooden hatstand standing in the far corner. The walls were plastered with posters from previous shows; the dressing table looked like a shrine, adorned with greeting cards and photographs tucked into the frame of the mirror and wall surrounding it, with a long, white feather boa hanging over its corner. A large glass vase of flowers sat amongst the trays and boxes of makeup and hair adornments that had spilt onto the surface. Isabelle sat on the painted wooden chair in front of the dressing table and peered at the photographs and cards.

'This lady looks very beautiful in her costume,' Isabelle remarked, pointing to one of the photographs of a dancer in a spectacular costume and headdress. 'Is she a dancer here?'

'Yes, that's Sylvie. She is the *étoile*, the star of the show,' Claudia replied.

'I am going to be an *étoile* one day,' Isabelle said, tossing her head and giving her hair a flick before picking up a hand mirror to gaze at herself.

'I'm sure you will,' Claudia replied, chuckling. 'But you know, there's more to it than beautiful costumes. Dancers must pay attention, or they won't stay dancers and become stars. It's as much about working alongside people as doing your own thing – listening to instructions, for example.' Isabelle looked at Claudia's reflection in the mirror. She was smiling at Isabelle meaningfully, eyebrows raised. Just like Kate and Olivia looked when they tried to make a point to her. 'Come on,' Claudia pulled the chair back, forcing Isabelle to stand. 'We'd better get a move on; there are lots more to see yet,' Claudia added, standing in the doorway and beckoning her to follow. 'And then you can decide if you still want to be a dancer when you're grown up.'

They continued down the dimly lit corridor. Halfway down was a door, slightly ajar. Isabelle peeped around it as Claudia went on ahead. Inside was a large room, the walls covered in mirrors, each with a long ballet barre running its length. The musty smell Isabelle had noticed in the auditorium was stronger down here, mixed with the smell of sweat, cheap perfume and hairspray. She wrinkled her nose.

'This is the practice room,' Claudia told her, coming to join her at the door. She pushed it wide open. A pair of soft-toed ballet shoes had been discarded in one corner; the soles were worn right through. 'Many hours are spent here, just practising and practising, before each performance. There is very little time off.'

'Oh, but it's worth it cos they get to wear the pretty costumes!' Isabelle remarked wide-eyed.

'They only wear the costumes for the performances, not all the time. It's hard work,' Claudia said, looking from the room to Isabelle's wrinkled nose and twisted pout, 'for a short spell of glamour,' she concluded.

Claudia pulled the door closed and ushered Isabelle on ahead. Still, the musty-sour smell seemed to follow them, and Isabelle was glad when they reached the end of the corridor to the side of the stage.

Squeezing past props, parts of the scenery and through a shoebox-sized entrance, Isabelle stepped out from the wings onto the great expanse of the stage. She stopped and turned as she caught sight of a gold-painted staircase resting on the stage's back wall. Isabelle stepped backwards, her eyes focusing on the top of the broad staircase; it stopped at the base of a picture of an exquisite white and golden palace painted on the backdrop.

She stood for a moment, spellbound. Isabelle had seen images like this in Olivia's magazine, but this was real life! She was aware of the heat radiating from the downlights shining on her as she turned to face the front of the stage. The thick red velvet curtains edged with gold braid, had been drawn right back, giving her a clear view of the auditorium, which stretched out from the stage below. Rows of red upholstered wooden seats were arranged on a blue patterned carpet, filling the space. Towards the rear of the auditorium, stacked vertically above, were three galleried seating platforms wrapping around the auditorium and stretching up to the domed ceiling. On each of the levels were further red upholstered seating areas. Her heart was thumping as she stood in wonderment at the vision in front of her. She would see this one day when she was an *etoile* – except every seat would be full.

'Don't go too near the edge; otherwise, you'll end up in the orchestra pit!' Claudia warned, giggling.

Isabelle walked towards the edge of the stage and peered over. 'Oh yeah. It's a long way down!' Isabelle giggled.

Claudia chuckled. 'So, how does it feel being all on your own on that big stage?' she shouted from the wings.

'A little scary, I think,' Isabelle replied with a nervous giggle. 'But this is what I want to be – a dancing girl on this stage,' she added, pirouetting on the spot.

'Well, just remember what I said – it's not all sequins and stars; it's sweat and tears, too. Come on, we'd better dance our way to the foyer now in case my friend rings with news of your sister's whereabouts,' Claudia replied, laughing.

'Oh, do we have to?' bemoaned Isabelle.

'Yes, we have to,' Claudia replied, turning off the leading lights and plunging them into near darkness. 'Come on and stay close.'

Isabelle trailed behind Claudia through the auditorium to the double wooden doors at the end. Claudia flicked on the lights. Isabelle stood at the top of the staircase leading to the magnificent foyer below. It was bathed in light from the chandeliers and the stunning ornate golden candelabras.

'Could we just have a quick peek up there, please?' Isabelle asked, pointing to the stairs leading up to the next level.

'Okay, just a quick look, though,' Claudia agreed.

Isabelle raced up the first flight of stairs and entered through the first door. It opened out onto a curved section of tiered red velvet seating.

'*Oh, là là!*' Isabelle exclaimed.

'This is one of the galleries; look at the view from here,' Claudia said, pointing towards the stage.

Isabelle skipped down the steps leading to the first row of the seating. Sitting on one of the seats, she folded her arms and placed them on the shiny brass balcony railing in front of her. Then, resting her chin on her arms, Isabelle leaned forward to look down onto the auditorium and across to the stage.

'We are so high up,' she exclaimed. 'One day, I *will* be on that stage,' she added determinedly, turning to Claudia.

'Well, if that's what you want to do, you have to follow your dreams, don't you – but remember to listen and learn along the way. Then you won't get lost again,' Claudia replied, giving Isabelle a gentle nudge.

'Oh, yes!' Isabelle replied, smiling broadly, her eyes shining with excitement. 'I'll remember that.'

***

Raimond followed the bus route in his car, heading where he suspected Isabelle had disappeared after remembering her confiding that she would be a dancing girl like the ladies in Olivia's magazine one day.

'And 'ere we are!' Raimond said out loud as he pulled up in front of the imposing building of the *Folies Bergère* in Rue Richer. He turned off the engine, got out of the car and gazed momentarily at the imposing building. Raimond had been to several performances at *Folies Bergère* over the years. He loved the glitz, glamour and especially the risqué shows they put on. Thoughts of them brought a smile to his face, but today, the theatre appeared closed and deserted. *So, now what – where can she be?* he thought.

Raimond walked up the steps at the front of the building. He noticed that the foyer lights were lit; he tried each of the glass entrance doors. They were all locked. Raimond cupped his hands around his eyes and peered through one of the doors. He caught sight of movement on the stairs at the back of the foyer; he blinked his eyes to refocus. Yes, he could just about make out the outline of someone coming into view… a young girl was descending the stairs, followed by someone else.

Raimond banged on the glass. *'Isabelle! Isabelle!'* Raimond shouted through the glass door.

Chapter 36

Kate couldn't settle. Everyone had gone home and she'd made several trips into the now empty gallery. She'd re-arranged some of her paintings and then returned them to where they were. Phillipe had rung earlier to see how the exhibition was going. Kate had told him of Isabelle's disappearance but not of Stephen's news; she wasn't quite ready to explain that to anyone yet. She hadn't even accepted it herself. She'd also declined his offer to come and help look for Isabelle. If anyone could find Isabelle, it was Raimond. Even so, Kate was anxious and paced the floor, wondering what else she could do to occupy herself. At the same time, she waited for Madame Schmidt to look in to see if there had been any news. Olivia was still driving her to distraction with constant telephone calls of *'any news yet?'* Kate got up and made herself yet another cup of coffee. She sat down, placing it on the table alongside the row of cups lined up – some still full, some half empty.

It was getting dark. Where *could* Isabelle be and why hadn't Raimond rung? It was all her fault; Kate chastised herself. She hadn't paid Isabelle enough attention; she'd been too busy balancing her own life – and where had that got her? A failed marriage and a failed relationship with Stephen, and now a little sister who had run away. What a mess! Her thoughts were suddenly interrupted as the door into the gallery staff room flew open.

'Kate, Kate, I'm back!' Isabelle cried, rushing into the room, flinging her open arms around Kate, and burying her head into her big sister's chest.

'Oh, thank goodness! Where have you been? I have been so worried about you!' Kate gasped, struggling to stay on her feet. After a moment, she gently disengaged Isabelle, holding her out at arm's length.

'I'm sorry, Kate. I didn't mean to worry you,' Isabelle replied, hanging her head and looking down to the floor.

'But you *did* worry me. *WHERE HAVE YOU BEEN?*' Kate shouted before she could stop herself as all the fear and irritation of the last few hours spilt over.

'Hush, she's back safely now; time for questions later,' Raimond said quietly, placing his arm around Isabelle and Kate's shoulders and giving them both a reassuring squeeze. 'I'll take 'er back to the hotel in my car and you can follow in yours,' he added.

Kate took a deep breath and consciously stopped herself from leaning thankfully into Raimond's arm. 'Of course, you're right. As you say, the important thing is that Isabelle is back home safely,' she conceded. 'So yes, let's go back to the hotel; it's been a long, long day,' she added, trying to stifle a yawn.

***

'I made Kate very cross, didn't I?' Isabelle asked Raimond as he drove her back to the hotel through the heavy traffic.

'She was worried about you. I was worried too,' Raimond replied.

'Will you tell Kate where you found me?' Isabelle asked. 'I might get into more trouble if you do,' Isabelle added sheepishly.

'No, I won't tell. It will be our little secret. But promise me you will never run away again?' Raimond answered sternly.

'I promise. Cross my heart,' Isabelle replied. 'Claudia thought you were my Papa,' she added as an afterthought, giggling.

'If I were your Papa, I would give you a big spanking for running away!' Raimond replied sternly. 'I say in jest,' he added after a moment or two, winking at her and then laughing out loud.

***

It was gone past nine o'clock by the time Kate tucked Isabelle up into her hotel bed. Isabelle snuggled down and let out a big yawn.

'I'm very sleepy,' Isabelle confessed.

'I'm not surprised, young lady.' Kate replied, kissing Isabelle's forehead, 'You've had a big adventure today.'

'I'm sorry I worried you, though,' Isabelle added. 'I didn't mean to run off; it just happened, and… I didn't think you would miss me.'

'Of course, I would miss you! Why would you think that?' Kate asked, astonished.

'Well, you've been so busy lately with the Château, the art retreat and your exhibition. I know these things are more important than me, but it makes me feel a bit lonely at times,' Isabelle began to sob.

'Oh, Isabelle. That's not true; nothing is more important than you!' Kate replied, drawing Isabelle into her and feeling Isabelle's little body trembling as she sobbed quietly. Kate realised then how very alike they were. She had been a bit lost, lonely and a little afraid herself at times. Clearly, Isabelle had been, too. She, of all people, should understand how Isabelle was feeling right now. *It would be different from now on*, Kate resolved.

'Do you mean that? That the Château, the art retreat and the exhibition *aren't* more important than me? Promise?' Isabelle asked in a tearful voice.

'I promise. And I want you to promise me something?' Kate replied.

'What?' Isabelle sniffed.

'I want you to promise me that you won't ever run away again and, when you are feeling lonely or upset, you won't be afraid to tell me?'

'I promise,' Isabelle replied.

Kate settled Isabelle back under the duvet and turned out the bedside light. 'Goodnight then and sleep tight.'

'Don't let the bed bugs bite,' Isabelle answered with a giggle.

With Isabelle settled into bed and Olivia minding her, at Raimond's suggestion, she went with him to the hotel's dining room for dinner. Kate had been dubious at first about how hungry she was but acknowledged she was ravenous as she tucked into the Steak au Poivre that had been placed in front of her. Little wonder, she'd not eaten anything since breakfast, she realised.

'With everything else that has been going on today, 'ave you managed to set up your exhibition?' Raimond enquired.

'Yes, thanks. It was a little stop-start, but I had some help – a nice work-away volunteer named Marc. Madame Schmidt organised it for me. She's also been popping in and out all day to see if I was okay. Thank goodness the exhibition doesn't open until tomorrow,' Kate replied.

'And… Stephen…' Raimond asked hesitantly. 'Has Stephen been in touch? As I was leaving the Château, he said he would ring you….' he added.

'Er… er… yes, he has rung,' Kate replied, her cheeks beginning to flame red. She hesitated. 'He rang earlier asking if we had found Isabelle.' Kate stopped. How on earth was she going to explain what Stephen had said?

'Why you 'esitate? Is there a problem at the Château?' Raimond asked.

'Well… no… but… you might as well know. By the time we return to the Château, Stephen will be gone,' Kate replied, avoiding Raimond's curious look by studiously cutting her steak into small pieces.

'Gone? Gone where?' Raimond probed.

'He's been offered another job and they need him to start immediately. That's all I can tell you,' Kate replied, sipping her wine, her mouth suddenly gone dry.

'I find this 'ard to comprendre,' Raimond responded, leaning back in his chair. 'He agreed to be Estate Manager and is now taking another job?' he added, frowning.

'Why the concern? I would have thought you would be pleased to hear that he's leaving?' Kate said sarcastically. An attack was always a good defence – wasn't that what they said?

'I did not like 'im, that's true, but he is good at the job. So, what are you going to do now?' Raimond asked.

'I don't know. I will have to rethink that role when I get the chance.' She'd had plenty of chance to think about it, but she wasn't ready to share her thoughts with Raimond just yet. 'By the way, you never did say where you found Isabelle?' Kate asked Raimond, whom she guessed was hungry too, as he'd almost polished off his steak already.

'I find 'er in the city,' Raimond replied with his mouth full of food.

'But whereabouts in the city, was she?' Kate pressed.

'I know the city, so it was easy,' Raimond replied nonchalantly. He shrugged in that particularly gallic way Kate had come to learn meant she wouldn't be told any more details no matter how hard she probed. Nevertheless, she continued.

'But how did you know where to look? Paris is a big place!' Kate questioned.

'I just knew,' Raimond replied, tapping the side of his nose with his finger.

Kate *was* grateful he'd found Isabelle, but she also found him so infuriating at times! Why couldn't he tell her how and where he'd found Isabelle instead of making a big mystery of it? Then she remembered how Olivia had said Isabelle was close to him and talked to him. Maybe he felt like a father-substitute to Isabelle? Perhaps she should let them have their little secret since she was sure she could trust Raimond to always have Isabelle's best interests at heart.

'Well, either way, thank you for coming to the rescue. I don't know what I would have done without your help,' Kate declared, sighing and accepting defeat. She really didn't have the energy for games tonight.

'I very fond of Mademoiselle Isabelle… and you,' Raimond replied, suddenly his own cheeks colouring as he reached out for Kate's hand, which was resting on the table.

Kate was taken aback. The heat that had been beginning to subside in her face was now coming back in full force. *Was he fond of her? Really?* For a moment, she softened, then she rallied again at the image of him and Angeline giggling at the top of the stairs. 'Well, thank you, Raimond, but I thought it was Angeline you were fond of?' she replied sarcastically.

'Angeline – l'amour? Pah! Non. She like my little sister!' Raimond replied, laughing out loud.

'What about when I saw you coming out of the Marquis suite the other day? It didn't look like you were treating her like a little sister then!' Kate said indignantly, then pulled herself together abruptly. What was wrong with her? She was acting like a scorned and jealous lover!

'Ah, non. I was teasing 'er with the spider I 'ad in my 'ands. Angeline saw it in Marquis Suite and asked me to catch it,' he replied, chuckling.

Kate bit her lip – could it be that she'd had hold of the wrong end of the stick all this time? That perhaps behind Raimond's cold and belliger-ent behaviour *was* because he was attracted to her after all? Some men could be gruff and awkward like that because they couldn't be what they wanted to be – gentle and romantic. In turn, she acknowledged that often she'd been antagonistic towards him because of Angeline. Could it be that he was attracted to him, too? Staring at him from across the table, she realised that she didn't really know him or herself anymore.

It was time for her to find out about herself – and to understand how Raimond might fit into that, too.

Chapter 37

'I think we should have a big party for Isabelle's eighteenth birthday!' Kate had announced over breakfast one morning. 'What do you think, Isabelle?' Kate asked, turning to Isabelle. 'We'll invite James and Elisabeth and all your friends.'

'Err… I suppose… if you like …' Isabelle replied. She wasn't much of a party girl, but she would look forward to seeing her brother and sister and her darling nieces and nephew. Isabelle was very fond of the children, especially now that they were that much older and no longer ankle-biters, as James had pointed out. But a big party?

'Don't you have an exhibition soon after my birthday?' Isabelle asked, looking for an excuse to get out of it.

'Yes, I do. But I think I know which paintings I'd like to exhibit. Maria has already offered to help set up the exhibition at the Gallery, so it won't interfere with organising your party. As I told you years ago, you always come first,' Kate replied, patting Isabelle's hand. So, Kate's notion of holding a party for her eighteenth had become a fait accompli. Still, Isabelle supposed it would keep Kate happy, too.

'What are you planning to exhibit this time?' Isabelle asked. Now that she was older, she took an active interest and was very proud of her sister's work.

'I plan to show the latest paintings I've done of dancers. I might call the exhibition *Allons-y et rêvons* – Let's go and dream',' she replied. 'Do you approve?' Kate added.

'Nice. I like that. Will you include that big painting of me hanging in the Winter Salon?' Isabelle quizzed.

'Of course. That will take centre stage,' Kate replied, nudging Isabelle's arm and laughing aloud.

'Ah! Fame at last!' Isabelle replied, chuckling.

'Right. That's settled, then. We will start planning the party today. Madame DuPont and Angeline, you'll help, won't you?' Kate asked.

'Oui, Madame,' they chorused excitedly in reply, then turned to each other and grinned. Isabelle had noticed how well they worked together lately; they were rarely heard screaming at each other these days. Peace had reigned at last, even if it had taken nine years for that to happen! But it also meant Isabelle could no longer play one off against the other to get her own way, as she used to when she was younger. Isabelle supposed this was due to Madame DuPont appearing to finally take more of a back seat, leaving Angeline in charge of the kitchen. She guessed Madame DuPont must be well over retirement age, not that anyone had ever been able to pin down *exactly* how old she was.

'Don and I will help, too,' Florence sang out.

'I can assist as well!' Raimond added.

'Looks like we have a party team in the making then,' Kate said, smiling happily. 'I'll telephone James in Australia later this evening to see if he can come; it's his offseason over there, so hopefully, he can. I'll also telephone Elisabeth. It's a busy time for them at the Camblez, but she may get away with the children and leave Robert in charge. It would be lovely if Nellie could come, too. She's been a little lonely since Edward passed away,' Kate added, ticking them off on her fingers as she listed them. 'So that would make twelve of us already. How about your friends?'

'Will there be room for them?' Isabelle teased Kate, then when she saw Kate's apologetic expression, added, 'Only joking. I'll give you a list.'

Seeing her sister flushed with excitement at the prospect of holding a party and the family descending on the Château, Isabelle decided not to tell Kate that she may have other plans.

***

Kate awoke early. As she lay in bed, she thought about how much her life would change once Isabelle became the Chatelaine of Château des Vieilles Tours; now, she was about to come of age.

Kate had initially felt trapped after her mother and Maurice had been killed in a car accident. She had been named in their Will as guardian of the Château and Isabelle until Isabelle reached eighteen. Instead of following her own dreams, she'd had to make do with her mother's – and Isabelle's.

It had been hard, but on reflection, whilst they had been difficult years at times, the last few had been fulfilling, too. And now, at age forty-five, Kate finally savoured the thought that she could do as she wished with her life. She smiled happily at the prospect of what she had planned.

As the morning sun streamed through her bedroom windows, her thoughts also turned to Raimond. After Stephen had abruptly walked out of her life, Kate was flattered when Raimond expressed his ardent feelings towards her. Still, after days of soul-searching, Kate had to admit that she'd not felt the same romantic connection to Raimond as she'd had towards Stephen. Instead, after a highly emotionally charged, volatile start to their relationship, Raimond had become her friend and ally over the years. They'd formed a strong partnership and a solid, platonic friendship. Raimond had also become her confidant. He offered her advice when called upon to do so – and conversely when not asked for! Kate smiled again at this. In recent months, he'd listened patiently as she shared her dreams and plans of what she wanted to do once Isabelle took over the Château. In many ways, she'd found more than a best friend in him – she'd found a soul mate.

'With Isabelle running the Château, I will have more time to paint and to exhibit my work,' Kate had said to Raimond one day. 'I've rung Maria and asked her to reserve me a space in her new exhibition just after Isabelle's birthday. Then I'll see where that leads me,' Kate added.

'Bonne idee. But what of the art retreats? Who will run these?' Raimond asked.

'Florence can handle the retreats; she loves running them. Anyway, I sometimes feel I'm just in the way,' Kate replied, laughing. 'I don't mind; it's given me more time to do my paintings and run around with Isabelle to her dance classes.'

'I think we've all 'ad turns running Mesdemoiselles Isabelle around!' Raimond laughed. 'And vice versa,' he added.

'That's very true,' Kate giggled. 'It's been a bonus having Florence and Don living here full-time in the apartment above the stable block. Renovating that area was a good idea of yours; it meant that they'd always been on hand to help. They've also been a steadying influence for Isabelle over the years,' Kate added, smiling.

Raimond beamed. 'I can't take all the glory. The Marquis 'ad planned many years ago to renovate that stable block for guests to stay in. I still 'ad the plans he 'ad drawn up and so was 'appy to see 'is plans through.'

'It's also been a double bonus having Don working in the garden full-time. The gardens have never looked better and the potager garden has kept us fed. Also, Don seems to have finally managed to turn Sébastien's lackadaisical ways around; he's quite the budding gardener these days. Our lawns are a credit to him!' Kate added. 'Yes, Isabelle will have a good team around her to help her when she takes over.'

'That is so but...' Raimond replied, stopping in mid-flow.

Kate was too preoccupied to notice; she was too wrapped up in her own thoughts. She'd fulfilled her obligations and they'd all helped her. She knew they'd all carry on helping Isabelle. In fact, they'd all come a long way since over a decade ago when life had changed dramatically and it was all about to change again. A tinge of excitement raced through her as she thought about all those long-shelved dreams she could now pursue, with Isabelle gradually taking over as Chatelaine. But in the meantime, she must focus on the party!

Chapter 38

Kate stretched, reaching out for her notebook and pencil on her bedside cabinet and consulted her list of things to do. As she started making notes on the list, there was a knock on her bedroom door.

'Come in!' Kate called.

'Bonjour, Madame Kate!' Madame DuPont said, walking towards Kate's bed, carrying a tray with a pot of coffee, cup and saucer, a selection of pastries on a plate and the morning's mail.

'Bonjour,' Kate replied, looking surprised as Madame DuPont rested the tray before her on the bed. 'Breakfast in bed? What's this all about?'

'It will be animé, animé today with the family coming. So, I thought you might like a treat before it gets too craazee.' Madame DuPont replied, flinging her hands up into the air.

'Thank you, Madame DuPont. As you say, it will be crazy here when everyone descends,' Kate laughed. 'I'll just have a quick look at my mail while I eat this delicious-looking breakfast, then I'll get up and give you a hand with the finishing touches on the rooms and see what help Angeline needs,' Kate added.

'Pas d'urgence, I'll see you downstairs when you are ready,' Madame DuPont replied as she withdrew. 'Angeline is big and strong and can cope,' she grinned – and was that also a wink Kate saw as she closed the door behind her?

Kate shuffled through the pile of assorted envelopes until she reached the small manilla one. She studied it; it wasn't the usual mail she received. Her name and address were typed on the front of the envelope, but there was no 'return to sender' information on the back. Nevertheless, she hurriedly tore it open. Inside was a syllabus from The Royal College of Arts, London.

'What the…?' she said out loud. Kate flicked through the glossy pages, reading the course outlines. Then she remembered, 'Ah! Elisabeth! That's who is behind this!' Kate exclaimed. Elisabeth had been pressing Kate to make plans for when Isabelle took over the running of the Château, leaving her, finally, free to do something of her choosing.

'Remember what I told you years ago? *Follow your heart, decide what you want to do and go for it.* So? What's it to be?' Elisabeth had asked.

'I don't know. When you asked me that last time, I promised I would bite the bullet, be brave and go out and find that missing link in my life. Then fate stepped in and Mother and Maurice were killed,' Kate replied.

'Well, soon you *will* be free to follow your heart,' Elisabeth had reminded her. 'Unless you're happy to bury yourself here and become an old maid....'

'Hey! Respect your elders – not so much with the *old* maid if you please!' Kate laughed out loud.

'Seriously, what *would* you like to do?' Elisabeth pressed.

'I don't know, really. Since I've never had any formal art training, it might be nice to go somewhere to study art. Maybe Italy, London or...'

Elisabeth had *definitely* been behind this! Kate could begin to feel a flicker of excitement rising inside her. This added to the thrill she'd felt earlier at her impending freedom. Kate studied each course outline, trying to decide which one she might like to do. It would feel strange to live amongst the hustle and bustle of London or any other large city after living in rural France and the confines of the Château for the past ten years, but how exciting! *Would Isabelle manage here without her,* she wondered. *Of course, she'd manage!* Isabelle would have Raimond to support her and the rest of the staff – and Florence and Don. She would finally be free to do what she'd wanted all those years ago!

Kate looked at her watch. 'Gracious, look at the time; it's time I got up!' Kate exclaimed as she swung her legs out of bed, reaching for her clothes on the wicker chair beside her.

'Je ne sais quoi,' Kate heard Raimond say as she entered the kitchen.

'What don't you know, Raimond?' Kate asked.

'Madame DuPont is asking for the final numbers for the caterers tomorrow,' Raimond replied.

'Oh, excusez moi, Madame DuPont. Here is the final list; I've just printed it off,' Kate said, handing it to Madame DuPont.

'Merci, Madame Kate. I'll telephone the caterers and let them know,' Madame DuPont replied.

Isabelle burst noisily through the kitchen door. 'Any coffee, Angeline?' she sang out.

'Si. cara, coming up!' Angeline replied brightly.

'Grazie. I need bucketsful today, so keep it coming,' Isabelle replied, slumping down on the chair.

'What makes you think you'll need bucketsful of coffee?' Kate asked, placing her arms around Isabelle's shoulders.

'All these people about to descend on us. Do we really have to have this party tomorrow?' she asked, pouting.

Despite being eighteen tomorrow, Isabelle could still act like an eight-year-old at times, Kate thought.

'Yes, of course, we are going ahead with the party. It will be lovely to see everyone: James, Elisabeth, Nellie and the children, plus your friends. You will have a wonderful time; wait and see,' Kate replied reassuringly.

'If you say so,' Isabelle replied, clutching her cup of steaming coffee with both hands, taking a large mouthful.

'And I've got something for you. Bring your coffee with you and come with me upstairs,' Kate added, beckoning to Isabelle.

Isabelle got up from her chair. As she was about to go out of the door, Madame DuPont called after her.

'Oh, Mademoiselle Isabelle, I have a letter for you.'

'Oh?' Isabelle backtracked and took the envelope from Madame DuPont. She scanned the front of it before stuffing it in her pocket. 'Merci!' she replied.

'What is it?' Kate asked.

'Oh, just something I sent away for,' Isabelle said, shrugging. 'Come on! What was it you've got for me? You know I love surprises!'

On entering Kate's bedroom, she signalled for Isabelle to sit on the bed. Kate reached into her wardrobe and pulled out their mother's jewellery box. Sitting down beside Isabelle and opening the box, Kate turned to Isabelle. 'There are several pieces of our mother's jewellery I will pass onto you sometime, but I'd like to give you this piece for your eighteenth birthday. I think your Papa would have liked you to have it to mark your coming of age. It's the ring he gave our mother as a sign of the betrothal of their future life together. It belonged to his mother, your grandmother. It was also our mother's birthstone.' Kate placed the ring in the palm of Isabelle's hand.

Isabelle looked down at the ruby and diamond ring in her hand. Then, picking it up, she slipped it onto the fourth finger on her right hand.

'Oh! Thank you, thank you!' Isabelle gushed. 'It's *sooo* beautiful. I will treasure it always,' she added.

'It is stunning, isn't it? And it suits you very well. I'm giving this to you today as I thought we could go into town later this morning and go dress shopping for your party. The beautiful red dress Mother wore the night your Papa gave her this ring won't fit you – you've grown too tall. I thought you might like a new one, anyway. What do you think?' Kate asked.

'Oh, yes, please, I love dress shopping now; Olivia was a good teacher,' Isabelle giggled. 'Sorry,' she paused, 'I know you hate it,' Isabelle added, pulling a face.

'As it's your birthday, I'll make myself like it just for today,' Kate laughed.

'Thank you for making my birthday so special. I know I haven't always shown my gratitude for all you have done for me, but I am grateful, truly. I don't know what I would have done without you all these years. I still miss Papa and Mama *soooo* much, though,' Isabelle said, tears welling up in her eyes.

'Shh… I know. I'm glad we have each other; it's still hard for me some days, too. Especially when I think of the years of separation from Mother and then finding her, only for her to be snatched away again,' Kate replied, pulling Isabelle towards her.

Holding each other in a close embrace, Isabelle sobbed quietly while Kate stroked her hair until her sobs subsided.

'Come, dry your eyes. We've got a shopping spree to get ready for. Maybe if we have time, if you don't try on too many dresses, a spot of lunch, too?'

Isabelle nodded her head vigorously. 'Oh, yes! That's a great idea!'

'As long as we're back here to welcome the family,' Kate added brightly.

'Sounds like a plan! Maybe I'm looking forward to this party after all,' Isabelle replied, blowing her nose and dabbing her eyes. 'I'll see you downstairs in about half an hour. I need to pop up to my room and tidy myself up,' she added as she left Kate's bedroom.

Kate sat staring absent-mindedly at the open jewellery box in front of her. Today wasn't the day to talk to Isabelle about her plans to go to London to study at the Royal College of Art. Maybe she would leave it until the day after the party.

Chapter 39

The party was in full swing. Guests were standing around, drinks in hand, trying to make themselves heard over the loud music.

The whole family had arrived to celebrate her birthday. The Château was bursting at its seams, forcing Isabelle to share her bedroom with her sister Elisabeth. She had arrived from Guernsey with her children: 'baby' Fleur – not that she was a baby anymore, but the name had stuck; and the twins, Annie and Petey, and their mother's long-term friend, Nellie. Her brother James had flown in from Australia with his partner Meaghan. Isabelle had giggled at her brother's Aussie twang when he'd greeted her on arrival. What a far-flung and diverse family she had!

Anxious to have some time to herself, Isabelle took the opportunity to slip away unnoticed. She crept around the outside of the Château and in through the Garden Room's side door. She could re-read the letter she was clutching before anyone else could pounce on her to wish her a Happy Birthday.

'I can hardly believe it – eighteen!' they were all saying to her, and she could hardly believe it herself. But little did they know, she was not only turned eighteen, but she was also about to embark on life outside the confines of the Château. The only life she'd known for the past eighteen years.

Isabelle sat cross-legged on the old, well-worn sofa. She could hear the muffled sound of music coming from the terrace as she sat, fingering the long white envelope balanced on her knee. This was the first opportunity she'd had to study the letter and make significant plans. Plans that would take her away from here….

After the death of both of her parents, Isabelle's destiny had already been marked out for her. She recalled that tragic summer just over nine years ago. Her world had crumbled around her that day. She'd been left bewildered, lost and unsure of her future, with Kate as the only lifeline to cling to, not realising at that time Kate had her own struggles to contend with. She realised that now. So much water had flowed under the bridge in the years in between. So many changes and yet so much was still the same. And here she was today, eighteen and about to take up her birthright, officially becoming the Chatelaine of Château des Vieilles Tours. There was no denying that Kate, sacrificing her own dreams, had turned the Château into a happy and secure place for her to call home. Yet … Isabelle let out a loud sigh and frowned at the prospect. Telling Kate wouldn't be easy; she had so much to thank Kate for – not least this party.

'How am I going to tell Kate?' Isabelle demanded of the world at large.

'Tell Kate what?' a voice said from behind her.

Isabelle spun around to discover Raimond standing in the doorway. 'You made me jump!' Isabelle exclaimed.

'What are you doing 'ere? You should be at your party!' Raimond asked.

'I know, but… I got this letter yesterday,' Isabelle replied, handing it to Raimond.

Raimond skimmed the first page and then handed it back. 'My engleesh is still not too good; what does it say?' He asked.

'I have been invited to attend an audition next month at The Royal Ballet School in London,' Isabelle replied breathlessly, trembling with excitement.

'Is this the study you tell me about before?' Raimond asked.

'Yes! You didn't tell Kate, did you?' Isabelle queried.

'Non! Of course, I don't tell. But I hoped *you* would,' Raimond looked sternly at her from under his eyebrows.

'I… I meant to, but I thought, what if it comes to nothing? Then I'd stir everything up for nothing too, so….'

'Hmm, I thought you did the audition before?' Raimond interrupted her before she could explain herself further.

'That was a preliminary video audition I did at the studio. That's why I asked you to take me, not Kate, that day,' Isabelle chuckled.

'So, what does this mean? Do you move away from here?' Raimond asked, frowning.

'Yes, but not until next year,' Isabelle replied. 'If I get it, that is. I might not.'

'You will,' Raimond nodded with certainty. 'And I will miss you,' Raimond said quietly, placing his arm around her shoulders.

'I'm going to miss you, too. You've been like a Papa to me,' she replied, tears pricking her eyes.

'Hmm, well… now you must tell Kate – and then come back to your party.'

'In a moment. You go on. I'll be there soon,' Isabelle replied with a smile.

Isabelle watched as Raimond exited the door, closing it quietly behind him. She would miss him, indeed. He was the first person she would run to, especially when she was a child when she'd felt Kate didn't understand her. He always understood – well, at least he pretended to, even if he hadn't, which meant just as much to her. She could share her secrets with him – like when she told him of her silly notion that she wanted to be a dancing girl like the *Folies Bergère* girls in Olivia's magazine. She remembered how he'd scoured Paris looking for her when she went missing and had found her at the *Folies Bergère* theatre. And he'd kept her secret for all those years and not told Kate where she was found. Yes, she would miss him!

And what about Kate? she thought. Well, Kate was a much better Chatelaine than she could ever be. She could still do her painting and her exhibitions. It would all be fine, Isabelle reasoned with herself.

'Oh, well. Here goes nothing.' Isabelle launched herself from the sofa and out of the door of her hidey-hole, her long elegant legs making nothing of the walk through the house into the Winter Salon.

She stood for a moment underneath the portrait of herself, striking up the same pose as in the painting. *This is my destiny, my dream and I'm going to follow it.* Not noticing she had company – until Kate put her arm around her.

'Madame DuPont told me the return address on that envelope you got yesterday.' Kate remarked while staring up at the portrait of Isabelle, looking every inch a prima donna. 'Is that why you've been avoiding me all morning?' she added.

'Oh Kate, if only you knew how much I want to do this. This is my dream….'

'I know a little about dreams myself, you know,' Kate smiled down at her, 'and how sometimes they have to wait. Or become other people's instead.'

'Are you saying I can't go?' Isabelle's expression became mutinous, like it had when she was a child. She tried to straighten it, but for the moment, she felt like that rebellious, angry child again – the one who'd run off when Kate had had her first exhibition in Paris. 'I'm sorry I snapped, but please, I have to do this. Do you mind very much?'

'No,' Kate sighed. 'It means we both have a long way to go to achieve our dreams, but this is the first step towards yours,' Kate added, smiling.

***

Much later, after everyone had gone to bed, Kate stood alone in the Winter Salon. She stared at the cold shaft of light that the moon was casting over the painting of Isabelle. The picture appeared different – distorted, not as energetic and free. It was still beautiful but somehow darker, colder. Much like her life now – dreams inside her that might never come to fruition after all. That had always been her life – to dream, to hope and then to make other people's dreams come true instead. Maybe that was as good as fulfilling her own dreams in a way, she reasoned. She imagined Isabelle dancing on stage, taking a bow to rapturous applause. The thought made her swell with pride.

She wandered out the door, onto the terrace and away from the Château. Isabelle would join the Royal Ballet School next year. In the meantime, she had a year to do what she wanted. A year? Well, that would have to be enough to gather all the memories and sights she wanted to paint and bring them back here with her. She turned and looked back at the Château, standing so serenely in its backdrop of Don's carefully manicured gardens and Sebastién's gently flowing landscaping. Inside, she visualised the elegant rooms and cosy nooks, home to the loving souls living there – the ones she called her family. She smiled and the moon shone a little brighter; after all, as Auguste Rodin once said,

"The main thing is to be moved, to love, to hope, to tremble, to live. Be a man before being an artist!"

And she could do that just as well at a Château in France as anywhere else in the world.

About the Author

B.B. Jones is a British author. Her books include The Chatelaine trilogy series. She lives on the Hampshire border in England with her partner and Bombay cat 'Pyewacket'. She has connections to many different areas of the world, including England, Guernsey, Australia and France. When she's not volunteering for various charities and planning grander designs for her woodland and herb garden, she enjoys researching history and plotting her next adventure – whether it be literary or a trip around the U.K. or worldwide.

Instagram: bbjones.indie_author

The Chatelaine series

The Chatelaine series tells the story of Annie and two of her daughters. It spans a period of over fifty years. It follows the three women as they face the challenges of living and loving in the twentieth century, whilst remaining true to both their obligations and their dreams.

The Chatelaine: Annie

The Second World War brought dramatic changes to everyone but none more so than Annie. At just nineteen, her world falls apart. When both the man she loves and the child she bears him are ripped from her, together with the only world she knows.

For a time, she can't imagine being someone other than a frightened girl in the grip of tragedy, but moving to Guernsey to start a new life as the war ends, neither can she anticipate the way her story will unfold, or the drama – and love – it will contain.

A new love and a new family bring her hope and healing and a respected business until unexpected death sweeps what she believed to be a certain future away from her again. But Annie hasn't bargained for fate and the power of love, to change everything – from families to fortunes – to a challenge. Even she couldn't have imagined for herself; becoming a Chatelaine…

The Chatelaine: Kate

Six years on and Le Château des Vieilles Tours and its residents are happy, healthy and thriving – all except for one, Kate.

Always the 'bridesmaid' and never the 'bride', Kate's world is less than contented until a glimmer of hope looks set to replace all the disappointments of her failed marriage and her confusion with her place in the world. A wonderful opportunity beckons – until it is dashed by a twist of fate, and tragedy, and far from being set free, Kate is instead imprisoned by her obligations and her past.

Once upon a time, she would have done anything to be the Chatelaine and a mother, now she only wants to escape…

The Chatelaine: Isabelle

The baby of the family, Isabelle has always got what she wants. A child of the twentieth century and all the opportunities it brings. She's lucky to have the luxuries of both her historic family home and the excitement of a fast-moving future. She also has Kate – ever-present and ever-reliable, until she isn't.

When Kate decides it's time for her little sister to take on the mantle of the Chatelaine and free Kate to live her own life at last, how will Isabelle juggle the responsibilities of the past with her plans for the future – plans which have nothing to do with the Château?